A Queer Kind of Umbrella

George Baxt

A PHAROAH LOVE MYSTERY

George Baxt

SIMON & SCHUSTER
New York   London   Toronto
Sydney   Tokyo   Singapore

Simon & Schuster
Rockefeller Center
1230 Avenue of the Americas
New York, NY 10020

SIMON & SCHUSTER and colophon are registered trademarks of Simon & Schuster Inc.

Designed by Hyun Joo Kim

Manufactured in the United States of America

1   2   3   4   5   6   7   8   9   10

Library of Congress Cataloging-in-Publication Data
Baxt, George.
    A queer kind of umbrella: a Pharoah Love mystery / George Baxt.
        p.   cm.
    1. Love, Pharoah (Fictitious character)—Fiction.   2. Afro-
American men—New York (N.Y.)—Fiction.   3. Gay men—New York
(N.Y.)—Fiction.   4. Police—New York (N.Y.)—Fiction.   5. New York
(N.Y.)—Fiction.   I. Title.
PS3552.A8478Q44   1995b
813'.54—dc20   95-17055
ISBN: 0-684-81496-X

For Joan and Robert Markell,
in memory of those rotten free options

A Queer Kind of Umbrella

CHAPTER 1

Very few people in New York City have heard of a street on the Lower East Side named Catherine Slip. It is only two short blocks in length and one finds there some derelict tenements that are habitable though there are those who say they shouldn't be. There are a few shops, one that deals in back-issue magazines, another that sells tobacco and stale candy bars and one that trades in men's accessories at incredibly reasonable prices. They never seem to do much business but somehow they manage to survive. Actually, the three deal in a variety of drugs and illegal guns. Their owners are all Asians, variously middle-aged and untrustworthy, with noisy, nagging wives and noisy, undisciplined children. The police are well aware of the illegal doings behind the storefronts but never move to put a stop to them. The proprietors are valuable informants. That is, on occasion they come up with some very good leads on the smuggling trade with China—a trade that deals in heroin as well as humanity. They can also direct you to the very accessible prostitutes inhabiting the tenements and are on agreeable terms with several assassins for hire who give money-back guarantees. The three live in comfortable apartments on the Upper West Side of the city and subscribe to cable TV. Their wives are a nosy bunch, and detective Pharoah Love refers to them affectionately as *oriyentas*.

An abandoned garment factory dominates the seedier end of Catherine Slip. To the naked, innocent eye, the factory looks abandoned. The windows and doors are boarded up, or seemingly so. But just about everybody knows or suspects that behind the shabby exterior there is a beehive of activity. The factory is the domain of the powerful and omnipotent Kao Lee, Chinatown's number-one godfather. Here again, the police know what's going on. They have their informants who have informants of their own, all this in addition to the three shopkeepers down the street. Upon entering the warehouse, one faces an impenetrable steel wall that rises and descends by the simple method of a finger connecting with a button. The machinery is so advanced and sophisticated that the police know attempting to raid the premises, should they have a mind to, would be rewarded with failure. Yet members of the police force come and go with amazing frequency. Kao and his lieutenants are aware when they are on the premises, and the police are aware that Kao is aware. It's a charming game they play because they need each other. Kao needs their protection and the police need their information, though they are well aware they are frequently misinformed and misled. The police are convinced their cooperation will eventually lead them to bringing about the collapse of the various syndicates and gangs smuggling Chinese aliens into the country. The police have the cooperation of New York City's FBI's

Asian Organized Crime Task Force. They have their sleuthing cut out for them. Murders and kidnappings among the Asian community are proliferating and no longer exclusive to Chinatown. Actually, New York now has three Chinatowns: one on the city's Lower East Side, the most celebrated and erroneously romanticized one, with its delightful shops and superb restaurants, one in the borough of Brooklyn and an even larger one in the borough of Queens.

Behind Kao's iron curtain there were all forms of illegal gambling: roulette, blackjack (vingt-et-un or twenty-one), sophisticated slot machines and so on. There was also free food and drink and pretty waitresses who were also pretty smart. There were the necessary dealers and pit bosses of various persuasions, and all were answerable to Lena Wing, an incredibly beautiful woman of an indeterminate age and very determined ambitions. If she couldn't rule the world she would be content to own an upper-class and very expensive restaurant anywhere in the city that would prove profitable. She answered to only one person, and that was Kao Lee.

On occasion she took over the deal at a blackjack table as she was now doing. She was very deft with the cards as she faced six gamblers. Three were Chinese boys in their twenties with a seemingly endless supply of cash. Two were middle-aged ladies who played daily, never cracked a smile and occasionally, when a dealer felt benevolent, won some money. The sixth gambler was a man in his mid-thirties who had been a frequent visitor for the past three or four months, played a cautious game, always knew when to double down on ten or eleven points and enjoyed bantering with Lena when she seemed in the mood. His name was Albert West; he was a detective with the local Fifth Precinct, having been transferred there several months ago from the Midtown Precinct on the Upper West Side.

On the table in front of Albert were three cards faceup, and they totaled fifteen. If he signaled for a fourth card, it would have to be no higher than a six or else he'd be above twenty-one and have to forfeit his chips. The department allowed Albert to lose so much a visit, but with Albert it was the principle of the thing. He couldn't stand losing money even when it wasn't his. Albert was taking a long time in deciding to draw or not to draw the fourth card. As dealer, Lena had drawn two cards, one facedown and the other faceup, which was a ten. Albert and the other players had to gamble if the card facing down was a low one. If it was an ace, which counted eleven points, they were sunk, as Lena would have twenty-one. If she had anywhere from a seven to a ten, she was still in a position to beat them. Lena and the other gamblers now had one thing in common, their growing impatience with Albert's procrastination. Finally he moved a finger indicating he would take another card, a very daring gesture with a count of fifteen. But Albert was feeling lucky. Earlier he had found a penny with its head up, put it in his shoe for good luck, which explained the devil-may-care expression on his face. Lena dealt him a six. Albert's face took on a beatific glow. Lena's face was inscrutable as she continued the play.

One of the women and two of the young men lost to Lena's count of twenty. She smiled as she added chips to Albert's two, which were worth five dollars each. Albert said, "It sometimes pays to live dangerously, right, Lena?"

"That depends on what you consider dangerous." Her voice was low and cultured and seductive.

"Haven't seen the big cheese lately. What's he up to these days?"

"Kao's a very busy man. You always ask the same question and you always get the same answer. I'm never sure what's occupying Kao from hour to hour. He could be getting a massage or shooting pool or on the phone to his broker." She was professionally shuffling the four decks of cards before resuming play. A waitress was taking drinks orders from the other players while the women gamblers were repairing their faces. "As a matter of fact, I think he's having his horoscope read. I saw his astrologer going up to the office a little while ago."

Albert feigned shock. "I can't believe Kao believes in that mumbo jumbo."

One of the women gamblers tapped Albert's wrist. "Young man, astrology is not mumbo jumbo. It is an exact science practiced in all Asiatic countries—"

"And Egypt," interjected her friend.

"And Egypt," came the echo, "for many centuries. Hitler was a great believer in astrology."

"Fat lot of good it did him," commented Albert.

"It caused him, as you put it, a fat lot of good for many years until Winston Churchill consulted an astrologer who could duplicate the information Hitler was receiving."

"Is that a fact?"

"It's not only a fact," insisted the woman, "but it's history. Toscanini and Marlene Dietrich and Nancy Reagan swore by their astrologers."

"I wonder how often they swore at them," mused Albert while his eye caught a familiar face at the bar, Harry Jen, one of Kao Lee's lieutenants. Jen was in his late twenties and stocky, with eyes too tiny for his chubby face. He blinked his eyes a lot as though to reassure himself they were still attached to their sockets. Lena followed Albert's gaze and when she saw Harry Jen, Albert could tell from the look on her face the stocky man was not high on her list of favorites. "You gave yourself dead away."

Lena's eyes shifted to Albert as she completed shuffling the four decks. "Concerning what?"

"Harry Jen. Not one of your favorite people."

"Just another pretty face." She indicated a yellow card on the table near Albert's elbow. "Cut the deck."

• • •

In Kao Lee's comfortably furnished office, he sat on a sofa facing the diminutive Madame Khan, who sat in an easy chair studying Kao's astrological chart. On the coffee table between them was a pot of jasmine tea, a plate of almond cookies and teacups. Madame Khan was one of those Asian women who seemed ageless. She was simply but smartly attired, and her brown attaché case rested against her chair. Madame Khan's reputation in her field was impeccable. She was consulted by other professionals, especially one woman who in addition to her column in one of the tabloids also had a telephone service. She dispensed such advice as "Today is a good day to clean house" or "Serve your spouse something special tonight" or occasionally "Mercury is in retrograde, so don't bake a cake, it will fall in." Madame Khan had received offers to write a column but she considered that sort of commercialism degrading and beneath contempt. She had an army of disciples who paid her handsomely for consultations, and Kao was terribly impressed when at one time she asked to use the phone, punched the buttons and then said into the phone quite distinctly, "Sell Viacom *now*" and hung up. Madame Khan was kind and benevolent about those whom she considered her inferiors, and did not envy those who were pocketing hundreds of thousands of dollars yearly for their newspaper columns and phone services.

Madame Khan set the chart aside and painstakingly polished her eyeglasses with a small cloth she dug out of her attaché case. She smiled a sweet smile at Kao, a man she knew to be a ruthless and dangerous person but, more impressively, seemingly totally fearless. He was of medium height and at the age of fifty still had jet-black hair combed back from his forehead and as sleek as a raven's feathers. His body was sinewy and muscular from regular workouts in his gymnasium. He waited patiently for Madame Khan to conclude her ritual and get down to the nitty-gritty. She asked him to refill her teacup, which he dutifully did.

"Well, my dear"—she spoke in a soft and gentle voice—"since we consulted last month, there have been significant changes in your chart. My dear Gemini, you now have Jupiter over you." He restrained the urge for a quick peek at the ceiling.

"What does that mean?" he asked in a voice that betrayed an addiction to strong tobacco.

"Jupiter is your protection." She stressed *protection*.

"Protection from what?" He sounded annoyed.

"Now don't be petulant, Kao." She sipped some tea. "Let's not kid ourselves. You of all people are in significant need of protection. You have enemies everywhere. And you can never be sure as to when they might strike. Now"—she riffled a few pages—"may I remind you Gemini is an air sign. . . ."

Kao shifted and crossed a leg. "What about water?"

"I'm coming to that. Will you please relax?"

"I *am* relaxed. I'm impatient."

"Impatience will someday be your undoing, so just shut up and listen." She cleared her throat. "Right now, you are a Gemini with Libra rising."

"Is that good?"

"Very good. Gemini and Libra are quite similar and very compatible. You have the Moon and Venus in Taurus. . . ."

"Sounds like they might be crowding each other."

She flashed him an unpleasant look. "Mars is in Cancer, and happily for you, the Sun and Mercury are in Gemini and"—she added triumphantly—"Saturn is climbing. Mercury and the Sun are your two main planets. They give you discipline. Mars gives you action. There is a great deal of action indicated."

"What kind of action?"

"What I should have said is 'activity.' "

"I always have activity. What I need right now is action."

Madame Khan consulted the chart closely. "Yes, Kao, there is action." She added solemnly, "Perhaps even more then you're prepared for."

Kao was lighting a cigar, and Madame Khan was waving the smoke away. He stubbed out the cigar in a jade ashtray and apologized for forgetting she loathed cigar smoke. "My forebears were almost all destroyed by opium. You and your kind are killing yourselves with cigars. Filthy habit."

"Would you go back to the action?"

She set the chart aside on the table and leaned forward, her hands folded in her lap. "There are women who are a threat to you."

His eyes narrowed. "Names."

"The charts never provide names. There are women in your life and among them there are a few who pose a threat to your future well-being."

"There are many women in my life."

"I understand." She unfolded her hands and leaned back in the chair. "You have your work cut out for you."

Kao poured himself fresh tea and sipped. "I thought Jupiter was floating above me as protection."

"It is. If it wasn't there, things would get much worse."

"How bad is it? Come on, sweetheart, what's there you're not telling me about?"

"I'm telling you everything I see. There is danger in the water. Were you planning a cruise, something like that?"

"No. But I have an interest in a freighter heading this way."

She said matter-of-factly, if not somewhat smugly, "Then that's where the trouble could lie."

Kao smiled. "I know you know an awful lot about me that you didn't read in the chart."

"I don't have to. It's in the newspapers. There have been so many exposés in the newspapers."

"They haven't exposed all that much. I let them learn only as much as I want them to learn."

"Smuggling Chinese aliens. Holding them to ransom when they can't pay the full sum. Kidnapping their relatives. Demanding extortion and tribute from restaurants and small businesses. Really, Kao, you're much too modest."

"You want a piece of the action?" He was nibbling an almond cookie.

She was gathering up her papers. "I get as much as I need from you."

He watched her gathering the papers and neatly returning them to the attaché case. "You mean this is all you've got to tell me?"

"I can only tell you what I chart. Now, really, Kao, it isn't as though the stars will foretell something momentous every day of the week. The heavens move slowly, and I can only operate at their pace. Let me remind you of the danger in water."

"You don't have to. It's sunk in."

"And women."

His eyes twinkled. "Does that mean you?"

"Indeed, I'm a woman. I don't think I've ever been a threat to anyone. On the other hand, should you misinterpret my reading of your chart, then indirectly I am indeed a threat. I hope not. I rather like you, Kao, despite the fact you're a scoundrel."

"That's for starters. I'm never sure when you're kidding me."

"You can be sure I'm not kidding when I'm reading your chart. I hope you know by now I'm quite ethical."

"Madame, I have the utmost respect for you." He was seated at his desk writing a check for her. "Don't spend this all in one place." He tore the check from the book and handed it to her. Without looking at the amount, she folded it in two and dropped it in the attaché case. He stood and, taking her by the arm, walked her to the door. She looked about the room and clucked her tongue.

"This room lacks color, Kao. You have a colorful ancestry. You need more Chinese-style decorations here."

"You mean like a dragon on the wall and arrangements of joss sticks with a seated Buddha holding in his lap a smoking tray of incense? I can't stand the stuff. I like this room the way it is."

"To each his own." He opened the door for her and with a gentle "Ta ta" she walked across the outer office where one of his lieutenants sat, a young man named Nick Wenji.

"Hello, Madame," Wenji greeted the small woman. "You tell him anything interesting?"

"That depends on what you would consider interesting." Her eye had been caught by the contents of an umbrella stand. "What a beautifully carved handle!" She lifted a green umbrella from the stand to better examine the carved handle. Wenji almost hurtled across the room to rescue the umbrella. Startled by the suddenness of his retrieving the umbrella, she asked wryly, "Is it a precious heirloom?"

Kao came to Wenji's rescue. "It's one I thought I'd lost several days ago. And here it is in my umbrella stand! Now how do you explain that?"

"I'm sure you'll think of something," said Madame Khan as she pulled the door shut behind her.

Wenji replaced the umbrella in the stand. "She tell you anything interesting?"

"Never mind her. Has there been contact with the freighter?"

"They expect to make the checkpoint as scheduled. They want to be sure the small boats will be there to unload the cargo."

"They'd better be there."

Albert was seated at the bar with Harry Jen, pleased at having won over two hundred dollars at the blackjack table.

"Lena must like you," said Harry as he signaled the bartender for a fresh beer.

"You telling me the table's crooked?" asked Albert archly.

"I ain't telling you nothing you don't already know. Casinos ain't in the business to lose money. What are you drinking?"

"Diet Coke," said Albert virtuously.

"If your buddy Pharoah Love were here, he'd make some smart-assed crack about sissy drinks."

"He's not here and I'm thirsty."

"Come to think of it, we ain't seen Pharoah around for a long time. Couple of months? Where you hiding him?"

"I'm not hiding him. He's off on a cruise."

"Oh yeah? Where to?"

"He wouldn't tell. He didn't want the chief tracking him down." Albert lowered his voice. "Got anything for me?"

"There's a new cargo in any day now."

"Where's it due?"

"Somewhere near the Rockaways. I'm not sure. The freighter's the *Green Empress*. Kao's nephew Michael is one of the enforcers on board. Pretty big cargo, over three hundred, I think."

"That's a lot of fortune cookies," Albert said.

CHAPTER 2

For a vessel with a name as exotically regal as the *Green Empress*, the freighter looked as though it had been recently salvaged after years of moldering on the ocean bottom. The boat was as tired and forlorn as its human cargo, over three hundred Chinese primarily from China's Fujian Province. They were mostly males ranging from sixteen to forty years old, with a handful of women who had stoically accepted daily mistreatment since the vessel had embarked on its perilous journey over two months ago. Somehow all had managed to survive on one meal a day of rice or noodles with a bit of rotted vegetables or putrefied meat. The hygienic facilities were barely adequate, and the ugly stench from below decks was nauseating. Every member of this cargo of illegal aliens had paid a minimum of five thousand dollars in Chinese currency for the privilege of space on the freighter. Another twenty-five thousand had to be paid upon arrival in the United States. It was hoped that relatives and friends would pay this. They and their families had toiled long hours, scrimped and saved for this rare privilege to escape to the freedom of the United States. Some, like Tisa Cheng, the eighteen-year-old girl who nursed an ambition to be a great movie actress, were fortunate enough to win a free ride. Tisa's sponsor was Michael Lee, a nephew of the powerful criminal Kao Lee. He became enchanted with Tisa, who appeared nightly at a sleazy café in the coastal village of Pusan, where the *Green Empress* was docked. Michael was one of five enforcers assigned to the freighter. Actually, he had volunteered for the assignment in the interests of learning the smuggling operation firsthand. His uncle was impressed and was beginning to see in his nephew a possibly worthy successor to his throne, if and when he chose to abdicate, or was murdered, which was the more likely prospect. Kao Lee was not fated to win any popularity contests.

A month earlier, Michael and a male friend, a light-skinned black named Archie Lang, or so he called himself, sat at a table in the café as Tisa Cheng did her best to entertain the motley clientele. She played a mandolin and, with what was presumed to be the help of a badly tuned piano, did her best to sing what Archie Lang presumed to be a Chinese interpretation of "Melancholy Baby." The young woman seated on the piano stool had a vacant expression that Archie recognized as drug induced. Occasionally her head drooped, and Archie expected she might fall off the stool momentarily. The condition of the pianist didn't seem to faze Tisa Cheng. She was enthusiastic and anxious to be a crowd pleaser. Archie Lang wasn't pleased. He winced as Tisa flatted a note and the pianist struggled to remain upright. Michael looked at his suffering companion and smiled.

"Tune out, Archie," he advised good-naturedly, "no need to suffer so. Have another beer."

Archie turned to him. "You really dig this chick?"

"I go for the girl, not her voice."

"You think it's a good idea importing her to the States?"

Michael shrugged. "If it doesn't work with us, I can set her up in a sweat shop or a massage parlor. Her English isn't too bad and she's a pretty smart kid." Then he suddenly changed the subject. "Archie Lang isn't your real name."

Archie smiled, displaying two rows of even, white teeth that belonged in a television commercial. He was a handsome man, thought Michael, probably in his late thirties or early forties. "Archie Lang is as good a name as any."

"How long you been in the Orient?"

"Too long. Like I told you the night we got acquainted," which was approximately three nights earlier, "I never expected to spend all this time in the Orient."

"You went to a lot of trouble to strike up my acquaintance. Why?"

"When I got the scuttlebutt that the *Green Empress* was yours and was heading Stateside, my juices bubbled." Michael signaled a waiter for fresh beers. "I know I can level with you. I can't fly back or sail on a liner."

"I suspected you were in trouble."

"Real bad trouble. That's why I started hanging around here. I heard there was steady traffic in illegal alien smuggling here and that was music to my ears." Tisa Cheng was now challenging what might have been "Honeysuckle Rose," although she was delivering the usually upbeat number at a funereal pace. "I figured, with any luck, I could get a berth back to the States."

"Archie, this freighter is no yacht. It's going to be a very long and very miserable voyage. These illegals could become troublesome because there's nothing for them but misery, boredom, a little bit of hunger. I'm one of five enforcers assigned to this teakettle. Five isn't enough to keep over three hundred illegals in order. I can't keep an eye on Tisa all the time. I've got a lot of work to do. I'm considering taking you on as her bodyguard."

"You won't be sorry." Archie tried not to sound too anxious.

Michael eyed the man professionally as the waiter brought the beers. "Assure me I have nothing to worry about where your possible interest in Tisa is concerned."

Archie leaned forward. "As William Shakespeare wrote, 'This above all, to thine own self be true.' And I am very true to myself. I'm not much for chicks." He poured himself the beer, took a healthy swig, grimaced and said, "They should pour this back down the throat of the horse it came from. When do we sail?"

"Late tonight with the tide. You share a cabin with the enforcers. They won't trust you, so try not to turn your back on them too often."

"What's not to trust?"

"In the first place, you're not Asian. In the second place, they'll be told you're Tisa's protection. They're not going to like the idea of Tisa to begin with. The only thing that I'm counting on to keep them in line is the fact that my uncle is a very powerful and very dangerous man." He told him briefly about Kao Lee.

"Formidable," said Archie, giving the word its French pronunciation. "Ain't uncle got no kids of his own?"

"A couple of girls. They're somewhere on the West Coast. They distanced themselves from their father a long time ago. They're not in touch, especially since their mother committed suicide."

"Oh boy."

"Very unhappy lady." Michael was staring ahead at nothing in particular. "My uncle's hobby is seduction."

"You telling me he always scores when he wants a chick?"

"When you're Kao Lee, you don't ever miss. He's very rich and very persuasive and not unattractive. He's very fond of me, which is very nice for me. I didn't have to volunteer to undertake this voyage but I wanted to impress on him my interest in learning firsthand every facet of his operation."

"He your father's or your mother's brother?"

"My father was his younger brother. He was Kao's partner."

"You sound as though he's quit the business."

"He's dead." Michael's voice was flat, a monotone. "He was murdered." Archie said nothing. "He was killed on a crowded street in Chinatown. The autopsy revealed a pellet of ricin, which is a deadly poison that paralyzes the nerves, in the calf of one of his legs."

Archie was fascinated. "How'd it get there?"

"Shot from some form of weapon. The pellet from the heat of the calf releases the ricin. Sometimes you die right away. Sometimes it takes a few days."

"Maybe your father was killed earlier than you think."

"Possibly. But he died on that crowded street. Delancey Street. He lay in a doorway for hours. Unidentified. Just another doped-up chink as far as passersby were concerned. Finally somebody sent for a patrol car. The cops recognized him. Everybody knew my father. He wasn't like Kao. My father told jokes. He loved to entertain. When he was alive, there were always dinner parties at our house. He was very much in love with my mother. He took great pride in her beauty and her intelligence."

Archie said warmly, "I see you take great pride in her too."

"Yes. I still do. Even though she married my Uncle Kao."

Archie waited a few moments before speaking. "Well, there's a howdy do."

Michael smiled. "Something tells me we're going to find out an awful lot about each other before the *Green Empress* docks. My other buddies aren't much for conversation. Where in the States you come from, Archie?"

"There's a borough in New York City called Brooklyn. And on the coast of Brooklyn there's a body of water called Jamaica Bay. Along Jamaica Bay there's a little community called Canarsie, named for the Canarsie Indians, which was a tribe of redskins and not a baseball team. Canarsie was mostly populated by the Italians and the Irish, with a soupçon of Jews to add a little flavor. My family was very distinctly a minority. For a long time we were the only blacks to settle there, though in time some city housing units were constructed and there went the neighborhood. And in case you give a damn, there were no Asians whatsoever."

"And when did you fall into a life of crime?"

"When I got lucky." His smile was as inscrutable as any Asian's.

Tisa Cheng slipped into a chair next to them and took a sip of Michael's beer. Then she put a hand over his and said, "I can't wait to reave this rousy joint." She obviously had trouble with her *l*s, an impediment usually reserved for the Japanese. Archie decided that on the voyage he would do his best to remedy the condition.

Michael informed her, "Archie's coming with us."

Her face lit up. "Oh yes?"

"He'll look after you when I'm too busy."

"Tisa can take care of herserf," she assured Michael. "Stirr, I'm rear grad Archie is coming with us. Here comes American sairor."

It was one of Michael's enforcers. He whispered something as he knelt beside Michael. Michael nodded and then said to Archie, "Show time. Get your gear. We're sailing in a couple of hours." He placed some bills on the table.

Archie said, "I'll be a few minutes." He hurried away to his tumbledown hotel. Michael sent the enforcer with Tisa to carry her belongings, and then strolled briskly along the pier to where the freighter was docked.

In his hotel room, Archie Lang tossed what he owned into a duffel bag along with his Glock 9mm handgun and several rounds of ammunition. He didn't expect to have to use the gun, but on these tricky expeditions one never could tell. He'd been warned by his partner, Albert West, to whom Archie was better known as Pharoah Love, ace New York detective, there'd been rumors of mutinies and killings on earlier smuggling trips. One freighter had foundered and sunk in the notorious Bermuda Triangle, many knots off its course. Pharoah stared at himself in the cracked mirror of the sagging dresser. He wondered what the crew and cargo of the freighter would make of his ponytail and the earring in his left ear, depicting Jesus and Moses with an arm around each other.

He said to his mirror image, another Shakespearean quote, " 'Now voyager, set thou forth and sail,' " and added some words of his own, "And may God have mercy on your soul and protect you from the evil spirits."

Eight weeks later Pharoah thought God had chosen to ignore him—this cruise was a remake of *Mutiny on the Bounty*. Conditions were egregious, to be kind. The aliens were on a starvation diet because not enough food had been stored for the voyage. But there was always enough for the ship's personnel, and the enforcers and Pharoah stole apples for Tisa, who was an apt pupil and had conquered her *l* liability in a very short time. They learned to turn a deaf ear to the entreaties and cries of distress from the female aliens suffering physical attacks, and in time those cries for help were subdued and then muted, as though the ladies had taken among them an oath of stoicism. After all, their parents and grandparents had suffered similarly during the great Japanese invasion of five decades ago and survived.

Michael's four enforcers soon tolerated and accepted Pharoah when he convinced Michael to teach him some useful Chinese phrases.

And from Michael, Pharoah learned a good bit more than that. After the first few weeks at sea, Michael realized there was very little for him and Tisa to talk about, and when not wondering what to do with her when they landed, he sat on deck with Pharoah, telling him about Kao's vast criminal operation. Pharoah knew about the Warehouse, of course, having frequented it with Albert. It was his job to try and learn as much as possible about the Warehouse operation when he and Albert had been transferred to the Fifth Precinct. Their old chief, Walt MacIntyre, had been good enough to phone Christy Lombardo downtown and tell him what a lucky chief of detectives he was. Lombardo appreciated MacIntyre's kind words until he was confronted with Albert and Pharoah in the flesh. Albert would do just fine, but this clown with a ponytail and an earring in his left ear (Mother of God, Moses and Jesus hugging!), blue jeans and a T-shirt on which was printed IN CASE OF EMERGENCY, GIVE HEAD! This was the celebrated Pharoah Love, who had more honors and citations than any other detective. But in time, Lombardo got used to the fancy packaging on this extremely gifted cop.

Pharoah absorbed Michael's information like the sponge he'd been trained to become. He recognized Michael was in his own way a true innocent, about as cut out to be a gangster as a TV news anchor. Michael never once suspected Archie Lang might be a plant. Pharoah never asked too many questions. He rarely had to. Michael droned on in his rather dull monotone, a stream of consciousness waiting to wash over the first sympathetic listener it came across. Frequently, Pharoah wished he'd been carrying a wire and recording Michael, but aboard the freighter that would have been instant suicide.

Pharoah learned about Kao Lee's number-one strong-arm man, who in the past would have been called the Hatchet Man, Nick Wenji. Nick danced constant attendance on Kao Lee and was handsomely rewarded. Nick's big frustration was Lena Wing, who was literally his uncle's second in command. Lena had big ambitions to be a famous restaurateur, and she had exacted a promise from Kao Lee that he would see to it her ambition would be fulfilled. Pharoah was fascinated with Kao Lee's addiction to astrology and expressed a wish to meet this shrewd and feisty Madame Khan, who intimated she was a descendant of the great Genghis Khan.

When Michael began discussing Kao Lee's relationship to the Greek shipping owner Cylla Mourami, Pharoah's heart skipped a beat. Cylla Mourami was the daughter of the notorious international play-boy Ari Mourami, who died of a heart attack when he heard Onassis had won the hand of Jacqueline Kennedy. On his death, Cylla inherited the whole shooting match, the vast Mourami empire, a shipping empire that covered the world. Pharoah reasoned the *Green Empress* was probably one of her fleet, albeit a poor relation. Pharoah asked one of his rare questions. Could Cylla Mourami possibly be one of Kao Lee's silent partners?

Michael laughed. "She's not all that silent. She does a lot of yelling. Yeah, I think my uncle's into her for something. He insists she's got a spy planted in the warehouse telling her everything that's going on. And that could be any of a number of people working for my uncle. Like maybe Harry Jen, one of the pit bosses who's a real slimeball. He's Lena Wing's very unfavorite person."

"What about Lena?"

"Lena's no mole. That's not her line. For whatever Lola wants, Lola gets, substitute Lena. I told you what she's after, and she's going to get it"—he paused—"or else."

"Michael?"

"Yeah?"

"Can I ask you something personal?"

"Shoot."

"Do you like your uncle?"

Michael said in his monotone, "He is very generous to me."

Pharoah thought, But that doesn't have to mean you like him.

They sat in silence for a while, Pharoah watching some seagulls doing somersaults in the sky. Seagulls. That meant they weren't too far from land.

Cylla Mourami. It was rumored she was the bankroll behind a chain of gay bars in New York City. If so, was Kao Lee in on the deal? What, wondered Pharoah, was Kao's possible involvement with the massage parlors in the city? As fast as the police closed them, another would surface somewhere else. He heard Michael say he had to speak to the captain and watched him as he crossed to the other side of the ship.

It would soon be time for dinner, and Pharoah dreaded going below more than he dreaded the cuisine that would be offered. If ever he deserved a citation, this gig was it. He thought of Albert West, who in his way, although a damned good detective, was as much an innocent as Michael Lee. Pharoah chuckled, remembering what a dyed-in-the-wool homophobe Albert had been when he met him. Well, time, circumstances and Pharoah Love soon remedied that unfortunate condition.

The boat was slowing down. Michael returned. "Why are we slowing down?" asked Pharoah.

"We may be in trouble."

CHAPTER **3**

Christy Lombardo, Chief of Detectives in the Fifth Precinct, was not a happy person. His world, the police department, was in a state of chaos. Twenty-six officers in Harlem's Thirtieth Precinct had been arrested and charged with felonies, extorting money from drug dealers, breaking into and robbing their apartments, beating them up brutally. It was not a nice way for policemen to behave; that their victims were slimeballs was no excuse. A policeman had to set a good example as a representative of his precinct. He had to help old ladies across the street even if he suspected their shopping bags hid some form of dope. When unarming a teenage felon, he had to be gentle and make nice and perhaps apologize for strong-arming them.

He should declare as income on his yearly tax reports all the thousands he extorted. He shouldn't be so stupid as to buy expensive cars and houses and flaunt his ill-gotten gains. Christy Lombardo wistfully longed for the good old days when the most a policeman could be held accountable for was taking an apple from his friendly neighborhood fruit stand.

Christy was also not happy with the circumstances that involved Pharoah Love. In cooperation with the FBI's Organized Crime Task Force, the NYPD had allowed Pharoah to go underground to the Fujian Province in China and try to infiltrate the Chi Who gang. The Chi Who ran the smuggling of illegal aliens operation, and the FBI and the police knew Kao Lee ran the Chi Who, but they couldn't get the goods on him. But they trusted their informer, Harry Jen. He'd been feeding them for a long time now in return for some pretty fancy payments. He was smarter then the crooked cops. Harry Jen didn't buy a fancy car or an elegant house. He didn't even have a mistress. He bought mutual funds and government bonds, using a broker who worked out of Staten Island. Harry Jen felt very comfortable in his job as one of the Warehouse's pit bosses. He knew he wasn't very well liked, a situation which he had learned to cope with since his childhood in China, when children threw rocks and mud balls and garbage at him because he was so ugly. While in his young teens, a sympathetic aunt who was also terribly ugly pitied the poor young unfortunate and bought his passage to America. As he left the miserable hut in which he dwelt with his ugly parents and six repulsive siblings, all boys, in addition to several pigs, goats and chickens, all eight of his relatives took turns kicking him a fond farewell.

Christy Lombardo was always kind to Harry Jen. He wasn't all that repulsed by the chubby face with its abnormally tiny eyes. It didn't bother him that Harry was a chronic perspirer, perpetually dabbing at his face with either a handkerchief or a tissue. When you're a police informer you usually have a good reason for perspiring. His eyes moved from Harry Jen to Albert West, who was the third occupant of Christy's office. Albert was also unhappy, but not for the same reason as his chief. He knew some of the police officers under arraignment and always suspected they were rogues. He was unhappy about Pharoah Love. Not a word in over two months. The FBI hadn't heard anything either.

Harry Jen was explaining with patience. "There is no way for Pharoah to contact you from the boat. You certainly understand that. And if there's been no word from him since his last communication from Pusan, then he must be on the boat."

Lombardo said, "If he was dead, we'd have heard something by now. I mean that ponytail and that nutty earring are bound to warrant an investigation if he's bought it." He paused. "We'd certainly have heard from Interpol. Look, Albert, Interpol told us he's probably on the freighter because there's been no sign of Pharoah in Pusan since the *Green Empress* departed. Harry, you trying to tell me Kao Lee's had no word from his nephew in all this time?"

"Oh not at all. Michael is in constant touch by wireless. But to my knowledge, there's been no word of Pharoah." He added smoothly. "Wasn't Pharoah to represent himself as a felon wanted by the U. S. police? Well, Michael wouldn't be about to report his presence on the boat." He mopped his face with a handkerchief. "Patience, gentlemen, patience. The boat is due any day now. Albert, remember that day at the bar in the Warehouse when Lena let you win a few hundred?"

"What was that?" asked Lombardo suspiciously.

Albert explained hastily. "She won it all back a couple of hours later. What about that day, Harry?"

"I asked about Pharoah's whereabouts. You said he was off on a cruise somewhere. I thought we played the scene rather well for the benefit of the bartender and anyone within earshot. Especially me, getting across I had no idea where Pharoah was. Well, as you know, the bartender reports to Kao, as does everyone who works there. There has been no mention of Pharoah in the club since. If there has, I haven't heard it. We checked and double-checked that Michael's never met or seen Pharoah. He works mostly out of Kao's office in SoHo. Forgive me for repeating this, but Kao is very protective of his nephew. After all, he's married to Michael's mother. And Kao was very impressed when Michael volunteered to be the number-one enforcer on this trip. There are those of us who think Michael is the heir apparent to Kao's dynasty."

Lombardo said to Albert, "What's biting you?"

"Me? Do I look as though something's biting me?"

"I've seen that look before. You brought it with you from uptown. You show that look usually when Pharoah's said something that bugs you. So out with it."

"Are we so sure Michael's never seen Pharoah before?"

Harry Jen looked as though he had just been stabbed. "I told you it was checked and double-checked. Now, come on, Albert, Pharoah is not easily forgettable. If Michael recognized Pharoah, then Pharoah's dead."

"Don't say that," yelled Albert.

"Stop yelling!" yelled Lombardo.

"Yes, stop yelling, it makes me nervous." Harry's little eyes were blinking, looking like trapped fireflies. "One has to be logical, Albert. If Pharoah's dead, we would have heard something from Interpol."

Lombardo leaned back in his chair. "Albert, I'm not intentionally upsetting you, but the Orient is notorious for people disappearing without a trace. But, Albert, my money's on Pharoah. If there's some slipup and he's caught in a tight situation, he'd manage to wiggle out of it. He's got the hips for it." Lombardo laughed. "He's on his way home. I feel it in my bones. Okay, Harry, you can skip out through the basement."

Along with the other rats, thought Albert. He wondered again what Kao Lee would have done to Harry Jen once he found out the chubby slimebag had been betraying him. He stared out the window and sighed, not having heard Harry Jen depart.

"What's that sigh about?" asked Lombardo.

"I was thinking of Harry Jen."

"You in love?"

Albert shot him a look. "I was thinking what Kao Lee will do to him when he finds out Harry's on our payroll."

Lombardo looked at the ceiling. "Oh, in the good old Chinese tradition, he'll probably have him drawn and quartered. And then he'll torture him."

"Gee, Christy," Albert said solemnly, "so you do have a sense of humor."

Christy laughed. "Albert, ever since you and Pharoah transferred down here, I've been dying to ask you some questions."

"Go right ahead. My life is a partially opened book."

"What made you decide to become a cop?"

"I have no memorable answer to that one. I studied law though I didn't want to be a lawyer. I thought maybe I'd apply to the FBI, but then there were things about them that didn't sit well with me. So I decided to try and join the force. I did. I guess I was a pretty good cop. It wasn't long before I was promoted to detective."

Lombardo sat forward, his elbows propped on his desk. "I just don't get you and Pharoah."

"What do you mean? He's my partner. We're a good team."

"Which comes as a big surprise to me and just about everybody else. You're a damned good team, and you shouldn't be."

Albert tried not to look uncomfortable. He suspected what was coming. "Why shouldn't we be?"

It was Lombardo who was uncomfortable. "Well, you're straight." A brief pause. "Well, aren't you?"

Albert parried, "Have you any doubts? And if you do, does it bother you?"

"Well, it's no secret Pharoah's gay."

"Pharoah doesn't like secrets. He also takes great pride in himself and his achievements on the force. I don't believe there are any demerits against him. I know he's been outrageous in the past and will undoubtedly be just as outrageous in the future. But whatever he does, he won't do anything like beat up dope peddlers, rob them, break into their houses . . ."

"Okay okay okay! Enough! Don't rub salt in my wounds!"

"Why your wounds?" Albert looked closely at his boss. "Who do you suspect?"

"You're too damned smart!"

"It's a simple deduction, Christy. They trap rogues up in the Thirtieth, that means there are rogues all over the city. You've got to have them here because Chinatown's crawling with gangs." He enumerated swiftly. "There's the Tung On, Born to Kill, the Ghost Shadows, the Green Dragons, and so on. The Feds insist the Fuk Ching is wiped out once they took its leader, Ah Kay, into custody. But how can they be sure? You know and I know there are still pockets of survivors carrying on the Fuk Ching tradition. They're still involved in smuggling illegal aliens and you know they're out there trying to collect old debts. And they call themselves posses. And we're having a hell of a time trying to get them to circle their wagons."

"Albert! I'm impressed! Still waters *do* run deep."

"As Pharoah would say if he was here, and I wish he was, Christy, cut the crap. We were transferred here because you needed the help. Pharoah and I have been doing our homework. Chinatown's the scene of one gigantic shakedown. And what a variety of victims. Drug dealers, dealers in stolen goods, carjackers, restaurants and factories that are hiring the illegals and paying them coolie wages, massage parlors, gambling houses like the Warehouse and much worse."

"The Warehouse's days are numbered."

"So what? It or an unreasonable facsimile will pop up down some other mean street, and Chinatown's got a lot of mean streets."

"And a lot of mean people." Christy looked at his wristwatch. "Ah! Teatime! How's for a suck of Old Grandma?" He produced a bottle of bourbon from a desk drawer. "You're looking pale, Albert. You need a transfusion. Get some paper cups."

Pharoah was tense. Michael Lee and he were on deck in the prow of the ship, Michael staring through a pair of high-powered binoculars.

"Any sign of them?" asked Pharoah.

"Nothing. Not anything." He lowered the binoculars and looked at his wristwatch. "They should have been here an hour ago." He was waiting for the small ships that were to transport the illegals to a carefully chosen secluded inlet on the Long Island shore. It was a frequently used landfall, property owned by Cylla Mourami.

Pharoah tried not to sound too anxious. He thought of breaking into song or doing a time-step but dismissed both ideas as excessively frivolous under the circumstances. "What happens if they don't show up?"

"I wire for instructions."

"How much longer can you wait?"

"If I have to, I can wait until before dawn. We need the darkness to land these people. They're to be dropped at a stretch of isolated beach."

"And then what?"

"There'll be trucks waiting to transport them to any number of drop points."

"How about that," said Pharoah solemnly. "And they never get caught."

"Not yet."

Pharoah saw several of the crew members on an upper deck watching them. He was grateful the wind was blowing in the opposite direction. "The crew don't look too happy."

"Would you after two months of what they've been through?"

"They knew what to expect. You pay them top price, don't you?"

"A lot of them are illegals paying off what they owe Chi Who. Most of them will be paying off forever, unless they come into a sudden windfall, and that pipe dream is highly doubtful."

"Not even if they get a pop at *Jeopardy?*"

Michael didn't think that funny. He was looking through the binoculars again. "Goddamn them!"

Pharoah had a sudden inspiration. "What about the lifeboats?"

Michael lowered the binoculars. "Outside of the fact that there aren't enough of them, you'd be safer dog-paddling."

"This is no way to fill me with confidence." Pharoah asked, "What do you do if the ships don't show up?"

"I'll run the boat aground." Michael's expression was grim.

"But that could kill a lot of these slobs!"

"I've got no choice. If I don't do it, the crew will do it. There's no way to stop them."

"Don't you have guns and ammunition?"

"Archie, I've got guns and ammunition, and they'll be as effective as a mosquito attacking an elephant." He looked at his wristwatch again.

"I'm going to send a message to Kao. We have a special code for an emergency, and by God my uncle better have a solution up his sleeve." He handed Pharoah the binoculars and hurried away. Pharoah looked to the upper deck. The number of crew there had increased. He thought of his duffel bag and his Glock 9mm hidden in it. Or hopefully still hidden in it. Surprisingly, there had been very few robberies during the hellish journey, or else if any had occurred they had not been reported. There was precious little worth robbing on this tub, except for the apples he stole to give to Tisa Cheng. Oh God, he thought, there's her to worry about. Then he thought, With any luck, she's a strong swimmer. She's lived on water all her life, she has to know how to swim.

He lifted the binoculars and was again met with disappointment. He thought of Albert West and wondered if he was worried about not having heard from him in all these weeks. Of course Albert would be terribly worried. I'm his best pal, his buddy, his partner. He's probably in a church right now lighting a few candles for me, except, damn him, he's a lapsed Catholic.

Now he was thinking about Kao Lee, the murdered brother Zang, Michael's father, and Zang's widow, who was now Kao Lee's wife, Michael's mother. Pharoah thought, I am faced with a true Chinese puzzle. Nests within nests. Truly, 'tis a puzzlement.

Tisa Cheng was at his side. He hadn't heard her approach, so deeply was he involved with his own thoughts. She arrived as silent as a breeze. "Is it serious?" she asked.

"Is what serious?"

"The predicament."

"What predicament?"

"I'm not a fool, Archie Lang. I saw Michael going into the wireless room, and the crew are quite troubled by our lying at anchor here and no sign of the ships to transport us to land." Her hands were on her hips, the picture of a very determined young lady. "Why don't we take a lifeboat and get the hell out of here?" No longer the sweet young thing who couldn't pronounce her *l*s.

"Michael says they're not reliable."

She bristled. "If he knew that, how dare he let us set sail on this broken-down wreck?"

"You didn't seem to think it was all that broken-down when you first boarded her. It was your magic carpet to paradise. You couldn't

stop kvelling about how at last you were on your way to the good old
U.S. of A."

She looked perplexed. "What's kvelling?"

Pharoah was thankful she had conquered her *l*s. He dreaded the
thought of hearing her say, "What's kverring?" "It means expressing
joy and pride in something."

"What language is it?"

"Yiddish."

"What's Yiddish?"

"A frame of mind."

Michael was back. "We're to hang in another couple of hours. It's
still light. My uncle thinks they might be waiting for darkness."

"Let's take a lifeboat," insisted Tisa, which did not endear her to
Michael.

"I don't think the crew would like that."

"The hell with them! You're the boss around here. Don't you have
a gun?"

"Tisa," said Pharoah.

"What?" she snapped.

He folded his arms. "I think, believe it or not, I'd like to hear you
sing."

CHAPTER 4

Harry Jen scowled at the light drizzle that began when he was meeting with Christy and Albert. The precinct adjoined an abandoned brownstone. Harry hurried from the precinct basement into the brownstone's basement, a path he frequently traveled and was therefore familiar with. He was prepared for the stench and the rats and the possibility of a squatter or two. He made his way carefully across the brownstone's basement to a door on the opposite side that led to an alley dividing the brownstone from a supermarket. Harry hurried into the supermarket through an emergency exit that opened into the alley. So far so good. He slowed his step and examined fruit and vegetables, a casual shopper like all the others. Five minutes later he was out on the street, standing under the supermarket awning. He was dabbing his forehead with a handkerchief. Just another sweaty Chinatown citizen out shopping, about to brave the drizzle. He looked at his wristwatch. He had a date uptown. The subway would get him there with time to spare. Despite the drizzle, there was fairly heavy pedestrian traffic. There always was. He braved the wetness, feeling rather good about himself and his life. He made good money as a pit boss and was paid equally well by the police and the fancy lady uptown with whom he had a rendezvous.

The fancy lady uptown was Cylla Mourami, who had been taught by her late father to trust no one except her lawyer and her financial advisers. She had to trust them, or as her father so delicately phrased it, she'd be up the Aegean without a paddle. There was nothing modest about the interior of her East Sixty-sixth Street town house, situated between Fifth and Madison. It was over a century old, solidly constructed the way town houses were a hundred years ago. It contained the usual accoutrements of the superwealthy. Magnificent furniture and furnishings, paintings valued in untold millions, Old Masters and some older mistresses, and through her connection with Kao Lee, some fine Oriental trappings dating back to the Ming and Han dynasties. Like so many wealthy people more concerned with her business life, Cylla wasn't quite sure of how much wealth was housed under the mansion's roof. She often promised her lawyer, Hiram Wiggs, that she would order an overall inventory and appraisal, but always postponed it for one reason or another.

The Mouramis came from a long line of Hellenic peasants. It was her great-grandfather who went into shipping and sowed the first seeds of the dynasty that emerged in a surprisingly short space of time. There were stories about his being a pirate that Cylla's father repeated with relish. Mourami senior, who was coarse and vulgar and ate with the same fingers he used to pick his nose, made up stories about his grandfather and had even hired a writer to perpetuate the legend with a book about the old man, *Gifts Bearing Greeks*, a surprisingly charming pack of lies that sold surprisingly well.

The Mourami drawing room had been photographed for *Architectural Digest* and *Vanity Fair*, and it was Cylla's favorite room. Cylla and her lawyer, Hiram Wiggs, sat patiently while waiting for a maid to finish pouring tea, a daily four o'clock ritual unless Cylla was occupied at her company's offices in the World Trade Center. Cylla was in her late thirties and had inherited her mother's sharp features and strong bones. She had learned to make the most of what she had, and so other women referred to her looks as "interesting." Men were attracted to her wealth but not too often to her. She never had an interest in marriage or children and as an only child was spared the nuisance of nieces and nephews. Sex was of little interest to her. Instead, she sublimated with an abnormal passion for the opera influenced when she was a young girl by the late Greek soprano Maria Callas. Cylla maintained a box at the Metropolitan Opera and had a superb collection of CDs, LPs, seventy-eights and tapes. There was always music in her house, as her father insisted there always should be. Tea was accompanied by *Ariadne auf Naxos*, though Hiram Wiggs would have preferred Aretha Franklin or Peggy Lee. Having served the tea, the maid departed quickly and silently.

Their conversation resumed at the very point the maid had interrupted it. Hiram Wiggs spoke. "To repeat, in case during this brief intermission you've forgotten, you're sailing into dangerous waters."

"You don't want me to sever my ties to Kao Lee because they're so highly profitable."

"He's a dangerous adversary. Nobody wants an enemy like Kao Lee. You know he's ruthless. He murdered his brother because he wanted his wife, and now there's the suspicion he'd like to be rid of the wife."

Cylla made an unpleasant noise of derision. "Why the hell people bother to get married any longer I'll never understand. Marriage is as obsolete as the bobby pin. And those idiots who divorce and then remarry! Masochists, every bloody one of them." She put her cup and saucer on an end table.

"Cylla . . ."

"What?"

"You must order the ships to meet the *Green Empress*."

"He has not paid me my share of the last two shipments." Her eyes were blazing. "I'm in the hole for much too much and I'm not going in any deeper."

"Kao's nephew is on the ship."

"He's not my worry."

"He will be if something happens to cause his death. If the ships don't rendezvous as expected, Michael could very well run the freighter aground. That will mean the Coast Guard. Police helicopters. Newsreels. Television coverage. The kind of hullabaloo you don't need or want."

"That's Kao's worry."

Hiram got to his feet, agitated. "Damn it, Cylla. That freighter is part of your fleet!"

"It should have been scrapped years ago when I wanted it and the others scrapped. But it was *you* who talked me out of it. They were still seaworthy, you insisted. They can be used for smuggling illegal aliens. Big new business. Every little punk chink in Chinatown was into smuggling. Thirty-five thousand dollars a head." Her hands were gesticulating all over the place and in every direction. Her olive skin was tinged with traces of blazing red anger. "So I listened to you because my father taught me to trust my lawyer, and you were my father's lawyer to boot. Why did I listen to you? I didn't need the money. I didn't need it then and I certainly don't need it now!" She scowled at her cup of tea. She thought for a moment. "I'll offer to buy Kao out."

Wiggs snorted. "He won't sell."

"How do you know? It's obvious he's hurting. If he can't pay me, then he's not paying a lot of other people. We know the Warehouse is hanging by a thread. The only thing about Kao we can trust is Harry Jen, the little pig."

"Don't be ungrateful, Cylla. He has served you well. And as to offering to buy Kao out, what does he have that you want or need? His gambling house? His whorehouses? The smuggling? Don't be ridiculous, Cylla. Up until the recent deficiencies, you did extremely well by Kao Lee. At the time, therefore, my advice was sound advice. It was highly profitable. Now, dear girl, calm down and listen to reason."

She refilled their cups with a steady hand and then settled back into her armchair. "I have calmed down and I'm waiting to hear some reason."

He said quietly, "Kao is headed for a fall. A very big fall."

"You sound so sure of yourself."

"I am very sure of myself. We have the same astrologer."

"Oh please! Not that mumbo jumbo again!"

"Madame Khan is a respected practitioner. I trust her implicitly. And, Cylla dear, for the right price, she can prove very useful. She tells me everything she tells him, and from time to time she tells him things I want her to tell him."

Cylla smiled. "You adorable scoundrel."

Wiggs smiled back. "I learned at an early age how to fight fire with fire. Find your adversary's weak spots and go to work on them and continue to work on them. Astrology blinds Kao Lee. He believes everything Madame Khan tells him. And I believe everything Madame Khan tells me about him."

"You must be paying her a great deal, you poor sap."

"I'm a rich sap, honey. A very rich sap. Madame Khan supports a very large clan of Khans here and in Asia. She has large holdings in Hong Kong that have to be taken care of before the Chinese reclaim it. She has holdings in Shanghai and Macao."

"Hey! Why don't I?"

"For crying out loud, Cylla. You have holdings everywhere but Tibet and Miami. You have holdings in places missionaries haven't heard of. Madame Khan gave Kao Lee a reading today. What she told him was a pack of lies because she didn't dare tell him the truth. She drew up a phony chart, read it to him and he bought it because he buys everything she tells him. The truth is, Cylla, Kao Lee is in for a hard time, a very hard time. His planets are about to turn against him."

"Sort of like a sit-down strike?"

"Let things ride out. Send the ships to the *Green Empress*."

"I can't now."

"Why not? There's the phone."

"They're dispersed. I ordered them out of my marina."

"My dear Cylla. This is awful. You're sending over three hundred innocents to their deaths."

Cylla contemplated the enormity of the situation. Then she said, "I'm sure some of them can swim. Don't you think?"

"Ouch!"

Harry Jen felt a sharp pain in his thigh as he entered the subway station. He leaned against a wall looking from right to left and back again. The pain smarted. Harry rubbed his thigh. It didn't help. In agony, he climbed the stairs back to the street. The rain had stopped and the pain was lessening. He pulled his handkerchief from his pocket and mopped the perspiration. On the opposite side of the street, he did not see Nick Wenji, under a green umbrella, hailing a cab to take him downtown. Harry was beginning to feel faint. He mopped his brow again and hailed a cab. He gave the driver the address of Cylla's town house. He slumped back against the seat. The driver looked in his rearview mirror and hoped the fat chink wasn't going to get sick and throw up all over the back of the cab.

• • •

Cylla was pacing back and forth in the drawing room. Hiram Wiggs sat at a table on which rested his briefcase and several documents. Cylla looked at her wristwatch. "Harry should be here any minute now."

Wiggs said, "I don't like that man. He's much too oily."

"True, but he's reliable," countered Cylla. "There's the doorbell." It was a very melodious doorbell, "The Cry of the Valkyries." She examined herself in a wall mirror and Hiram Wiggs watched her and wondered why she had to look her best for a lowly informer. He heard the butler shouting for help, and he and Cylla hurried to the foyer. Harry Jen lay on the floor, face drenched with perspiration and contorted in agony. She asked the butler, "What happened to him?"

"I don't know, madam! I opened the door and he must have been leaning against it. He fell in."

"Shut the door!" commanded Cylla. Hiram and the butler dragged Harry to one side, and the butler slammed the door shut. Cylla knelt at Harry's side. "Harry! Harry! What happened?"

"My thigh," he mumbled, "my thigh." He groaned as his head lolled to one side.

Hiram asked, "What do we do now?"

Cylla was standing and thinking fast. "You have to get him to a hospital."

The butler asked, "Shall I dial 911?"

"No!" cried Cylla. "You have to get him out of here. No 911. No police." She said to the butler, "Get a cab. Hurry." The butler went into the street in search of a cab. Cylla said to Wiggs, "The two of you take him to New York Hospital's emergency room. Say he collapsed on the street." She opened the door to a hall closet and found a raincoat. "This is for the butler. Hide his uniform."

Harry Jen was having difficulty breathing. Wiggs said, "Christ, I think he's dying."

Cylla said with impatience, "He picked a fine time to die." The butler returned. The cab was at the curb, its motor purring. He put on the raincoat.

The butler and Wiggs had a struggle getting the chubby Asian on his feet. Cylla said, "If there are any questions, just say he was here for an interview as houseboy and suddenly collapsed."

"Good thinking," gasped Wiggs. Cylla ignored the compliment as she held the door open and watched Wiggs and the butler haul Harry Jen down the front steps and into the taxi.

Cylla shut the door and went back to the drawing room. She aborted *Ariadne auf Naxos* and, by way of a requiem for Harry Jen, selected the Oriental-themed *Turandot* as the replacement. *My thigh. My thigh.* She could not wipe from her mind the agony in Harry Jen's voice. The awful look on his face. The heavy perspiration. If he had been stabbed, there should have been blood, but there was no blood. She did a breathing exercise to calm herself. She carefully arranged and rearranged her troubled thoughts until they were neat and orderly. Now it all seemed exquisitely clear to her. Harry Jen was the target of an assassin. Kao Lee must have had proof Harry was divulging secrets about him and ordered him done away with. Undoubtedly Harry was also a police informer. God, the police had so many of them, Cylla wondered what would happen if they all got together and unionized.

The *Green Empress.* Harry Jen. Were they omens of Kao Lee's downfall or a lot of trouble for Cylla Mourami? Patience, she told herself, patience. It will all soon fall in place and in good time. She began another breathing exercise.

The Coast Guard had been alerted. A freighter was foundering off the coast of Long Island's Far Rockaway Beach. Boats and helicopters were rushing to the rescue. The media was alerted. Television and radio crews tore out to the area that had once been one of New York City's most popular summer beach resorts. A small army of reporters and photographers were on their way. It had been a dull week of the usual: middle European civil wars, massacres by machete in central Africa and another serial rapist on the loose on the Upper West Side. But here was a freighter reportedly carrying a human cargo of illegal Chinese aliens—there were bound to be some juicy scenes of bodies washing up on the shore and a great shot of the freighter itself going down for the last time. Nothing as spectacular as the sinkings of the *Lusitania* and the *Titanic*, but these days one couldn't be too choosy.

Albert West and Christy Lombardo were in an unmarked police car with a siren on the roof caterwauling like a banshee out of hell. Although Far Rockaway was out of his jurisdiction Christy saw no reason for them not to be there as curious spectators.

"That son of a bitch better be okay," said Albert speaking fondly of Pharoah Love.

"That son of a bitch had better be among the passengers," said Lombardo.

"There's that too," said Albert. "By the way . . ."

"What?"

"What direction is Far Rockaway?"

The *Green Empress* was listing to one side. It had struck a sand bar shortly after Michael Lee ordered the boat grounded at gunpoint. He at least recognized his responsibility to Tisa Cheng and ordered her to stay at his side. She was too frightened to even think of disobeying. Pharoah had disappeared below deck to retrieve his duffel bag. He had to fight his way down against a frightening onslaught of terrified Asians fearful of dying a watery death. They scratched and clawed at each other, punched and kicked and crawled over each other. His clothes torn, his face bruised, his ponytail a near shambles, Pharoah made it to the cabin he shared with the enforcers. He found his duffel bag and hastily rummaged through its contents. The Glock 9mm was there. Pharoah pulled it out and tucked it in his belt. There was nothing else he wanted. The bag stank. The boat stank. Pharoah could hear screams from above and hoped Tisa Cheng was safe with Michael Lee.

Topside, the enforcers were loosening a lifeboat. They got it free and over the side, but as they attempted to climb in, the lifeboat tipped and two enforcers hurtled downward into the icy, forbidding waters. Overhead, police helicopters flashed light on the scene while news helicopters had a field day recording the tragic excitement below. Onshore there were ambulances and rescue crews trying to be of some help. Four Coast Guard boats stood at the ready to rescue as many illegals as possible.

The panicking Asians in the water tore at each other's faces and some who couldn't swim pulled others down to a watery grave. A young woman cried for help but her pleas fell on seemingly deaf ears. Michael Lee wondered what had become of crazy Archie Lang. He grabbed Tisa by the hand and led the frightened woman to the main deck, where there might be the hope of utilizing one of the remaining lifeboats. They were a good distance from the shore, and some of the hardier victims decided to try and swim for it.

So did Pharoah Love.

Albert West and Christy Lombardo had to argue with a young cop before he accepted their shields and let them through the police lines. They had to fight their way past the press and onlookers and local residents who were crowding the beach. It was an overcast night, and the half moon and the stars were of little use as far as illumination was concerned. Albert shouted in Christy's ear, "We'll never find Pharoah in this mess!"

Christy said nothing but pushed onward toward the shoreline. He could see arms flapping in the water at a distance, which meant some brave souls were desperately trying to make it to the beach. Stupid sons of bitches. The Far Rockaway undertows were notoriously dangerous. He himself had lost a brother out there years ago when they were kids. "Oh my God!" cried Albert. "Look! Look at the bodies floating face downward! They're dead!"

"Or disinterested," said Lombardo, wondering why the hell they had bothered to drive out here in the first place.

The Coast Guard were doing a commendable rescue job, especially considering the fear and hysteria they had to deal with. One young sailor had the good fortune to rescue three pretty young things in a row. The third, Tisa Cheng, was particularly delectable, but unfortunately, she referred to the man clambering up the Jacob's ladder behind her as her boyfriend.

Michael and Tisa along with the other survivors on board sank to the deck breathing heavily and grateful for the postponed reunion with their ancestors.

"Archie!" Tisa sobbed the name. "I wonder where's Archie!"

Michael also wondered as he stared around at the other survivors. There couldn't have been more than thirty or so. The Coast Guard spotlight was sweeping the water for more survivors. Perhaps the other boats had picked up his enforcers. He knew nothing of the unfortunate incident with the lifeboat. Tisa put an arm through his and he was gentleman enough to pat her hand reassuringly. He had to believe he had done the right thing in grounding the boat. It would be a while before he'd know what the body count would be, but whatever it would be, he would have to live with it. He fought back tears. He thought of his mother. He thought of Kao. He wondered what he'd do with Tisa. He wondered about the police and didn't worry too much because his uncle had powerful political connections. Then his thoughts returned to Archie Lang. Had he survived? Was Archie Lang safe?

Pharoah Love alternated between dog paddling and floating on his back toward shore. He knew the danger of hypothermia but knew if he kept his body moving, the risk of hypothermia was minimized. He thought of Esther Williams and sang "Baby, It's Cold Outside," which had been featured in one of her pictures. He sang "Pagan Love Song" and for a little amusement warbled "By a Waterfall." By way of a memorial to some of his former shipmates who he was sure hadn't been fortunate enough to survive, he sang "I'd Like to Get You on a Slow Boat to China."

Joke's over. He was cold. His limbs were beginning to feel numb. Dear God, any death but drowning in the waters off Far Rockaway. Pharoah Love deserves a choicer location. Acapulco. Marbella. Copacabana. God help me, Laguna Beach. But this? What if they never find my body? What if I'm eaten by the fish? The crabs? The eels? He'd been floating on his back and he was exhausted. He forced himself into an upright position. He was breathing heavily, and then he was laughing.

He was standing up.

I made it, by Christ, I made it. He sloshed his way out of the water onto the beach, where he sank to his knees. He then sat, breathing heavily. He wondered how far it was to the nearest subway station, even though he didn't have a token. He got to his feet and wandered toward the crowd of people on the beach in the distance, guided by the helicopter spotlights. The Glock 9mm was still safe inside his belt. Thank God. Very expensive issue.

Albert West and Christy Lombardo walked from corpse to corpse as they had been laid out on the beach. The local police had been sympathetic and helpful when Lombardo described Pharoah Love to them, his ponytail, his earring. But nobody alive or dead so far fit his description.

Then Albert saw two civilians assisting a sorry sight staggering between them. Slowly they came closer and the light was better. Albert gasped, "Pharoah?" Lombardo's head shot around. "Pharoah?" yelled Albert as he and Lombardo started running.

"Oh thank God!" cried Pharoah, "oh thank God!" He told his Good Samaritans, "They're from the mother house." Then he mustered his strength and yelled, "Quick, babies, quick! Get me to a Big Mac and a double pistachio milk shake before I *plotz!*"

CHAPTER **5**

In the taxi in which Hiram Wiggs and Cylla's butler, Goren, were transporting Harry Jen to New York Hospital's emergency room, the lawyer was very swiftly going through Harry Jen's pockets, transferring Jen's wallet and anything that might help identify him to Wiggs's pockets. Goren said nothing. He was a silent butler. He'd seen Harry Jen several times before and suspected he was of dubious character. At the hospital, Wiggs sent Goren into the emergency room for a wheelchair or a gurney. A gurney was provided with two attendants who quickly and professionally moved Harry Jen out of the taxi and onto the gurney. As they hurried Harry Jen up the ramp that led into the emergency room, the lawyer hustled the butler back into the taxi and directed the driver back to Cylla's town house, where Hiram rewarded him with two twenty-dollar bills. The driver winked at Wiggs, a very willing conspirator, and took off as Wiggs and Goren entered the house.

Cylla was in the drawing room sipping a very dry sherry as she listened to taped selections from *Der Rosenkavalier.* She thanked Goren, who withdrew to whatever sanctuary town houses offer butlers. "Any problems?" she asked Wiggs.

"None. I think he was dead when we arrived. Don't worry. They can't trace him back here. I emptied his pockets." Wiggs placed the contraband on the coffee table.

"What about the cabdriver? He could be a problem."

"I gave him a forty-buck tip. The way he winked at me I thought it was a prelude to a marriage proposal." He sank into an armchair and exhaled. "I think I rate a large vodka on small rocks. Have you heard from Kao?"

"He's called twice. I instructed the maid to tell him I was out to dinner."

"Cylla, meet him head-on." He meant business.

"Meaning?"

"Tell him straight out why you canceled the ships for the rendezvous. There's no point in beating around the bush. Kao can be dangerous, but so can you."

"Damn Harry Jen. I demanded his presence because I wanted to know how much the police knew about my affiliation with Kao Lee."

"I'll take care of the police. It will be the usual line: I'm your lawyer and I arrange all your business transactions. I arrange deals in your name all the time. You haven't all that much of a head or patience for big business. You pay your executives generously to handle the shipping business. You dutifully attend board meetings and meetings with your lawyer and your financial advisers. You are an international phenomenon and if you had to keep tabs on everything that is in your name, you'd suffer frequent breakdowns."

He finally paid attention to the glass of vodka over ice she had placed on the coffee table. He took a healthy swig and then settled back for a moment to treasure the joy of the liquor beginning to course through his veins. "Ah," he said softly, and then again, "Ah," and they heard the phone ring. "If it's Kao Lee, I'll speak to him."

Goren entered carrying a phone. "Are you in to Mr. Lee?"

Cylla told him Hiram Wiggs would speak to him. Goren plugged the phone cord into the wall near Wiggs and placed the phone within the lawyer's reach. Wiggs cleared his throat and braved the phone. "Hello, Kao. This is Hiram Wiggs. Cylla is unavailable."

In his office in the Warehouse, Kao Lee shouted into the phone while Nick Wenji stared at the television set where the *Green Empress* disaster had preempted the scheduled programming. "That damned woman!" yelled Kao Lee, "that miserable bitch! She's responsible for this! Turn on your set, God damn it and see for yourself. The freighter's aground! It's listing! It could break up!"

Wiggs instructed Goren to turn on the set while he calmly asked Kao Lee, "What channel?"

"Every channel!" shouted Kao Lee.

Cylla Mourami was appalled by what she was watching. She couldn't believe herself responsible for the tragedy. The TV cameras spared nothing, the human flotsam and jetsam struggling in the ocean, the screams of agony and despair and the cries for help. Much of what she was watching was a replay of events shown earlier, but still, it was powerful and sickening.

"My nephew! My wife's son! He was on the boat! I have no word of him! If he's dead, I swear I will destroy Cylla!"

Cylla took the phone from Wiggs in time to hear Kao Lee's threat. She said sharply, "You should have thought of that when you were shortsheeting me! You owe me hundreds of thousands! I held back my ships to teach you a lesson!" What he was shrieking was almost gibberish. Cylla shouted back. "I didn't put your nephew on the ship, you did! I don't understand a word you're saying, you damn fool! Cool it! There's always a good chance your nephew's been rescued!" She paused. "Kao, I didn't personally lease you the ship. I know next to nothing about my company's transactions. And once my ships are leased, I don't question how they are to be used or what cargoes they're to transport. I haven't the vaguest idea what you're talking about. Me traffic in illegal alien smuggling?" She laughed, the mean and ugly laugh she usually reserved for displeasure with her hair stylist. "Kao, I'm a very respected pillar of society. I rub elbows with the mayor and the governor and the president of the United States. And you're a notorious gangster, the Chinese godfather, a ruthless racketeer."

Lena Wing was now with Kao and Nick. She asked Nick, "Who's he talking to?" Nick told her. Lena folded her arms and waited for Kao to conclude his tirade at Cylla. It ended abruptly as he slammed the phone down. He lit a cigar. Then he addressed Lena and Nick. "I want you to get the word out fast. To everybody in the Chi Who." He hit the desk with his fist as he said with machine-gun rapidity, "Collect collect collect collect. Get every nickel owed us by the families of all the scum on board the freighter. I don't care if they died or survived. A deal is a deal and it must be honored. They don't pay us, then we kidnap them or their kids or their mommas and their poppas and hold them to ransom. No mercy! You hear me? No mercy!" He was on his feet, waving the obscenely long cigar like a baton. "The Fuk Ching! They knew how to collect!"

Lena Wing said, "Fuck them, they're wiped out. The Feds have Ah Kay, and there's no hope of their getting their act together again."

"I don't give a damn about Ah Kay. Just another snotty kid who ran lucky for a while. I'm Kao Lee!" He thumped his chest. "When I yell, all Chinatown dances." He stared at the set with its muted sound, turned down when he phoned Cylla Mourami. "Get the word out. Pay or die."

Lena told him, "The Feds are putting all the survivors behind bars. They're going to deport them back to Fujian. I suppose some will seek asylum from political persecution."

Kao assured her, "They'll lose a lot of them. If they make it to shore, they'll slip away under the cover of darkness. Damn clever some of these people. I hope Michael's one of them. If anything happens to him, I'll never hear the end of it."

Lena asked, "And Harry Jen?"

Nick spoke softly. "He's no longer with the firm."

"That's the trouble with this organization," said Lena, "nobody ever gets to give two weeks' notice." Her voice darkened. "And Cylla Mourami?"

Kao was back seated at his desk. "She'll take careful handling." He stared at the lit tip of his cigar. "And I'll do the handling."

Hiram Wiggs did not consider cheese, fruit and crackers a proper dinner, but that's what Cylla provided. It was the most expensive cheese, fruit and crackers Cylla's money could buy, but Hiram would still have preferred pheasant under glass or a one-pound sirloin steak smothered in mushrooms and onions or at the very least some Chinese take-out, which, under the circumstances, had been an unfortunate suggestion, which Cylla vetoed vehemently. "With Harry Jen dead, we'll have to find a replacement," said Cylla as she very carefully cut a luscious green pear into sections and then helped herself to a soggy wedge of rich Camembert cheese.

"What about Lena Wing?" asked Wiggs, nibbling cheddar and wondering what mice saw in it. "She wants to own a restaurant of her own. I think she'd find an offer to back her very tempting."

"That's just what this city desperately needs," said Cylla, lacing each word with venom, "another effing Chinese restaurant. Let's let it ride for a while. Kao will be very busy for a while sorting out the disaster." She sat back as she chewed slowly. "He's going to make some stupid moves."

"You think so?"

"If what you say about his finances is true, then he's bound to be desperate."

"Oh, it's true all right. He's made some financial blunders in Asia that have him staggering. He's no match for those money wizards in Hong Kong and Shanghai." He brushed a crumb from his vest. "I think Kao answers to somebody higher up."

"Of course you don't mean Buddha," she said wryly.

"Cylla, everybody has to have a beginning. You're one of the lucky ones. You inherited and thanks to me and your financial advisers, you're in splendid condition. I had a mentor. A very shrewd Jew who taught me his tricks of the trade because he believed in me. He's dead now, but in his lifetime, I never let him down and he left me his business. But then there are the self-made types like Kao Lee. Twenty years ago he was a small-time hood, a hatchet man who murdered on assignment."

"Brrr. A chill's just gone up my spine."

"A very splendid spine, if I may say so."

"Now that you've said it, forget it and get back to Kao."

"Kao the hatchet man. He got his start in San Francisco with the notorious Black Fang. Some very imposing mysterious deaths are attributed to him. Then he got a taste for kidnapping. Wealthy merchants, restaurant owners and such. In time, his business was beginning to get too big for him, so he sent for his younger brother, Zang. Zang arrived from China with his lovely wife, Rhea, and their infant son, Michael. The family thrived. Zang had a pleasant touch of the bloodthirsty in him. This pleased his brother tremendously. When things got too hot in San Francisco, Kao moved fast. He headed them all to New York after first moving his monetary assets here. It was a smart move but he didn't know it at the time. New York was in the depths of one of its usual real estate recessions and Kao began buying up just about everything in sight, including the infamous Warehouse on Catherine Slip. But Kao overextended himself and needed an investor to cover him."

"And with his usual luck, he found one."

"It is said brother Zang, of all people, found this mysterious investor. It was this person who thought up the scheme to smuggle illegal aliens, a scheme needless to say that appealed to Kao's greed. There was soon an epidemic of smuggling operations, but it seems there were so many Chinese desperate to escape their homeland shackles that everyone prospered. But in time Kao, like some of the others, needed fresh injections of cash, and I brought you into it. But long before your entrance, my dear, while Michael was still a child, Kao fell madly in love with Zang's wife, Rhea."

"Rhea for ostrich," said Cylla.

"Yes, Rhea for ostrich. But she didn't hide her head in the sand. Brother Zang died suddenly, somewhat mysteriously, and Rhea was free to marry Kao."

"She was in love with Kao?"

"I don't think so. But it was expedient on her part to marry him. Kao was rich and there was Michael to rear. Zang left her very little— Kao wasn't all that generous with his little brother."

Goren brought them small cups of espresso and then departed. "Kao was very fond of his nephew, now his stepson. Michael, amazingly enough, unlike Mr. Shakespeare's Hamlet, who was in a similar situation, was equally as fond of his very rich uncle, who then took him under his wing and groomed him as his possible successor. Michael, unfortunately, doesn't have all that much substance between his ears, but he's eager and game for just about anything. Which is why he volunteered to lead the enforcers on the *Green Empress*'s ultimate and not so very golden voyage. I mean, it's not as though he was

Jason in search of the Golden Fleece. Of course, this impressed Kao—the boy was showing he had balls by wanting the firsthand experience of those god-awful trips. I rather like Michael. I hope he's safe." He sipped his espresso. "I wonder what happened when the hospital called in the police to help solve the mystery of poor old Harry Jen."

In his walk-up apartment on West Fifty-fifth Street between Ninth and Tenth avenues, Pharoah Love soaked in a bathtub while Albert West and Christy Lombardo urged him to shake a leg so they could get back to the precinct downtown and get the latest on the *Green Empress* disaster. Pharoah's TV was tuned in to the CNN channel, which was promising to continue the coverage of the event for the remainder of the night. Christy had phoned his precinct to advise them as to his whereabouts and was told that Harry Jen had been murdered. "Shit," said Christy under his breath, but Albert heard him. Christy listened to the details and then said into the phone, "Let Kao Lee or one of his minions know, though I'm sure it'll come as no surprise. Maybe they'll even claim the body after the autopsy." He hung up and said to Albert, loud enough for Pharoah to hear while scrubbing away the filth of the freighter, "Harry Jen is dead. His body was dumped at the New York Hospital emergency room late this afternoon. Pockets stripped. They identified him through his prints. He was brought to the hospital in a cab—on which there's a tracer—by two Caucasians, described by the hospital attendants as middle-aged, one wore a raincoat and the other was smartly suited. Apparently, the attendant has an eye for good tailoring. Tracing the cab won't be all that easy unless we attach a reward to Harry, and Harry ain't even worth five bucks."

"Less," yelled Pharoah from the bedroom. "I heard he brought popcorn to his brother's funeral. Be ready in ten minutes!"

A few seconds later he stuck his head out the door. "What are you two dudes wearing? I don't want us to clash." His head disappeared, and they could hear dresser drawers opening and shutting and then a

closet door being opened and hangers being pushed back and forth as
Pharoah selected his attire for the night. Albert prayed it wouldn't be
the purple pantaloons imported from Italy at great expense and little
taste.

Christy said to Albert, "I had a feeling we were soon to lose Harry.
He was getting too cocksure. I also don't think we were his only
clients."

"Probably not. We know Kao Lee has some silent and maybe some
not so silent partners. They'd want to keep tabs on Kao. I know I
would if I had some dealings with him."

Christy was thinking aloud. "Brought to the hospital by two white
civilians. Stands to reason he dropped in on these guys."

"You think they offed him?"

"If they did, they'd be damn dumb to deliver him to the hospital.
They'd dump him in some alleyway or something." He thought again.
"New York Hospital. Upper East Side. Mostly a very classy neighborhood. Stands to reason Harry got it in the vicinity." He scratched his
chin. "I'll bet Kao has an idea who killed him, once he hears he's been
iced."

"Maybe Kao did it himself."

"Don't be daft," said Christy Lombardo. "Kao's the big cheese now.
He delegates his dirty work." He laughed. "Boy, does Kao have big
trouble now. The Feds have brought the curtain down on the Fuk
Ching gang. They'll be feeling their oats. They'll be after Kao's Chi
Who now."

Pharoah entered from his bedroom wearing Levi's with large paint
stains, the Levi's jeans torn at the knees. He wore a hot-pink T-shirt
on which was printed I'M A GOOD GIRL, LAST NIGHT DOESN'T COUNT.
On his head he wore a purple beret with a red tassel dangling from its
center. He had on a green blazer, which he wore over the T-shirt, to Albert's and Christy's relief. "Ta da!" cried Pharoah, flinging his arms
wide. They saw the Glock 9mm handgun tucked under his belt and

watched as—while whistling through his teeth—he went to a desk, took a tin cash box from a drawer, opened it and drew out a wad of bills.

"Is it dutch treat again, you skinflints, or is the department paying?" He didn't wait for an answer. "So chubby, sweaty Harry Jen finally bought it. Poor Harry. Is there anyone to mourn him?"

CHAPTER **6**

The dilapidated pickup truck wended its way arthritically toward the Queens-Midtown Tunnel. The woman at the wheel was named Hattie Reilly. She was transporting crates of fresh fish to the Fulton Fish Market. She had stopped briefly to watch the goings-on on the beach involving the stranded freighter, between gulps from a can of diet cola. There was a maelstrom of confusion as a number of the illegals, after debarking from the Coast Guard cutter, ran off in all directions. Michael held tight to Tisa's hand as he steered her toward several parked cars. The pungent odor of fish overwhelmed them, and they heard a rasping voice asking, "Hey! What's going on down there? What's all the fuss?"

"A freighter ran aground," Michael told her.

"Is that all? They're always running aground out here. Why all the helicopters and the searchlights? I thought they were maybe a movie company on location."

"There's TV cameras," said Michael, hoping he was a picture of innocence if a bit light on information. "We drove out here with another couple, but in all the excitement we've lost them."

Hattie eyed Michael and Tisa with suspicion. Tisa's damp hair hung in lacy strings while one of Michael's shirtsleeves was ripped. "Where you from?"

"Downtown Manhattan. Chinatown."

"I mean where you coming from now?"

"We were down on the beach. We were horsing around a little. Then we saw the freighter hit . . ." He paused in his improvisation. She didn't seem to be buying their story. She held the soft drink can in a tight grip while she studied their faces. "And then—"

Hattie interrupted. "Sonny, you're full of shit. It's a lucky thing you're feeding that line of crap to me and not to some crummy police sergeant. I don't like the police. They railroaded my husband up the river on a two-to-five rap for transporting illegal cigarettes up here from Virginia. I heard all about the freighter on my radio. You're off the freighter, ain'tcha?"

"I live in New York," said Michael.

"Sure you do."

"That's the truth." He bowed his head toward Tisa. "This is my fiancée." Tisa managed a smile.

"Cute. A little waterlogged, but cute."

"Maybe you heard of my uncle."

"I did if his name is Sam."

"His name is Kao Lee."

Her eyes widened in recognition. "That's real big time, sonny."

"Lady, if you drive us to Chinatown, I'll guarantee you'll be handsomely rewarded." Police cars were racing back and forth on the nearby road. Michael knew if they remained in the area much longer they were in danger of being detected.

"The *Daily News* horoscope, that Jillson broad, she said this would be my lucky day. I'm a Libra."

Michael was encouraged. "My uncle lives by the stars."

"Oh yeah?" She tossed the can away.

"He's a Gemini."

Her voice went up an octave. "No kidding! Gemini and Libra is very compatible." She thought for a moment. "Are very compatible. I should have married a Gemini, but I settled for a Virgo and . . ." She smiled. "Get in." They went around to the other side, and she opened the door for them. Tisa climbed in and sat between Hattie Reilly and Michael. "Christ," Hattie said as she revved the motor, "I can't tell if I'm smelling you two or the fish. Lower your window, sonny."

In the unmarked police car, Albert West and Christy Lombardo, who sat next to him, listened to Pharoah's story emerge from the backseat. They were headed downtown on the West Side Highway, where the traffic was unusually heavy. Pharoah's voice was heavier. He finally summed it up with: "Guys, I have read about human misery, I've seen it on the tube, I've seen it in streets, but I've seen nothing as miserable as what I took part in on the *Green Empress.*"

"You don't have to tell us, Pharoah. We know. We've read the testimonies of all the illegals we collared in the past."

"I hope the Lee kid made it. And Tisa Cheng. His girlfriend. He found her in a dive on the waterfront. She was singing, which is me being very polite. Very cute, though." He was staring out the window at the twinkling lights of New Jersey across the Hudson River. He was glad to be home, such as home was. Christy and Albert had told him of the shame brought to the department by over forty rogue cops. Miserable bandits hustling drug dealers out of thousands of dollars, covering up for them, warning them when raids were impending. Breaking into drug dealer apartments and robbing them of cash, jewelry, fur coats and appliances. A world gone mad, a city gone madder.

"Pharoah, you're too quiet all of a sudden."

"Gee, guys, do you remember when being a cop used to be fun?"

"Pharoah, there was never anything fun in being a cop. It's almost my twenty-fifth anniversary and I hunger for retirement."

"You'll go berserk," said Pharoah. "Your adrenaline will dry up. You might even go bad. You might start molesting teenage girls."

"Dry up!" muttered Christy. "Jesus, molesting teenage girls!"

"Okay, so molesting teenage boys. Albert, you turn off here!"

"All right, all right! I see it!" They made it onto Canal Street by the skin of their teeth.

A few blocks farther to the east, Hattie Reilly was steering her pickup truck toward Catherine Slip. By now she felt as though Michael and Tisa were old pals. "Say, listen, Michael, I'm thinking of bouncing my personal other. I'm fed up with him and I'm fed up with fish. How about your uncle?"

"What about him?"

"Has he got an attachment? You know. Girlfriend. Wife. Things like that."

Michael smiled. "He's got lots of girlfriends."

"Oh"— dejected—"one of those."

"And he's got a wife."

"That figures too."

"He's married to my mother."

"Jesus Christ!" she boomed, "it's a bleeding soap opera!" She slammed on the brakes. "You're home." She reached into her pocket and found a business card, which she handed to Michael. "That's me. Hattie Reilly. Whatever you do, don't send me no candy, no flowers, nothing that isn't negotiable." She stared at Tisa, who had been silent throughout the drive. "Well, kid, happy landing. It was real nice not talking to you." Michael opened the door on his side, got out and then helped Tisa. Hattie slid along the seat and pulled the door shut. "Michael." He looked up at Hattie. "My instincts tell me you're a nice guy, Michael. This smuggling crap is crap. I know you're both off the freighter and you're going to be dodging the boys in blue for a long time. Try something legitimate. There's no tomorrow working for your uncle. You're young, kid. That's your biggest advantage." She winked, gunned the motor and took off.

Michael took Tisa's hand and hurried her to the Warehouse.

"Hail the conquering hero!" shouted Pharoah as he entered his precinct with Albert and Christy. He asked the desk sergeant, "Darling, any messages?"

The desk sergeant, Rosten by name, made a show of shuffling papers. "Oh yeah. Eight from the Gay Men's Health Chorus, three from your doctor to tell you the bad news. . . ."

Pharoah pressed a fist to his forehead. "Oh God, I can't be preggers again!"

The desk sergeant continued, "And one from Tom Cruise saying he's sorry he can't make it."

"I warned him oxtails take careful preparation." He sauntered into Christy Lombardo's office, where Albert West was tackling the report on Harry Jen's murder. "What you reading, Albert?"

"The report on Harry Jen."

"It can't be. It's not perspiring."

Christy was studying a page from the coroner's office. "This is the coroner's preliminary examination," he said without looking up. Pharoah sank into a chair and sat with his feet stretched out in front of him. "He'll do a full one in the morning. Seems the morgue is running out of space. All them drowned Chinamen."

Pharoah dwelled again on Michael and Tisa. *All them drowned Chinamen.*

Christy looked up. "He found a small wound in Harry's right thigh. He probed around and found a ricin pellet."

"I've heard that song before," said Pharoah. "How do you shoot a pellet into somebody's body without being seen? You can't use a blowgun, they're too clumsy. A peashooter? Too risky, the pellet might leak in your mouth."

Albert asked, "Is that what those pellets do? They leak?"

"They dissolve," said Christy. "The ricin paralyzes the nerves. It can work as fast as this"—he snapped his fingers for emphasis—"or it can take a couple of days."

"So now we have to find us a killer who specializes in ricin," Albert said.

"They say you get quick results if you advertise in the *Times.*" Pharoah then added, "Although I think we'd get better results talking to Kao Lee." Albert had passed him the report on Harry Jen, and Pharoah was scanning it. "Pockets emptied of any ID. Why bother? There are fingerprints on file. Just about everybody gets fingerprinted at least once in their lifetime. Didn't cut out the jacket label. That's easily traced."

"Not always," contradicted Albert. "I had a lot of trouble with a stiff fished out of the East River. The label was some obscure tailor in Spanish Harlem."

"Snob." Pharoah stifled a yawn. He asked Christy, "Do you suppose I should check the morgue and see if they've got Michael Lee in one of their refrigerators by any chance?"

"Pharoah, if the morgue is preparing a list of the dead, it's going to read like a dim sum menu. Once they've rounded up all the illegals or at least the ones they can find, those people will hopefully be able to identify the bodies. By the time the voyage was over, they all knew each other pretty damned well."

"Yes, there was a lot of fraternizing going on—some of it forced. I can imagine what my pastor will say when I report that to *him*." He turned to Christy. "You don't expect me to start typing up my version of *Two Years Before the Mast* tonight?"

"Don't sound so pained," said Christy, "I'm not easily given to tears." His phone rang. He snapped into the mouthpiece, "Lombardo." He listened. "Don't tell me your suspicions, give me names, damn it! I need names!" He slammed the phone down. "Son of a bitch. I recognize the voice. He's called often enough."

"Looking for a date?" asked Pharoah with an air of innocence.

"No, asshole. He keeps telling me we got infections in the precinct. We got rogues. We got bandits." He leaned back. "Says Kao Lee owns one of them."

"Oh, that Kao Lee," bristled Pharoah, "he has one of everything!" He exhaled. "Why don't I have the guts to betray my fellow officers and become filthy rich and get caught and shamed and sent into cold storage for the rest of my life. Don't these guys think?"

"Pharoah, to go on to more pleasant things, you have a date with the Feds tomorrow. They want to hear everything."

"Nosy bastards."

"They're being very accommodating. Two guys will be here tomorrow morning at nine to play Twenty Questions." Lombardo recognized the look on Pharoah's face. It was the same look when the pizza parlor made the mistake of putting anchovies on his pie.

"Nine A.M.! They expect me to spend the night here? Don't they realize I've had an exhausting day? I've been shipwrecked and I almost drowned and all I've had to eat was a lousy burger and a milk shake."

There was a light tap on the door, and Lombardo barked admittance. Detective Hutch Casey came in and asked insincerely, "Am I interrupting anything?"

"Yes," said Pharoah, "I'm having a temper tantrum, and as usual, it's very unbecoming."

"So you're back." Casey held some pages in his hand.

"I'm back. And no hugs and kisses, please. I'm feeling terribly delicate."

Lombardo asked Casey, "What you got there?"

"A preliminary report on the *Green Empress*." He crossed to Lombardo and handed him the pages. Lombardo took the pages and placed them on the desk.

Lombardo asked, "Have you read it?"

"Not much to read yet."

"So tell me what there is so far."

"We were told there would be over three hundred illegals being smuggled in. The Coast Guard has rescued about a hundred and fifty. They're not too sure on the number. They were still picking some out of the drink when this report came in."

"Go on."

"So far, some fifty or sixty drowned. Again, they can't give a clear number. There are no numbers on how many escaped and are roaming around the island."

"Unless they have city maps and can make their way to Mott Street," said Pharoah.

"Unfunny," said Lombardo.

"I'm giving you a fact, Christy," said Pharoah, "some of them have street maps of New York. They also have the addresses and phone numbers of relatives and friends who are waiting to hear from them and to help them. They know where there are safe houses made ready for illegals with little six-by-ten cubbyholes constructed in basements for them to reside in. They know which sweatshops are eagerly waiting to hire them at a dollar an hour, if they're lucky. What restaurants will put them in as dishwashers and waiters for next to nothing an hour but all the moo goo gai pan they can eat. They're very lavish with food. They don't want their employees starving, just poverty stricken and at their mercy. They keep a lot of them prisoners in basements and attics in tumbledown tenements all over the city and the suburbs until the relatives fork over the rest of the money the illegals have contracted to pay. The women mostly end up at houses of prostitution and massage parlors, which are the same difference. Some of them are taught to kill unless they already know how." He paused. "With any luck, there'll be a political dissident or two to fill us in on what's really going on in China. Maybe a dentist or a doctor or a scientist hoarding a cure for cancer. Or maybe a pretty girl with no talent whatsoever but a burning ambition to be a Hollywood star." He stared out the window at a neon light advertising a coffee shop. "After close to two months, I began to understand what it must have been like for my ancestors coming over here on slave ships. But *they* didn't want to make the trip. These poor bastards did. I'll never get the stench of that boat out of my nostrils." He looked at the three men. "And now, guys, will you all forgive me?"

"What for?" asked Albert.

"For not sending any postcards."

CHAPTER 7

It took Rhea Lee just a few months to realize the only good thing about marrying her brother-in-law was she didn't have to alter the monograms on her clothing and linens. She sat in Kao's office clutching her alligator handbag, the TV flickering soundlessly behind her while Kao poured tea for both of them. Kao was having a bad day, and it wasn't in the stars. Or at least if there had been omens Madame Khan kept them from him. The *Green Empress* disaster, the telephone fiasco with Cylla Mourami and her lawyer, the weasel. Jupiter was supposed to be lolling over him as protection. He was beginning to doubt this, unless Jupiter was a pigeon in disguise and gaily using him as a target. He held out a cup of tea to his wife but she waved it away. He was thinking, Still a good-looking woman despite her age, a smart dresser and a mind like a steel trap. He supposed that kind of mind ran in the family. There was her sister, Wilma Joy, who owned a chain of women's dress stores stretching from coast to coast that produced the famous line of Wilma Joy dresses. They saw little of Wilma. She rarely traveled below Fifty-seventh Street, fearing she might contract the bends. Wilma was a genius, and Kao Lee agreed to this begrudgingly. Rhea was the comely one, not Wilma, and Kao considered himself a connoisseur of beautiful women.

He sipped his tea after first lacing it with cognac while wishing his wife's eyes would cease burning holes in his soul, if he possessed a soul. "I told you not to come here. I told you to stay at home."

"You tell me a lot of things except what I'd like to hear. You don't tell me where Michael is."

"I don't know."

"The police might know. Your spies could tell you."

"They haven't reported anything today."

"My son is all I have." Her voice broke, and for a moment he considered the magnanimous gesture of taking her in his arms and comforting her. But he was beyond any display of affection for this woman who had once captivated and bewitched him with a spell that caused him to murder his brother and take possession of his widow. Rhea fumbled in her handbag and produced a handkerchief that she dabbed at her eyes, an empty gesture, as her eyes showed no evidence of tears.

"I realize I mean nothing to you anymore," said Kao, hoping there was an appropriate trace of sadness in his voice.

"This is not the time for our monthly self-recriminations." Her voice grew stern. "You should never have let Michael join the cruise."

"I was very proud when he volunteered. Michael showed admirable bravery."

"Don't give me that crap. Michael is in many ways truly Zang's son. Zang was touched with a bit of idiocy and so is Michael. And so, come to think of it, are you." She crossed her legs, placed her handbag across them, and folded her hands atop the handbag. "I've asked you time and again and you never answer me. Are you sure there isn't insanity in your family?"

His smile was faint and enigmatic. "My dear Rhea, there is insanity in everybody's family. I have no reason to believe that mine was a special case and spared. Nor yours. There's your sister and her sudden rages. Wilma's a volcano that might any day erupt. There's yourself and your days of continuing silence."

"We ran out of things to say to each other ages ago."

They heard a buzzer, and Kao picked up his private line. "Yes?" He listened and gulped the remainder of his tea. "What about the rest of the crew? The enforcers. My nephew." Rhea leaned forward. "We'll talk again soon." He placed the phone back in its cradle. No cellular phones for him. No newfangled inventions. He actually still used the faithful abacus he kept in a drawer of his desk next to his Brazilian-made .38-caliber Taurus. He chose the gun because Taurus was the sign of the bull.

He shared his news with Rhea. "The captain of the *Green Empress* is dead."

"I see. The old cliché. He went down with his ship."

"On this occasion, not possible, the ship couldn't go down. It was aground on a sandbar. The lifeboat he commandeered sprung a large leak and sank, so we can say he went down with a part of his boat. Most of his crew died with him. My enforcers are also dead. There's no word of Michael."

"God," she whispered.

"The Coast Guard rescued over a hundred people. Michael may have been among them. He's smart enough to save his own skin. Of course, that could mean imprisonment for smuggling illegal aliens." He slammed a fist down on the desk. "Damn those bastards! There are ships sneaking illegals along the coast of Florida and Texas and the

Carolinas. They sneak them into Mexico constantly. All of a sudden they've stepped up their operations along the Long Island coast. That miserable bitch Cylla Mourami!" He slammed his fist down again. "Her treachery is at the bottom of this. Just because I owe her money she orders the small ships not to rendezvous with the *Green Empress*. This is on her head."

"Why didn't you pay her? You've been partners a long time. I thought you liked and trusted each other." He poured himself more tea. She studied his face. There were still laugh lines, though he rarely laughed. Certainly not in her presence. "Kao, are you having financial problems?"

"I always have financial problems!" He waved his arms over his head. "It takes a lot of money to run an empire. The Warehouse isn't making half as much as it used to. The word's out we're under police surveillance. So now the uptown and midtown swells don't come here anymore. All I get are the miserable little fan-tan players and the mahjongg players while my blackjack dealers mostly sit around and read comic magazines. Sometimes they don't even show up for work. Even the kidnapping and the extortion has fallen off. Do you realize I have over fifty businessmen, merchants and restaurant owners being held captive until their ransoms are paid? Well we're not being paid all that fast, and these sons of bitches eat. God, how they eat!"

"Oh, stop behaving like a demented bandit mandarin and release them."

"Never! It's against my principles. They are responsible for their relatives' passage and they must pay. Some of those I hold in thrall have been sequestered for months. Some of their families have stopped complaining to the tongs. They've stopped complaining to the police. They don't even run ads in our newspapers. It is as though they've reasoned it was Buddha's will that they not be reunited with their loved ones."

She mocked him. "Maybe it's Buddha's will that they haven't the money to pay the ransoms. I know what outrageous sums you demand."

"They keep you in elegant finery and luxurious surroundings."

"Cockroach infested!"

Lena Wing hurried in, excited and happy. "He's here! Michael's here!"

Rhea let out a cry of joy and jumped to her feet as Michael entered and threw his arms around his mother. Kao Lee hurried to Michael's side and clapped a welcoming hand on his stepson/nephew's shoulder. Rhea kissed Michael and emitted small cries of "My son! My Michael!" followed by "And who is this?" somewhat sternly. Tisa had slipped into the room unaware she looked like a drowned mouse.

Rhea quickly sized up what she wrongly supposed was the situation between Michael and Tisa. After all, she reasoned, after two months aboard a ship, she didn't blame Michael for bringing along female companionship. She wasn't a possessive mother.

Tisa bowed three times as was the custom in China and only Kao Lee was sizing her up with interest. Even under the filth his professional eye discerned a looker, despite what was obviously her insignificant breasts. When she bobbed up for the third time, he chucked her under her chin. "What is your name, little one?" Rhea flashed him a look that had a lethal potential.

"I am called Tisa," she said melodically.

Lena Wing saw the look Rhea flashed Kao and hoped Tisa guessed she might be called a few other things before Rhea was through with her.

"Tisa," echoed Kao. "It is so much like 'teaser.'"

Lena folded her arms and leaned against a wall. What an operator, she thought. Up to his armpits in deep shit, yet finds the time to go on the make. Well, why not? On his deathbed she saw her old goat of a grandfather trying to grope his nurse.

"Is Tisa all the name you have?" asked Kao playfully, while Michael silently thanked Buddha that this little albatross looked as though she'd soon be removed from around his neck.

Michael heard his mother saying, "Perhaps it was the only name her family could afford."

Tisa recognized the edge in her voice and quickly understood in Rhea Lee she had the nuisance of an adversary. She cocked her head to one side like a slightly addled canary and said softly, "I am Tisa Cheng. The Chengs are a very exalted family in Fujian." She paused and chose not to elaborate on this as there was the possibility Buddha might paralyze her or even strike her dead for such a huge lie. Her father was serving ten years with hard labor for rustling a pair of water buffalos and her mother was a laundress in a government whorehouse. "I am a singer of songs," she stated as Michael trembled, "and I play the mandolin. I am also a fine seamstress and a reciter of the poems of the great Li Po. I am also an actress and permit me to humbly say I won more than a little acclaim as *Lady Precious Stream*."

And, thought Lena Wing, on the seventh day she rested.

"Undoubtedly a redundant question," said Rhea to Michael, "but what do you propose to do with her?"

Kao interrupted brusquely, "First we must show our good manners and make Tisa Cheng welcome."

"Oh, how I desire to submerge myself in a long, hot bath." For a scary moment Lena Wing thought Rhea was going to volunteer to assist, but instead Michael's mother said to him, "I'm sure you want one too."

"And some food. We're both starving."

"Please," pleaded Tisa, "no apples."

"Apples?" Kao was bemused. "Why apples?"

"That's what Archie Lang stole from the galley for us. The food we ate was swill."

Kao asked Michael, "Who is Archie Lang?"

Michael spoke quickly. "A crew member we picked up in Pusan

when one of the captain's men took off unannounced." He could have kicked himself for not thinking of warning Tisa not to mention Archie Lang. "I saw Nick Wenji downstairs, but where's Harry Jen?"

"Sadly, Harry Jen has left us," said Kao with mock piety. "Perhaps he has had the surprising good fortune to have been sent to a greater pantheon."

"Like maybe the Loew's Pantheon," said Lena Wing dryly.

"You mean Harry's dead?" asked Michael.

"Very," said Lena. Michael's mouth formed an O. She said to Kao, "There are some rooms and baths available next door." Next door was a small hotel, which also doubled as a house of prostitution. Michael demurred, preferring the comfort of his own apartment on West Fourteenth Street, but Kao insisted he bathe and then return to Kao's office for a long talk.

Rhea told Tisa, "Lena will take good care of you."

"We haven't been introduced," said Lena to Tisa. "I'm Lena Wing. I look after things here, when things need looking after." She led Tisa out. Kao went to the door and shut it.

Rhea asked Michael sternly, "Who's the girl?"

"Oh, come on, Ma, I'm only human."

"There's human and there's human. Who is she?"

"She was an entertainer in a dive on the pier in Pusan. She's really a nice kid."

"Did you have to bring her here?"

"Well, Mom, you know the old expression. 'No tickee, no washee.' Me need washee and so I gave her tickee." He cast a sly eye at Kao. "I'm sure she can be of some use around here."

Kao asked, "Has she any talent?"

"On her feet, no."

Kao said gruffly, "We'll work something out. Rhea, I think you should go home."

"You always think I should go home." She looked at her wristwatch. "It's too late for *Barbara Walters*. Anyway, Michael, it's a blessing you're safe. You've been away so long, it would be nice if very soon you reserve some time for me."

"Absolutely, Mom, I promise." He kissed her, and she left without a parting word for Kao. Michael told Kao about Hattie Reilly, the Good Samaritan. Kao assured him he'd send her a check, taking Hattie's business card from Michael and dropping it on the desk.

"Now, listen, Michael. Running the boat aground was a serious error. I'm having enough trouble with the cops as it is."

"It was in the captain's orders, the ones you gave him. It distinctly said if the ships don't rendezvous, scuttle the boat."

"Scuttle, not run her aground! Scuttle means to sink a boat!"

"So the captain was trying to sink the boat and landed on a sandbar instead." He shrugged his shoulders with his hands outstretched. "Kismet!"

"Bullshit! I've got lots of *tsurris*, Michael. Cylla Mourami is acting up. Harry had to be iced because he was stooling for the police *and* for Cylla and God knows who else. Maybe some of the other gangs. It's getting way out of hand. Way, way out of hand. I can't get any of the ransoms paid. With all those illegals that are drowned or in custody, I'll have to renege on my promises to the restaurants and sweatshops. I can't supply the labor I promised."

"And we don't dare lose face," said Michael, not without some irony.

Kao hit the desk with a fist. "The hell with face. We don't dare lose money!"

Pharoah Love stifled a yawn in Christy Lombardo's office. Albert West and Hutch Casey were there along with the precinct captain, Oswald Schmidt, whose name prompted Pharoah to imagine he was descended from a long and irregular line of SS police. Actually,

Schmidt was a good-natured man who treated his men fairly, was usually reasonable and did his best to weed out bad cops who depressingly enough of late were not only proliferating but becoming brazen about it. Only that afternoon in a private meeting with Christy, Albert and the few others in the precinct he could trust as being above suspicion, he pleaded, "Tell me, for crying out loud, tell me, how can Persky afford a Cadillac convertible? And what's with McClelland and that condo in East Hampton?"

"Don't forget Baskin taking his family on a Caribbean cruise. He even asked for extra time off." Christy added glumly, "And I gave it to him."

"We can't take any more of this bad press," insisted Schmidt. "If they start investigating this precinct and come up with our own filth, I could be out on my ass."

Christy tried to look at the bright side. "Maybe these guys will resign. They've got to know there's a whistle-blower in the woodpile."

"Resign hell! They're sure they've got it made!"

And now, hours later, Schmidt confronted the four men he trusted the most, even after asking Pharoah if he was dressed for a masquerade ball. "Now this goddamn *Green Empress* thing!" He turned to Christy. "Didn't Harry Jen say Kao was going to switch his landings to the New Jersey shore?"

"That's what he said. Unfortunately, he is no longer in a position to confirm it." He slapped a fist in the palm of a hand, a gesture borrowed from early gangster talkies. Pharoah grinned. He adored Christy Lombardo. He was such a model of an old-time cop. A delightful throwback who despite his protestations very obviously enjoyed his work. He couldn't envision Christy in retirement. If and when he retired, he'd be underfoot at his precinct making a nuisance of himself. He'd be better off getting killed in action. The trouble was, in his position, Christy didn't see action. He only detailed it. He heard Christy saying, "Pharoah, you did a great job with that trip. You'll impress those two Feds who are coming here tomorrow. But you've got to do more. You were buddy-buddy with Michael Lee."

"Very buddy-buddy. And that's all. Just buddy-buddy."

"Would it worry you to admit to him you were an undercover agent on the voyage?"

"Hell, no. The only reason he didn't recognize me as a sometime patron of the Warehouse is that he's been working mostly out of Kao Lee's so-called legitimate office on East Fourteenth Street. On the other hand, he's never seen me in my more memorable, flashier outfits such as the one I'm wearing now. He saw me only in jeans and a sweatshirt. Believe you me, for two months I felt practically anonymous."

"Kao Lee needs to be questioned. And it's legitimate. Harry Jen was one of his pit bosses. You're investigating his murder. It was undoubtedly ordered by Kao. I want you and Albert to handle this." He turned to Casey. "Something bothering you, Hutch?"

Casey was taken unawares. "What? No. Nothing's bothering me. I guess I'm a little tired."

Pharoah said, "Christy. You're talking like you know Michael survived."

Christy said, "Michael, and a little ortolan named, I believe, Tisa Cheng."

Pharoah fluttered his eyelashes. "You sly boots. Finding a replacement for Harry Jen so quickly. You sometimes move at a startling pace."

"Now, Pharoah, surely you've guessed Harry wasn't our only ringer at the Warehouse. Michael and the girlfriend showed up about an hour ago. They were rescued by a Coast Guard cutter, but in the confusion when landing on shore they escaped."

"Hurray for our side."

"Who's this Tisa Cheng?" asked Captain Schmidt.

"Captain, she is absolutely adorable. An entertainer. A chanteuse. I hope Kao Lee puts her on at the Warehouse. I can't wait for all of you to hear her rendition of 'Stout-Hearted Men.'"

CHAPTER 8

Later, Pharoah was alone with Christy in his office, Albert and Hutch having called it a night, a very long night. Christy poured coffee from a thermos. He said with a smile, "My wife still thinks of things like packing me a thermos and some sandwiches." He took a brown bag from one of his desk drawers. "There's a tired ham and cheese on rye and I think that obscene stuff on pumpernickel is tongue and relish."

"I'd relish some tongue," said Pharoah lazily. Christy handed him the sandwich, which was wrapped in tinfoil, and Pharoah felt as though they were costarring in a television commercial.

"Tell me about the trip."

"You'll hear it tomorrow when I tell the Feds."

"I want to hear it now without the Feds."

Pharoah unwrapped the sandwich. He lifted a slice of bread and stared at the meat and relish. Then as was his usual habit, he smelled it. "Guess it's okay," he muttered.

"What could be wrong with it?"

"Well, it's been in your desk all day, hasn't it?"

"Well, my desk isn't contaminated, for crying out loud!"

"I'm not saying it is. It's just that food lying around all day unrefrigerated can develop dangerous bacteria and that can result in diarrhea . . ."

Christy stormed, "So don't eat the fucking sandwich!"

Pharoah asked in a little boy voice, "Don't you want me to have it, Christy? I'm so hungry I could even eat you."

"Get to the goddamned trip!"

"It was a living hell. The passengers were fed garbage once a day. Worm-infested rice or noodles. Sometimes I saw the worms. Braised. The aliens were cramped together below decks, men and women together. Many of the women were raped." Listening to his own words, he shoved the sandwich aside, having lost his appetite. "There are undoubtedly better toilet facilities in deepest Mongolia, and as for showers, sometimes they worked and mostly they didn't. You soon get used to your own stench. But the stench of the others, that stays with you like an incurable disease." Pharoah returned Christy's sandwich to him.

"The boredom. That's what really gets to you, there were no Scrabble sets. The captain kept away from everyone. I assume he drank his way from Asia. The times we stopped to refuel there was no chance of going ashore. Some of the aliens wanted out but they had no hope. The crew locked them in until we were under way again. There were deaths, the bodies flung overboard. I didn't see them jettisoned but I heard the splashes." Pharoah stood by the window staring outside.

"Michael, the girl, the enforcers, the pilots. We were slightly better off. We had breakfast and dinner, mostly out of cans. I snuck into the galley during the night and stole apples. Those were for Michael, the girl and myself. I sang a lot to myself, not because I was happy, but to remind myself I was still alive."

"What did you learn from Michael?" Christy had rewrapped the tongue sandwich and returned it to the paper bag. Waste not, want not.

"Not as much as I was hoping to, but I did hear some choice items. One thing about Michael I find puzzling. It's obvious Kao Lee murdered Michael's father because at the time he had the hots for Michael's mother and was determined to get her. Kao had imported his brother and family to help out in the business. You know how it is with smuggling aliens, kidnapping, extortion and other exotica; it takes a lot of manpower."

"And a lot of concentration," added Christy.

"When Kao was in a financial hole, it was Zang, surprisingly enough, who came up with a mysterious angel."

"Why mysterious?"

"Because Michael claims nobody knows this person's identity."

"Isn't it Cylla Mourami?"

"Cylla's interest was arranged by her lawyer, Hiram Wiggs."

"Of the Cabbage Patch?"

"Of the Madison Avenue Wiggs. He's a heavy hitter. Big in raising political funds."

"For which side?"

"The one that has the most to offer. He and Mourami are very big with fund-raising. Their pictures are always in the *Times*'s Sunday Style section. They lunch at Mortimer's or La Cirque and are never seen slumming at Joe Allen's. Wiggs is a bachelor."

"Gay?"

"For his sake, I hope not. I've seen his picture. Little guy. I assume when he has sex with someone he goes up on them."

"What about Mourami?"

"Unmarried, and I don't know if she's gay or not. The jury's still out. But you know those Europeans, especially the Mediterraneans and the British. They can swing back and forth like a pendulum."

"Likewise Arabs." He winked. "Likewise American housewives in the suburbs. I read that somewhere."

"To continue, Michael gets the feeling that Kao's hurting financially. He hasn't been paying off of late. So he suspects he and Mourami ain't the bosom buddies they used to be. In fact, today he was positive they aren't because the ships that were to rendezvous with the freighter to unload the aliens never showed up."

"Mourami's ships, I suppose."

"Oh, absolutely. She owns lots and lots and lots of ships, all shapes and sizes. Some in excellent condition. Some in fair condition. Some in awful states of disrepair. The *Green Empress* is one of hers."

"There it is. She's in trouble!"

"Not so fast. The boat is leased to Kao Lee. It's not on loan. You know, she doesn't travel around examining the boats to check on their condition. The boats the freighter was expecting were due to come from a stretch of waterfront she owns along the Long Island coast."

"She owns a mansion in the Hamptons. Very secluded. Heavily guarded. Over the years, docks have been built stretching into navigable water."

"She probably paid plenty for some heavy dredging, though Michael says there's not enough depth for something like a freighter. Just darling little pleasure boats, the sort Joan Crawford used to cruise around in when she played party girls. Anyway the boats don't rendezvous, which means it's Mourami's way of sticking it in Kao's eye. The assumption is he's too far behind in her share of the take."

"Sounds to me that she's the one Kao answers to. She's the one manipulating the strings and calling the shots from backstage."

"I don't see it, Christy."

"Why not?"

"Smuggling, extortion, blackmail, murder. That's Machiavellian."

"Maybe Mafiavellian?"

"Oh, that's adorable, Christy. When I get home I must jot it down in my memory book."

"Piss off."

"No, Christy, the Mafia is clean where the Chinese racketeers are concerned. When necessary, they cooperate. But the unwritten law is they keep to their own turf. So the Asians don't open pizza parlors and the Italians don't open Chinese take-outs."

"Get back to Michael's father. Michael knows Kao murdered him and he isn't looking for an opportunity to avenge his death?" Christy now sat with his feet up on his desk. The precinct was surprisingly quiet for this hour of the night. Possibly the muggers were on a sabbatical.

"I think Kao's fate, as far as Michael is concerned, lies in his mother's hands."

"Do you suppose maybe Mama is the big bok choy behind Kao?"

"Maybe if this was a Monogram Picture, but no, not Mama. Her name's Rhea."

"A rhea's an ostrich," said Christy, which slightly impressed Pharoah. "Maybe that's a clue. Ostriches hide their heads in a hole in the ground, so maybe Rhea's the hidden brains."

Pharoah said with a tired sigh, "Ostriches poke around in holes in the ground looking for worms." He thought for a moment. "You've always suspected we weren't Harry Jen's sole means of support."

"So?"

"Maybe Kao don't tell Rhea much about what's going on in his rackets and she wants to know. Maybe she was slipping Harry a little something on the side so he'd tell her what's going on."

"It doesn't make me want to sing." Christy was tired and looked it.

Pharoah was on his feet and staring out the window. He was thinking hard. "See if this makes you feel like humming." He turned to

Christy, who was making notes on a legal pad. "Mourami's been paying Harry for information."

"Mourami and the lawyer. Whatsisname. Wiggs."

"Yeah," agreed Pharoah, "that's more like it."

"You mean that's more likely."

"Kao's gotten wise to Harry. Someone's tipped off Kao that Harry's on the take and up to no good. Someone in this precinct. Not a happy thought, Christy."

"But the obvious one. One of our bad guys is working for Kao. Who spends a lot of time at the Warehouse?"

"Oh, come on, Christy!"

"Oh, come on what? What?"

Pharoah slumped back into the chair he'd been occupying. "Albert spends a lot of time there. Or used to before I left. Come on, Christy. Not Albert. He's my partner. My best friend. Albert's not on the take. He's a college graduate. Come on, Christy, you're giving me butterflies."

"What are you blaming me for? You mentioned Albert, I didn't."

Pharoah asked, "Was Harry Jen here today?"

"He was."

"You were expecting him?"

"He always phoned before coming in, in case I thought meeting here was a bad idea. Then we'd meet outside of the vicinity."

"Harry was set up. Kao was tipped Harry Jen would be here at a certain hour. It was a cinch for Kao to assign somebody to tail Harry and ice him."

"Harry always took the same route out of here. The safest. Into the basement, then into the abandoned house next door and through that out to the alley where there's a door into the supermarket." He snapped his fingers. "Listen! Harry had an appointment uptown. He was heading uptown."

"Possibly to Mourami," said Pharoah.

"It was drizzling. Harry probably took the subway. His killer was carrying an umbrella. In the subway, he poked Harry with the umbrella."

"Shot him."

"Yeah. Shot him with the umbrella. An umbrella, for crying out loud. Is nothing sacred?"

"Don't jump the track. I think we're on to something, and it's got me wide awake. Hypothetically, it's this. Harry decides to continue on to his appointment. There's probably a payment due him, and Harry had every intention of collecting. He either takes the train after all or goes back up to hail a cab. He gets to Mourami's place and there he collapses. The ricin has begun to work."

"Pharoah, I love this scenario." Christy was rubbing the palms of his hands together.

"Yeah? Maybe I can sell it for a movie-of-the-week. Let's get back to Harry."

"I can't wait to get back to Harry so we can maybe be rid of him once and for all."

"Okay. Okay." Pharoah was back on his feet and pacing. "Harry's on the floor. I suppose he's in agony. Does ricin cause agony?"

"I don't know. I've never had any. I know it paralyzes the nerves and often the muscles."

"Sounds real nasty. So anyway, there's Harry laying on the—"

". . . Lying on the floor," corrected Christy.

"Stuff it! Lying. Laying. He's on the floor and he's a problem. He's probably sweating worse than usual. Wiggs is there with Mourami."

"Yes, yes. We can assume that."

"We have to assume it because we need him and one other Caucasian to deliver Harry to the hospital. Anyway, there's Harry on the floor. Maybe still conscious. But he's hurting. He's hurting, and Mourami is wringing her hands and moaning, 'Oy vay, he's got to be taken to a hospital.' Hey! Wait a minute! She probably has a butler!"

"Of course she does. She wouldn't be caught dead without one. Joan Rivers has a butler."

"What's that got to do with Mourami?"

"They're both rich and live on the East Side. So there's a butler. We need him. He's our second Caucasian."

Pharoah carried the conversational ball again. "So the butler being a stereotype, suggests he dial 911. But Mourami shrieks, 'Guttenyoo, no! No 911. We mustn't have the police here. I'm Cylla Mourami and how do I explain a dying Asian on my floor? So she sends the butler out to hail a cab, he brings one back to the house. He and Wiggs with Harry Jen between them hustle Harry into the cab."

"Wait," Christy said. "The butler's uniform would be a dead give-away."

Pharoah thought for a moment. "Maybe all this is taking place in the hallway, the foyer, the entryway or whatever the hell she has. Maybe when the butler answered the door Harry had been slumped against it and fell into the hallway."

"Perfect! It's like a movie."

"And every hallway has a coat closet, right?" Pharoah pantomimed opening the door to the coat closet. "So she opens the coat closet and there's something for the butler to wear to cover his uniform. Maybe a raincoat."

Christy took up the narrative now. "So they've got Harry in the cab, they direct the driver to New York Hospital. When they get there, one of them gets out of the cab to get a wheelchair or one of those rolling tables . . ."

"A gurney."

"Is that what they call them? How come?" asked Christy.

"How should I know? I was a school dropout." Pharoah thought for a moment. "It was probably the butler who went into the emergency room. Lawyers are no damn good in an emergency. Anyway, they get rid of Harry. Direct the cab back to Mourami's dump. Wiggs gives the rotten cabdriver a handsome tip . . ."

"Why a rotten cabdriver?"

"They're all rotten. And they're snotty too . . ." He crossed his knees, folded his arms and said, "Now all we have to do is prove it."

"Pharoah, this is a really good piece of detective work."

"If it works."

"We'll make it work. We'll lean on Mourami and Wiggs. I've got to bring down Kao Lee."

"If he's got money troubles, he's on his way already."

Pharoah watched Christy as he jotted some more notes. "Who do you suppose used the umbrella?" asked Pharoah.

"One of Kao's hatchet men."

"Probably Nick Wenji," said Pharoah.

"Wenji? Wenji? Has anyone mentioned him before?"

"He's a fixture in Kao's outfit. He's a runner. I'm positive a hit man. Sometimes he deals for Kao." He went off on a different track. "And there's Lena Wing."

"Oh yes, we mustn't forget Lena Wing. *Her* I've seen for myself. She's the hostess, right?"

"I suspect for a time she was Kao's girl. Albert's talked to her a lot. He sort of likes her. She's a very ambitious lady. She wants to own a restaurant. Something elegant with haute cuisine and linen napkins. A watering hole for all the swells and the celebrities and the politicos. Albert's money is on her. Outside of working for Kao, though, I don't see where Lena fits into the picture. I can't see her as a killer."

"Why not?"

Pharoah shrugged and then said, "I'm filing her under least likely suspect."

"Don't let her get lost in the file. She might have other fish to fry besides Kao." Christy glanced at his wristwatch. "Go home, Pharoah. Get some sleep. You've got the Feds here at nine A.M."

Pharoah clucked his tongue. "Oh dear."

"*Now* what?"

"I haven't a thing to wear."

CHAPTER **9**

While Pharoah and Christy were forming their deductions in Christy's office, Kao was interrogating Michael in his office. Michael was tired but he knew there would be no sleep for him until his uncle was satisfied. Uncle. Stepfather. Whatever. Kao was lighting a cigar when Lena Wing entered with glasses of beer for them.

"Good stuff," she told Michael, "we import it from Mexico." Michael took a glass as she set the other on Kao's desk.

"Not bad," said Michael.

"It's great," corrected Kao, "we've been smuggling it in through Texas for a couple of months now. Don't go, Lena. Sit and listen." She sat on a straight-back chair, crossed her knees and both men silently admired her shapely legs. Then Michael began his narrative. Kao had largely heard the same thing from previous enforcers. It was never much different. Awful food, stinking unhygienic conditions, women raped, men died and cast overboard, and so on ad infinitum. Michael's narrative had some color. Drunken captain who rarely left his cabin, Tisa Cheng and what a boost she was to his morale until he got bored with her constant harping on her career in America . . .

"And Archie Lang?" pressed Kao.

"He said he was wanted by the police on a felony charge."

"China or here?"

"Here."

"Then why did he risk coming back?"

"Homesick, I guess."

Kao puffed the cigar and then placed it in an ashtray. "What did he look like? How old is he?"

"Good-looking black man. Late thirties, early forties, I guess. He has a ponytail and he wears a sort of sick earring in his left ear."

Lena spoke. "Why sick?"

"It was a carving of Jesus and Moses with their arms around each other."

"Pharoah Love," said Lena.

"Why is the name familiar to me?" asked Kao.

"He's been in here. He's with the Fifth Precinct. He's been away several months. Now we know where he's been. I don't think you've ever seen him. You'd never forget him." She described, and not without a touch of humor, Pharoah and his notoriously outlandish getups.

Kao's face hardened as he stared at Michael. "You had no reason to suspect he was an undercover agent?"

Michael said with equanimity, "I had no reason to suspect he was anything but a criminal on the lam. He was good company. There was very little laughter on the freighter because there was very little reason to laugh. But Pharoah was mostly good-humored. He sang a lot, which was pleasant. He knew a lot of risqué songs from old Broadway musicals."

Kao said, "And between renditions, he asked questions."

"Yes, Uncle, he asked questions."

"And you obliged him with answers."

"They were innocent enough."

Kao puffed the cigar and then looked at Lena, whose eyes never left Michael's face. "There were many questions about me, I presume."

"I wouldn't say many. A few. The usual ones I get out of idle curiosity when people find out we're related."

"He asked questions about the smuggling."

"Yes."

Kao was warming up. "And was this business entirely mine or did I have silent partners?"

"I only knew about Cylla Mourami."

"You told him the ships that were supposed to rendezvous were hers?"

"Yes."

Kao leaned forward. "You never once suspected he was a plant?"

Michael was annoyed. "I had no reason to."

"Of course he asked personal questions," Kao stated. Lena Wing was beginning to wonder if through some supernatural power Kao Lee had been on board the freighter with Michael and Pharoah.

"Personal? Like what? Where did I go to school? Who was my favorite actor?"

"Don't be facetious."

"I don't know what you mean by personal. On board that hell ship after a while everybody got personal with everybody else. The aliens knew just about everything there was to know about each other after a few weeks at sea. You can't imagine what was going on. I'm sure some of those who died were murdered for their food. There wasn't a day or a night that I didn't expect a mutiny. Archie Lang, Pharoah Love, whatever the hell his name is, he kept me sane."

"You volunteered to undertake the voyage. I didn't force you. It never once crossed my mind to send you out. I still don't understand why you wanted the experience!"

"I thought you'd be pleased."

"I was. I don't deny that. But this Pharoah Love! He came all the way to Pusan to ingratiate himself with you to get on board. I wonder what he'd have done if you refused him passage."

"Why, he'd have stowed away," said Lena offhandedly. She met Kao's questioning look with a smile. "Mr. Love is a legend, Kao. I'm very friendly with his partner, Albert West."

"Oh yes. Albert West! I remember. You let him win two hundred dollars."

"It made him feel good. I got it all back. And more. He's a terrible blackjack player. Kao, we know the Warehouse is swarming with police. There's always three or four on the premises. They're always asking questions. They're always looking for information. Any idea who kidnapped the professor, or the professor's wife, or his children or the whole family, and where might they be sequestered? Or are they dead? And what about the doctor or the lawyer or their lovely daughters and handsome sons? Face it, Kao, you've plundered so many citizens of Chinatown I think you've lost track of your victims and where they're stashed."

"No I haven't. I keep meticulous records in my Grand Street office. I know who is where, how long they've been there, what ransom I've asked for each individual. I am very meticulous. You know that, Lena. True, I'm a little top-heavy with victims, but to release them without collecting *something* would make me a laughingstock. It would all get out of hand. If they can't afford to bring their friends and relatives here, they should leave them behind. I paid heavily to import Zang and Rhea and Michael. But I *paid*. The man who smuggled them here was far more ruthless than I am. Of course his system twenty-five years ago was nowhere as sophisticated as mine is today."

Lena suppressed a laugh when he said "sophisticated." Michael stifled a yawn. He longed desperately for sleep.

But there was no stopping Kao. Despite the hour, he was only beginning to warm up. Michael drank more beer while Kao expounded.

"His boat was a tanker. It had a Panamanian registration. Don't you remember it, Michael?"

"I was sick the entire voyage," remembered Michael. "So was Mother."

Kao pounced. "Pharoah Love questioned you about your family? Your mother? Your father?"

"Kao, sooner or later everyone questions a new acquaintance about their family. I know everything there is to know about Archie's family."

"Yes! Of course! Archie's family. But what do you know about Pharoah's family?"

"Well, if he fed me a line, I've got to hand it to him. It was a pretty good one."

"And what did you feed him?"

"I guess just about everything."

Kao's fist hit the desk, taking the others by surprise. Michael flinched and Lena Wing winced. "Now Pharoah Love is a serious threat to me."

Lena Wing said with reason, "Kao, don't be so optimistic. I should think by now Mr. Love has shared whatever he learned on the *Green Empress* with Albert and his chief and any number of other interested parties. They'll soon link Harry Jen to us if they haven't already. I suppose we should claim his body and bury it."

"Cremation is cheaper," suggested Michael.

"I've already phoned the police," Lena told them. "They're not releasing his body until after a full autopsy. And that's sometime tomorrow. And as to Pharoah and the freighter, he was planted there by the FBI's Asian Organized Crime Task Force."

"You know this for a fact?"

"On extremely good authority," she said while examining a fingernail.

"Lena, I sometimes think you enjoy making me feel as though I don't appreciate you enough."

"That's right. You don't." She folded her arms. "Your body and your mind are poles apart. Your body is of today, but your mind still exists in the nineteenth century. Like your ancestors who bound our feet and made us walk five paces behind them and cater to their every perversity. You consider women your inferiors."

"That's not so!" he protested.

"I'm about as close a thing as you've got to an executive in your organization and that's because most of your men are a bunch of lamebrains. Useful in certain particular ways but, in general, highly useless. Harry Jen never had an original thought in his entire lifetime and Nick Wenji is a laughable caricature of an underworld thug."

"Nick is very useful to me. Don't be so unkind."

"He does your dirty work. He's an old-style hatchet man except in his case he uses an umbrella. And I think the cops are beginning to wise up to that gimmick." Michael looked bemused and she explained the umbrella to him, though she thought he had known about it for quite a while. "What about Tisa Cheng?"

"Michael's Tisa Cheng?" Kao asked.

"Anybody's Tisa Cheng." She turned to Michael. "You're not in love with her, for crying out loud?"

"Hell, no. I was hoping you two would have an idea as to what to do with her."

"She is very sweet," said Kao.

"Adorable," said Lena, her voice as flat as the top of Kao's desk.

Kao was thinking. "She sings and plays the mandolin, eh?"

"There's singing," said Michael, "and there's singing. A belter she isn't."

"She's too pretty for a factory or a laundry. A masseuse, perhaps?"

"Not with those fingernails," said Michael.

Kao Lee was stubbing out the cigar in an ashtray as he said coolly, "I will take care of Tisa Cheng."

"I had an idea you'd settle the matter," said Lena Wing.

"The FBI," said Kao.

Lena said, "I was wondering when we'd get back to them."

"Yes, this Pharoah must be very good if the FBI borrowed him to send him undercover. You know everything, Lena, or seem to. Have we any Feds on the premises?"

"Probably."

He leaned back in his chair with his feet stretched before him, hands clasped behind his head and on his face an expression that might have passed as beatific. "They're really moving in on me."

"You sound delighted," said Michael.

"Delighted? No, I'm not delighted. I'm flattered." He thought a moment. "They brought about the ruin of the Fuk Ching, but the ruin was already under way. There was all that internal feuding. They thought they were invincible."

Lena Wing said, "Don't you feel the same way?"

"I used to, but I don't anymore." Michael was astonished at his uncle's honesty. "They've been closing in on me for a long time. Wrecking the *Green Empress* is another nail in the coffin. But I have something the Fuk Ching never had. I have alternatives."

Michael decided to take the bull by the horns. "The word's around that you're in financial trouble."

Kao chuckled. "I've been in financial trouble since the day I was born. For the first two decades of my life I was a self-made pauper." Now he was leaning on the desk, warming up to his favorite subject, himself. "Then I robbed a number of people and bought passage to

San Francisco, where I thrived. And by the time I got to New York, my reputation and my fortune was made. Financial trouble? Sure, there's always that. Like everybody else in this business, my credit is overextended, but they'll never ruin me. There's always a new smuggling ring cropping up when another is destroyed. Lena, you know how much competition I'm up against. A few of them are better organized than I am, but that's because we've been suffering brain drain around here."

Kao turned to his nephew. "That's why I've been grooming you, Michael. The trouble with you is, you lack too much in the scheming department. Like your father. He was terrible at scheming. For a while he took to reading the old Fu Man Chu novels to try to get a line on how to be a real villain. But they taught him nothing. Harry Jen I thought had possibilities, but they were mostly sweated out of him and he turned traitor. I've got Nick Wenji, but he doesn't have an original thought in him. But he's a good hatchet man. An automaton. Wind him up and he assassinates. But he's good for nothing else."

Lena Wing suggested, "There's a lot of potentials out there in the streets."

"Not for me. I don't like those kids. Carjacking and shaking down restaurants is where they belong. Michael, you're falling asleep. Go home. We'll talk again tomorrow. Michael!" He spoke the name sharply. Michael was on his feet about to say good-bye to Lena Wing. Kao's voice darkened. "Pharoah Love asked many questions about your mother and me? Your father? How he died?"

"I merely told him that after Father died, you and Mother fell in love through your mutual grief and married." Michael thought, Not bad if I must say so myself. It's almost lyrical.

"Somehow," said Kao, "I don't believe you." Michael shrugged. Lena thought of grand opera, but wasn't quite sure what aria she would assign each of them.

Michael said, "I knew you wouldn't and I don't blame you. You only believe what you want to believe. Good night, Lena. Good night, Uncle." And he went out the door.

Kao asked Lena, "You still care about him?"

"I'll always like Michael. He wasn't cut out for you and this business."

"He had potential," sighed Kao. "He could have been a contender. But like his father, too weak, too innocent, no balls."

"What happens next? Or won't you say until you've consulted Madame Khan?"

"I don't need to consult her yet. What happens is I wait and see how the Feds mean to show their hand. Then I see how deeply the police will go into investigating Harry Jen's death. Then there's the problems of the aliens they've incarcerated and the ones who escaped. Regardless, I have to deal with the people who sponsored them." He hit the desk with his fist. "Dead or alive, they must pay the balances. Contracts must be honored. And then there is Cylla Mourami to deal with. I know she was paying Harry just as the police were. I didn't think she'd order the rendezvous canceled."

"Very naive, Kao. From the moment you introduced us, I knew this was one strong lady whose path I would rarely cross again. Has Rhea met her?"

"A few times at the necessary social occasions."

"Did they like each other?"

"I never cared one way or another. Cylla was a partner. She has the ships I need."

"Past tense. Needed. What do you do now for ships?"

"Lena, I'm thinking the time has come to put an end to the smuggling business, before it puts an end to me."

"Give me my restaurant," she said in an insistent tone.

"There's no real money in restaurants. Say, have you thought of opening a modeling agency? You've got class. You could do real good at it."

"And who's my first client? Tisa Cheng?"

"You could do worse."

"I'd rather do better. I'm going to bed. Good night."

"Lena!" She had the door open and paused without turning to him. "You be good to that girl!"

"Or?" Lena asked. He said nothing. She left.

He made a phone call. After several rings, a familiar voice answered. "I didn't wake you? I hear the television. There's much to tell you. Much to discuss. I can be there in half an hour."

Pharoah Love lay in bed staring at the ceiling. He thought of Christy Lombardo and how well they worked together, complemented each other. There was a lot more work ahead. He thought of Malone and Rogers, the two FBI men he'd be meeting within a few hours and groaned at the thought of how humorless they would be. He thought of Michael Lee and if he had told Kao about Archie Lang. And if so, so what? On the other hand, if it had been deduced that Archie Lang was an undercover agent, there could be a contract out on him. And if so, so what?

I'll have to be more observant in public, thought Pharoah. Keep a sharp eye out for anyone in the immediate vicinity carrying an umbrella, especially if it's not raining. In England they carry umbrellas rain or shine out of force of habit. You never know when the skies are going to suddenly open in England. And in some places on the Continent. Pharoah thought of Paris, and for some reason this led him to Tisa Cheng. He'd once seen a Chinese belly dancer in Paris and wondered if the profession might hold some promise for Tisa. He wondered if anything held any promise for Tisa.

He elbowed the body lying next to him. "For crying out loud, Albert, stop hogging the blanket!"

CHAPTER 10

The FBI men, Malone and Rogers, from the look of them and the way they dressed, seemed better suited to the professions of law and dentistry. Malone wore a bowtie, which he thought gave him a very sporty look. Rogers wore a turtleneck knit shirt because he had a thick neck. They sat with Christy and Pharoah in the precinct's conference room. Pharoah did not disappoint Christy. Yellow trousers with purple stripes, a brown-and-orange sweatshirt partially hidden by a calico sport jacket. All he lacked was a string of pearls and an orchid corsage. The FBI interrogated Pharoah at length. From the way the two men spoke, Pharoah was glad he wasn't Kao

Lee. As far as Malone and Rogers were concerned, Kao Lee was about to take his place in criminal history.

The two interrogators struck Pharaoh as candidates for the roles of end men in a minstrel show. But they don't do minstrel shows anymore. Much too racist. A pity, these two FBI boys would have been perfect. They never overlapped their questions. When one stopped asking, the other stepped in. Pharoah had to jockey for position in order to supply them with information. The meeting lasted over two hours. In his office, Albert West was hoping Pharoah wasn't getting too sassy with Malone and Rogers. For starters, when Pharoah introduced Albert to the Feds before closeting them with himself and Christy, he blandly told them Albert was his gynecologist. Albert hurried away while Christy made some lame remark that Pharoah was always kidding. The Feds were what Pharoah referred to as belt-and-suspender men; they took copious notes in addition to using a tape recorder.

Before the two hours or more were up, Pharoah began to warm up to them. He had had dealings with the FBI on other occasions and also the CIA. There were more tics and twitches among the CIA than the FBI. Of course, the CIA were betrayed more often, but that's because they dealt with espionage, and espionage was more conducive to betrayals. Malone tugged at his shirt collar a lot. Christy asked him if he'd like the air conditioner turned on. When Malone asked, "Why?" Christy refrained from replying, "Just for the hell of it."

Rogers was very interested in Tisa Cheng. Was there any chance she might really be a dissident fleeing for her life? Pharoah asked if dissident was a brand of toothpaste. Christy resisted an urge to kick him. He wished the Feds would pack up and go.

Pharoah told them as much as he knew, or as much as he thought they ought to know. He knew this meeting wouldn't be the last. They'd find reasons to invite him uptown to their offices in the East Seventies just off Third Avenue for further questioning. Or to read and check the transcripts of their notes. Pharoah kept assuring Rogers that he was positive Tisa Cheng was apolitical. Once when he mentioned the Soong sisters, Tisa wanted to know what label they recorded for. It occurred to him later that her generation of young Chinese probably knew nothing of the great Chinese leader Sun Yat-sen, whose wife was a Soong. Madam Chiang Kai-shek was another Soong daughter.

Toward the end of the meeting Malone asked Pharoah, "You think Michael Lee didn't penetrate your cover?"

"I don't think so. Michael was truly capable of only one kind of penetration and that you can discuss with Miss Cheng when you catch up with her."

Malone flashed his associate a look. Rogers said, "Pharoah, you did a good job."

"Do I get an honorary FBI badge?"

Malone said, "You'll be receiving a citation."

Christy said to Pharoah with a straight face, "How about that?"

"Wow," said Pharoah.

Rogers asked Christy, "Have you any information as to when Kao is planning his next smuggling job?"

"Well, if I were Kao, after the *Green Empress* disaster, I'd slow down in that area and do some rethinking. Kao's into a lot of other forms of smuggling. He's bringing in beer from Mexico, stolen goods from South America and so on. He's doing constant battle with the other major Chinatown gangs such as the Tung On. Tung On is the most powerful gang in the area. They're also the most violent."

"We've got plenty on them," said Malone, "and every day we keep getting more. Trouble is, our informants don't seem to live long enough to spend their fees."

Christy said, "Your informants can't possibly belong to the Tung On. It's a rigid power structure, and they mete out swift punishment to maintain its influence. I suspect the information you're getting is secondhand. Kao Lee is supposedly a one-man operation, but we know he has partners. We also suspect he takes orders from someone who is even more powerful and frightening than he is but keeps a low profile, lets Kao take all the bows. But if Kao is hurting financially, how much longer can he keep the Chi Who from collapsing?"

Pharoah said, "Kao Lee and the Chi Who are two distinctly separate entities. Kao is in trouble personally. The Chi Who is an independent financial structure of its own."

"The Chi Who wouldn't rescue Kao?" asked Malone.

"They will, I suppose, if he's still of any value to them. Also, he knows where all the bodies are buried. I'm sure he has hidden records of every murder, every kidnapping, every attempt at extortion and probably in triplicate."

"What about Rhea Lee?" asked Rogers.

"What about her?"

"We have it on good authority she's no longer happy being Mrs. Kao."

Pharoah nodded. "That's an old story."

"Well," said Rogers good-naturedly, "twice-told tales are often the best ones. Maybe one of these days she'll do us all a favor and dispatch him to that great teahouse in the sky."

"When Kao dies," said Pharoah, "he takes his secrets with him. You want his secrets before he goes. And believe you me, unless there's a taxi cruising around out there with Kao's name on it, I think you'd better assume Kao's going to be around for a long, long time."

"What about you?" asked Malone.

"What about me?"

"If Kao finds out you're Archie Lang, you could have problems."

Pharoah stretched his arms and then said, "I've a hunch he spent a lot of time last night cross-examining Michael, I assume with the help of his henchwoman, Lena Wing. Lena is one cool cookie, she knows me, and if Michael gave an accurate physical description of Archie

Lang, then I have been identified. If so, why ice me? The damage has already been done. The freighter's wrecked. And Kao knows we're on to him and have been for a long time. We're his frequent patrons at the Warehouse, especially my pal Albert you met earlier. The place is very useful to us. We get a lot of information, a lot of tips. And," Pharoah added wryly, "sometimes they're true."

"Very tricky people these Chinese," said Rogers. "But," he added with a practiced smile, "I'm sure you know how to deal with them." The Feds said their good-byes, shook hands and lumbered out to the corridor while Pharoah groaned and crossed one ankle over the other.

"I'm beginning to wonder," said Pharoah, "where the freighter's concerned, was that trip necessary?"

Christy said, "In more ways than you realize. You found out a great deal about Kao from Michael. We know for a fact that Kao murdered his brother. . . ."

"You'll never pin the rap on him."

"Don't be so sure."

"After all these years?"

"It's not so unusual. We might get help. Rhea. Michael. If Michael had been killed, I think Rhea would have turned into our pet nightingale. Too bad."

"Aw, come on. Michael's a nice kid."

"Don't nice kids ever want to avenge their father's murder?"

"Maybe he does. But right now I think Michael is entertaining the long view. The thought of occupying the throne when Kao gets the boot." He smiled. "Then he'll off him or get somebody to do it for him."

Pharoah followed Christy back to Christy's office. On the way, he poked his head in Albert's office and said, "Won't you join the ladies, into one big lady?"

"Very old," said Albert. "I heard that line in London, in a revue called *Share My Lettuce*. Did you bring joy to the hearts of the Feds and carols to their lips? They looked like a pair of undertakers."

Christy sat at his desk and Albert sank into a chair while Pharoah bellowed out the door to anyone in particular to bring coffee for the three of them. Christy was reading a report that had been placed on his desk.

"Well, here's the bad news. Sixty-three bodies have been recovered from the drink. Two hundred and one are behind bars with all of them marked for deportation unless they can prove the right to political asylum. The rest are still at large, and they can't supply numbers because they don't know what the grand total was."

"Three hundred and twenty," said Pharoah. "But that includes the ones who died during the voyage, so there aren't that many clunking around on the loose. They'll turn up sooner or later unless they somehow got to New Jersey, which means they'll never be found."

"You're sure of your numbers?" asked Christy.

"That's what my new best friend told me," said Pharoah, "and Michael was the epitome of efficiency. Say, Christy, you suppose the Feds have some plants of their own in the Warehouse?"

"Everything's possible in this worst of all possible worlds. Does it bother you?"

"No, it's just if the quality of the information they're getting is better than ours, I'll get very jealous and very high-strung. I'm a terribly possessive person, surely you know that by now." Hutch Casey arrived with a tray of coffee and fixings. Pharoah glared at him. "No bagels? Beast."

Hutch set the tray on Christy's desk. Christy was busy with another memo. "Harry Jen got it in the thigh."

"As opposed to?" asked Pharoah.

"Ricin pellet in his thigh." He handed the memo to Albert, who was hovering over the desk. "He also had tumors in his colon."

"Maybe that's why he perspired so much," said Pharoah as he claimed a mug of coffee. "Anybody gone dibs on his body?"

"Yeah, Lena Wing. She asked it be sent to a crematorium."

"Which means Kao is picking up the tab."

"You know," mused Pharoah, "Harry must have a stash salted away."

"Don't start slavering," cautioned Christy.

"I don't intend to, but it's something like that that makes me think of life's injustices. Think of that money. Lying there in some hidden, dark recess. Gathering dust. In time, moldering and disintegrating. Never to be used for the betterment of the world. All my life I've dreamt of being kept."

"From doing what?" asked Albert.

Pharoah folded his arms and glared at him. "You have become a despoiler of illusions, Albert," he commented archly while Christy and Hutch Casey exchanged bemused looks. "Albert, have you never dreamt of immense wealth? Of being waited on hand and foot for the rest of your life? Of snapping your fingers and sending the lowly scurrying in all directions? Have you never dreamt of living in a castle in Spain?"

"No, I haven't," said Albert, a veteran of Pharoah's wild flights of fancy. "I have visited castles in many countries, and they are dank, damp and drafty. I have visited Spain but it didn't inspire me to set up residence. And I think we'd better start thinking of visiting, among others, Cylla Mourami and Kao Lee. We should be figuring out who the candidates are for replacement stool pigeon."

"Stool pigeon!" exclaimed Pharoah. "How quaint! I thought that expression died with Edward G. Robinson." He smiled at Christy. "You're the boss. Where do you suggest we start?"

"The men's. You both sound constipated." He shuffled papers on his desk. After a moment, he looked up. "Let's get nearer to closing the book on Harry Jen."

"We may never know his killer," said Pharoah realistically.

"I don't want you to know him, I want you to nail him."

"Albert," said Pharoah, "you got Mourami's home phone number?"

Albert picked up a phone. He dialed 0 for operator. He asked for a supervisor after identifying himself. The operator wasn't too sure about the identification. "You know Carlos Fuentes?" The operator knew him. "Connect me with him." After much clicking Albert heard a familiar voice. "Carlos? Albert West."

"Hey, Albert! Where you been keeping yourself?"

From the impatient look on Pharoah's face, Albert knew it wisest to keep the small talk to a minimum. Within a few minutes, he had Cylla Mourami's number. He jotted it down. Pharoah looked at the number.

"Awfully ordinary number for an out-of-the-ordinary woman." He looked at his wristwatch. "Almost noon. Maybe we'll be lucky." He dialed the number. On the fourth ring he heard Goren, the butler, speak. Pharoah identified himself. "I'd like to speak with Miss Mourami."

"I'll see if she's available," said Goren, wishing Mourami would lower the volume on the stereo. He was fed up to the teeth with *The Pearl Fishers*. Cylla Mourami was in the library, seated at her desk, an antique purchased in Greenwich, England, from a dealer who assured her that at this very desk Charles Dickens gave birth to *A Tale of Two Cities*. This dealer used to claim it was where Jane Austen wrote *Sense and Sensibility* until he understood that people who could afford to pay five figures for an antique desk had never heard of *Sense and Sensibility* let alone its author. Better yet, Dickens had a magical cachet. Everybody was familiar with Charles Dickens.

Cylla wore harlequin-framed eyeglasses in lieu of her usual contact lenses. She removed the glasses and set them aside as Goren approached. "Who is it, Goren?"

"It's a gentleman who says he's a detective."

"Oh, really. Not many detectives are gentlemen." Goren wondered how many detectives she had met in the past, here and abroad. "What does this detective want?"

"I gather he wishes to speak to you, Miss Mourami. Are you in or are you out?"

"Let me think a moment."

She stared out the window at her magnificent garden in the rear of the mansion where a beautiful fountain was providing baths for several serins. Near the fountain was the brilliant Brancusi and just a few feet beyond that was a superb Jacob Epstein. Farther back against a marble wall was the parvenu Myron Lipsky. Well might you ask, And who is or was Myron Lipsky? Myron was once an *is* but now he's a *was*. Cylla had read in the newspaper of the tragic suicide of this sculptor Myron Lipsky. Her father had advised her to always pursue the work of artists who she might hear are on the verge of death. The value of their work could easily double or triple or even quadruple in a very short time. So Cylla, letting no grass grow under her feet, presented herself at the late sculptor's studio, the address of which was conveniently printed in the newspaper. There she found his wife devouring a banana and obviously totally incapable of expressing the emotion known as bereavement. In no time at all, Cylla chose the work now reposing in her garden, the title of which was *Another Dawn* and depicted a man either hugging or strangling a woman. It was an incredibly ugly piece of work and Hiram Wiggs had offered to smash it to smithereens with a sledgehammer. But Cylla was firm about it and defended her taste and business acumen, and *Another Dawn* stayed in the garden, in one piece, untouched. It was Myron Lipsky's fifteen minutes, because Cylla was stuck with it. After ten years of pleading and importuning, no museum in the world would accept it as a gift.

"Miss Mourami?" Goren prompted.

"What?"

"Mr. Love is waiting."

"What? Oh yes, the detective." Damn, it was going to be one of *those* days. Yesterday the face-off, albeit by phone, with Kao Lee. Harry Jen's collapse practically at her feet. She'd had men at her feet but never in Harry's unfortunate condition. She thought of phoning Hiram Wiggs, then scrubbed the idea when she realized if this detective wanted to question her and she had her lawyer present, this Mr. Love would recognize immediately she had something to fear.

She stared at the row of phones on her desk. A red one was blinking. That was Pharoah Love, and undoubtedly rather impatient by now. She unclipped an earring from her left lobe, a large pearl surrounded by an arc of tiny diamonds and emeralds, placed it on the desk in front of her and then picked up the phone with her right hand while her left waved Goren out of the room.

"This is Cylla Mourami."

"What kept you, honey?"

"I beg your pardon."

"This has been a long wait. And not even some music to soothe my savage breast. But hark! What do I hear in the background! Goodness, it's *The Pearl Fishers*."

Cylla was taken by surprise. "You know *The Pearl Fishers*?"

"Not individually, but some of the music can send me into uncontrollable rapture."

Back in the office, Albert, Christy and Hutch Casey were frozen in place. The brazen bastard!

"How charming, Mr. Love. I had no idea detectives had time to enjoy opera."

"Oh, I'm not one of your ordinary detectives, feet on the desk, cigarette behind the ear, wad of tasteless chewing gum and the rest of the clichés. I'm the esoteric type. You must be dying to meet me by now."

"I'm never dying to meet anybody, Mr. Love. Now what's the reason for this call?"

"An old associate of yours. Harry Jen."

"Harry Jen?"

"Kao Lee's Harry Jen." He went for the jugular. "We know you do business with Kao Lee."

"I do?"

"You suddenly develop amnesia?"

"No, Mr. Love, I'm just impressed by your information. How do you think I can help you?"

"Invite me to your elegant mansion. I have a partner and his name's Albert West. You'll just love him. He's a saint despite the fact halos are in short supply. Miss Mourami, are you there? Are you tired of me already?"

Cylla laughed. "I was wondering if I should call my lawyer."

"If he plays bridge, great. Then we're a foursome. Otherwise, he's just excess baggage. We just want to talk, Miss Mourami."

"I haven't had my lunch."

"How's about Le Cirque?"

"How's about an hour from now, by which time I'll have eaten something." She told him her address.

Pharoah thanked her and hung up. He grinned at the others. "You three look as though you've got upset stomachs. Albert, we've got a date with the billionairess an hour from now. I think we're going to have some fun with Cylla Mourami."

"Is Hiram Wiggs going to be there?" asked Christy.

"Maybe yes, maybe no. She wondered if she should have him there, but you heard me going on about our having a bridge game and I'm so rusty with all those conventions. Christy, do you know the 'Goldberg Variations'?"

"Christ no!" The crazy names these bridge players give their conventions.

"Well, I shall go right out and buy you a CD. You're in for such a treat."

An hour later, Cylla Mourami, wearing a smartly tailored pearl-gray hostess gown, sat on the couch in her drawing room while Pharoah and Albert settled into easy chairs. Amid all the splendor, Albert felt like a poor relation. The drawing room reminded Pharoah of a lounge in the old Loew's Pitkin in Brooklyn. All the room lacked was a head usher, though Goren was a respectable substitute. Cylla told the butler to bring coffee. No drinks were suggested, as Cylla knew officers are not permitted to drink while on duty. Goren left as Cylla hoped her face betrayed no dismay at Pharoah Love's outlandish attire. Albert West, at least, wore a respectable blue serge suit that would soon celebrate its sixth birthday.

Pharoah said to Cylla, "You're overcome by my flamboyance."

She didn't bat an eyelash. "I'm not that easily overcome. As a matter of fact, I've been thinking of applauding."

"You see, Albert! The lady appreciates my showmanship." He continued, "Sad about Kao Lee."

Her eyes widened. "Is he dead?"

"I hope not. He's next on our list. What's that we're listening to? Not *Porgy and Bess!*"

Cylla said sweetly, "I thought you might like that."

"How'd you know I was black?"

"You thought I wouldn't check up on you before you got here?"

"I forget. You've got friends in high places."

"And lower," said Cylla. "Now what's so sad about Kao Lee?"

"To add to all his other *tsurris*, the bath he took yesterday." Her face told him nothing. "The *Green Empress*." There was still nothing to read in her face. "The boats didn't make the rendezvous. They were called off."

"I really don't know what you're talking about."

"Sure you do, Miss Mourami. Your boats. From your spread in the Hamptons. They were supposed to greet the freighter offshore and collect her cargo. No boat whistles, no orchestra playing 'Aloha Oy,' no natives diving for coins or flinging leis. Just a lot of scraggly, frightened Chinese people praying for sanctuary in the promised land, except the promise wasn't kept. We know the *Green Empress* was on lease from your fleet."

"Mr. Love, there are many ships out there on lease from my company. I have no idea what cargoes or passengers these ships carry, as they are no concern of mine. And as for Kao Lee . . ."

"You are heavily invested in his operation."

"I wish you had said 'heavenly' invested and then I could call you a liar. I don't deny that. Hiram Wiggs—he's my lawyer—oversees my interests, and only yesterday he told me I was one of Mr. Lee's investors. We watched the tragedy on television."

"Oh, he was here with you?"

"Why yes. We see a great deal of each other. He's one of my closest friends and associates. I told you. He oversees my interests, and I've got an awful lot of interests."

Goren wheeled in a cart of coffee and biscuits. "Forgive me for interrupting, I thought you'd want this right away."

"Of course, Goren. Please serve." They all took theirs black, and Goren was soon on his way back to the kitchen.

Pharoah placed his coffee on an end table at his elbow while Albert studied Cylla Mourami, wondering how it felt to be so filthy rich.

"Miss Mourami," said Pharoah, "let me take you by the hand and lead you into the light. You didn't just learn yesterday you were one of Kao Lee's investors. I'm not telling you anything you don't already know. You've known Kao a long time. You've socialized with him. You've met his wife and his stepson, who is also his nephew, which is one of the neater tricks of the week. I mean, talk about a dysfunctional family, this one belongs on daytime television at least, if not behind bars.

"I'll go straight to the heart of this meeting, much as Kao Lee's operations also interest us. You knew Harry Jen."

"Harry Jen?" She selected a biscuit and took a bite. The detectives would never know how it tasted like ashes.

"Please, Miss Mourami, let's not figure skate. Harry Jen. Chubby guy who used to sweat a lot. He worked for Kao Lee as a pit boss. Gambling. The Warehouse. Catherine Slip. It used to be one of Kao Lee's biggest operations and now it's fallen on hard times. Harry moonlighted a lot. He was a spy. He sold information about Kao Lee to the police and to you."

If she was about to remonstrate, Pharoah didn't give her a chance. He steamrollered ahead. "Maybe somebody else. We're not sure. We think there's a mysterious somebody behind Kao Lee who really calls the shots. Orders the murders and the kidnappings and the whorehouses and the illegal smuggling of both animate and inanimate objects. My God, but they're a busy bunch. But that's the Asians for you. Look how they've been taking over New York. Korean fruit markets on every corner. Head shops, dry cleaners, take-out restaurants, illegal gambling parlors, even my favorite Jewish delicatessen down on First Avenue is Korean owned. *Guttenyoo!*"

Albert West finally piped up, Pharoah having paused to draw breath. "We've been using Harry Jen a long time now. He was very good. We'll miss him. He was at our precinct yesterday. He told us he was on his way to an appointment uptown with a lady."

"And I'm that lady?"

"We think you are," said Albert.

"I can't deny that isn't a possibility. And if it was, is it a crime to pay a person for information? Why, I've read about these television exposé programs that pay large sums to people to appear on camera and expose themselves." She paused. "I don't think I meant to say that."

The three enjoyed a much-needed laugh and relaxation of tension.

"Gentlemen, without even the presence of my lawyer, I'll"—she screwed up her face—"what's the expression I'm looking for? Oh yes! I'll level with you." She looked pleased, as though she had just invented the wheel. "Harry Jen was also a runner for Kao, which is how Hiram and I got to know him. I'll skip the unnecessaries. We knew Kao was in trouble, and since he wasn't a public company, we had to know how he was and still is cheating on us. Harry Jen supplied us with some very valuable information, and I paid him well. Kao is personally in deep trouble and owes me a good deal of money." She was not about to tell them she was privately partnered with him in the smuggling. She didn't have to, they already knew, but Pharoah was not about to spring it on her, not just yet. "I knew my small boats were to rendezvous with the freighter and I rescinded the order. I was angry with Kao. I had no idea the captain would run the boat aground."

Truly curious, Pharoah asked, "What did you expect him to do? There was no way for him to refuel."

Cylla ignored the question. "My lawyer heard that there was a move afoot to depose Kao Lee. We don't know who is behind this, but I suspect, Mr. Love, it's your mysterious higher-up who is the most likely candidate. Well, after all, gentlemen, we had to protect my interest!"

Pharoah jockeyed himself into position. "Yesterday, your lawyer was here with you?"

"Yes."

"You were expecting Harry Jen?"

She thought for a moment, and then admitted Jen was expected.

"What I'm giving you is a scenario my chief and I worked out last night. I'd appreciate it if you'd cooperate and let me know how close to accurate we've come. It'll be a nice substitute for the applause I didn't get earlier."

"More coffee?" she asked, remembering she was also a hostess.

"Please, Miss Mourami, let's get on with it. Harry Jen arrived. He'd already been murdered but he was not yet dead." She sipped coffee. "Your butler went to the door. Harry was slumped against it. He fell into the entryway. Your butler yelled for you. You and the lawyer went to the front door, and there was Harry stretched out like a side of smoked salmon. You could see he was dying. You didn't want him croaking on the premises. Calling 911 was out. You didn't want the cops. What would the neighbors say? One of you thought of dumping him at the emergency room at New York Hospital. The butler got a cab, and the idea was for your lawyer and the butler to carry Jen out to the cab between them. Okay so far?"

"Not bad." She selected another biscuit.

"You had to do something about the butler's uniform. You found a raincoat in the hall closet. The butler wore it, and they took Jen to the hospital. Once there, they left him without asking for a receipt."

"Cute touch, that," said Cylla while pushing an errant piece of biscuit back in her mouth.

Pharoah asked her, "Aren't you curious as to how he was killed? Who killed him?"

"Well, I'm sure Kao had him killed. As to who committed the act"—she shrugged—"that could be any one of Kao's henchmen." She suddenly shuddered. "I wish I had never heard of Kao Lee."

"We know how he was killed." He told her about the umbrella and the ricin.

"How awful. Dear God, that could happen to anybody! It could happen to me!" They gave her a few moments to collect herself. Suddenly a small smile played on her lips. "It could even happen to Kao, couldn't it?"

Pharoah told her, "It happened to his brother, Zang. Michael's father."

"I've heard the story."

"Miss Mourami, the FBI is stepping up their crackdown on these Chinese gangs."

"I read the newspapers."

"Kao's gang is their current major target. The Chi Who."

"That may not be so easy."

"That's what the Fuk Ching thought. They thought they were invincible." He shook his head. "No longer."

"What more do you expect from me, gentlemen?"

"A pleasant smile would be appreciated," said Pharoah.

"Why, Mr. Love, you're not flirting with me, are you?"

"I never flirt," said Pharoah. "I'm too proud."

"You're cute, Mr. Love, you're very cute."

Pharoah turned to Albert and said mockingly, "And you say I have all the charm of a mongoose in heat."

"I've never seen a mongoose in heat," said Albert. "As a matter of fact, I've never seen a mongoose."

"What happens now, Mr. Love?" asked Cylla as she selected a lowly Hydrox that had somehow been added to the plate of fancy biscuits, never realizing it was out of its depth.

"You now become a part of our file. In time we'll be examining all the information we've received and then we'll draw a conclusion."

"Have you met Kao Lee?" she asked.

"I've seen him. But we've never been introduced."

"I'm right in assuming that omission is about to be rectified?"

"It's inevitable. Like death and taxes. I'm very friendly with his nephew, but I'm not sure he knows it." He assuaged the questioning look on her face. "I was on the *Green Empress.*"

She leaned forward. "You were there last night? You saw it go aground?"

"I was there last night and I *felt* it go aground. I sailed with her from Pusan."

"Oh?"

"Another of my infamous masquerades. I was Archie Lang, wanted by the fuzz for a serious felony and on the lam for a couple of years. That was the only time Harry Jen and I had something in common. I was a spy. For the FBI. On loan from the police department."

"That was very brave of you."

"Yeah. It reminded me of the first time I tasted sushi. Michael Lee was the head enforcer on the trip."

"An enforcer?"

Pharoah explained the routine of smuggling illegal aliens. He couldn't believe she hadn't been clued in early in her relationship with Kao Lee. But if she wasn't learning something new, she was giving a brilliant performance. He had her undivided attention as he recounted his nautical and not so nice adventure. Pharoah went into full detail: the atrocious conditions, the dreadful and insubstantial food, the animal behavior of many of the men, and how his good humor and endless store of show tunes drew Michael Lee closer to him.

"I've met Michael," Cylla told him. "Attractive. Good manners."

"Poor taste in uncle and/or stepfather," said Pharoah.

"Not terribly bright," added Cylla as an afterthought.

"He thinks he's next in line to occupy the throne."

"That makes sense. But if you people have your druthers, there'll be no throne to inherit."

"You can bet on that. Put your money on us."

"Do I come under the heading of guilt by association?"

Pharoah shrugged.

Said Cylla, "That gesture tells me very little."

Pharoah said, "I'm a master of the art of empty gestures. But although empty, they are sincere." He got to his feet, and Albert took the cue and joined him.

Cylla asked, "And what about Goren?"

"The bridge master? He died years ago."

"My Goren is very much with us. He's my butler." She was leading them to the front door.

"Well," said Pharoah, "he's just a small part player with minimal billing. Unless like too many butlers before him he turns out to be the least likely suspect."

"He's a very good butler, but he's hardly qualified to be a master criminal."

"Miss Mourami," said Pharoah as they entered the front hall leading to the front door, "master criminals exist only in fiction. There's no such thing in real life. There're villains and head honchos and cheap, petty crooks who wear Armani suits and swagger and strut like they're the kings of the hill. We've got an awful lot of them behind bars and we've got reservations for a hell of a lot more of them. I've locked horns with a very imposing share of them, if I must say so myself."

"And you will," muttered Albert.

Pharoah shot him a look. "Albert and I once collared a lot of Mafia biggies, what was left to collar after some poor, sweet, sick nut decimated most of them." They reached the front door. "Won't Goren sulk because he wasn't asked to show us to the door?"

"Goren is rarely afflicted by the sulks. If he is, he confines them to the privacy of his room. He's quite a lovely man. I inherited him from my father."

Pharoah was staring at the floor. "Is this where Harry Jen lay dying?"

"Yes."

"You don't suppose it deserves a plaque?"

"Oh God." Cylla looked rather ill.

Albert interjected swiftly, "Thank you for your cooperation, Miss Mourami. You've been very helpful."

Pharoah added, "And I'm sure, if necessary, you'll continue to be so in the future." Albert held the door open, and Pharoah sauntered out into the street. Albert followed him, shutting the door behind him. Cylla hurried to the library, sat at her desk, and pushed buttons in one of the phones that would soon connect her with Hiram Wiggs.

Albert steered the car toward Second Avenue, which would take them back to the precinct. "Very interesting lady," said Albert of Cylla. "If she hadn't inherited all that wealth, I think she'd starve to death."

"Her kind never starves," commented Pharoah. "Her mind's as sharp as her features. I'd hate to have her knifing me with that nose. You notice through the window those sculptures in her backyard?"

"The rich don't have backyards. They have terraces or gardens. Backyards are where mothers hang their wash out to dry. I noticed that abortion propped up against the marble wall."

"That's the one I meant. *Pfeh.* No taste. She's probably on the phone to Mr. Wiggs right now. Ah, Wiggsy, Wiggsy, I'll bet you're getting an earful."

• • •

Two in the afternoon and Tisa Cheng was still abed. The exterior of Kao Lee's hotel was drab and covered with graffiti, all of it obscene. The interior was another story. Tastefully furnished and elegantly decorated, all under the direction of Lena Wing, who had the individual rooms copied from a book of interior design that featured the unique creations of the late Syrie Maugham and the very late Lady Mendl. Both had been married to homosexuals. Syrie's husband had been the wealthy novelist W. Somerset Maugham, and Lord Mendl was the last of the British potentates who flaunted their wealth and their connections to royalty. Lena reserved a suite on the top floor for herself, a very well deserved bonus from Kao Lee. Tisa Cheng had one of the Syrie Maugham suites, adapted from a suite in the château in the south of France that belonged to the silent-film-serial queen Pearl White. Now an eighteen-year-old Chinese nitwit luxuriated in the replica.

The ceiling was mirrored, and Tisa gloried in the sight of herself stretched out like a swastika but with less meaning. She sang to herself a song her maternal grandmother had taught her. It was a paean to hope, to life and to the possibility of great wealth, and contained lines about four and twenty hummingbirds baked in a vast spring roll and told of swampy rice fields that would magically produce emeralds and amethysts and lapis lazuli. It promised plump little babies that would spring out of the top of a virgin's head. Man babies, of course, as girl babies were next to useless.

Oh, Grandmother, thought Tisa, fourth sister of the sixth aunt of the twelfth niece, if you could see me now. I have a protector. He is the mighty emperor of all Chinatown, Manhattan division. His name is Kao Lee, and last night he said I was now his empress. This beautiful suite will be mine forever, and I will reign alongside him and he shall lavish me with money and have Lena Wing introduce me to the wonders of Loehmann's and Macy's and Toys "R" Us, whatever they are.

She sat up, a cold expression on her face.

He shall rid himself of his nasty wife, Rhea. He has not said so in so many words, but she was not nice to me when we met last night, when she thought her son, Michael, intended to take me as his bride. Well, Michael shall never take me again. He is very dull in bed, and besides, he wheezes and sighs and snorts a great deal, much like the water buffaloes Father tried to steal.

Oh, Grandmother, for an older man, Kao Lee is so skilled in the art of making love. He whispers such filth in my ears, you'd be tempted to wash his mouth out with bitter almond extract. She giggled. Oh, Grandmother, it is so arousing and erotic. I have never known the blood to rush the way Kao Lee sends it coursing through my veins.

"Okay, sleeping beauty, rise and shine." Lena Wing entered briskly and crossed to the draped windows, pulling them back on their rails and sending daylight into the room. "You were talking to yourself."

"Oh no. Not to myself. To my adored and respected grandmother, O-Lan Shwa."

"I hope you reversed the charges. What time did Kao leave?"

"Oh, it was still darkness outside. That is why I have slept this late. I have always been an early riser, living on a junk that rose and fell in the water, filling me with nausea. Oh! What is this?"

A young black woman wearing slacks and a sequined blouse had entered carrying a breakfast tray. She set it down on a small lacquered table next to the bed. "Good afternoon," she said in an accent that betrayed her Bronx origins. "Kao Lee told me to look after you until you've learned the ropes."

"Ropes?" asked Tisa as she sniffed the scrambled eggs and bacon and home fries and rye bread toast and steaming hot coffee.

"Yeah, ropes, by which you try not to hang yourself. My name is Anna May Jefferson and my room is across from yours. If you hear a lot of thumping and giggling and gasping for breath, don't knock, because I'm otherwise occupied. Give it a half hour and then come back."

Tisa clapped her hands with joy. "Oh! You are my handmaiden! You will draw my bath!"

Anna May flashed Lena Wing a look, Lena Wing immensely enjoying the colloquy. Anna May put her hands on her hips and rasped, "I ain't drawing you no bath because I ain't got no crayons, and as for being your handmaiden, I leave you with two words, *fat chance.*" With which she turned and sashayed out of the room, leaving in her wake the sickly strong scent of heliotrope.

Lena stood watching Tisa, who obviously did not know what to make of the likes of Anna May Jefferson. Lena indicated the tray of food. "Eat," she commanded.

"No rice," said Tina forlornly.

"Rice is for weddings," said Lena, and explained the contents of the tray to Lisa. She drew up a chair and sat. "Don't let me spoil your appetite, but whatever Kao Lee promised you in the heat of his passion, don't hold your breath."

Tisa studied Lena's strong and beautiful face. "We are rivals?"

"No, honey, he's all yours and you're welcome to him. Make the most of it. The money, the gifts, the best restaurants, this room." She smiled. "But remember what that great Chinese philosopher Confusion said . . ."

"Confusion?"

"Yeah, he specialized in naive teenagers. Confusion say, Take all sugar with a grain of salt. Anna May will bring you some clothes. She's thrown out the stuff you were wearing. We'll get your hair done, get your fingernails manicured, then we go shopping for some new clothes, and the rest is up to your daddy."

"Daddy? My daddy is in jail."

"The one I'm referring to is doing his damndest to keep himself out of jail."

CHAPTER 12

That morning, Rhea Lee sat across the dining table from her husband. On her plate was a thin slice of buttered toast. In her cup was decaffeinated coffee. Kao was pigging out on kippers, ham, grits and eggs. He alternated mouthfuls of food with mouthfuls of piping hot coffee. Their silence was not unusual. Rhea always waited for him to finish eating before beginning her daily peroration. Suddenly, he pushed his plate to one side and lit a cigar.

"Your silence, this morning, is deafening."

"I want you to send Michael away."

She had succeeded in irritating him. "Now what the hell's that all about?"

"I don't want him to end up dead in the street like his father did. And I want him away from your influence. He was not cut out to be one of your toadies."

Kao mocked her. "Of course not. He's a prince. He was to the manor born. He is deserving of worthier than I have to offer." He snarled. "In China he'd be a miserable coolie pulling a ricksha! He'd be humbling himself on a street corner begging for coins. Or at the best, he'd be some whore's singsong man, pimping for her, living off her earnings, and proving to himself he's a man by beating her nightly."

"You shut up! Whatever he would be, it would be better than what you have planned for him. Letting him sail on the freighter. If he'd been caught, he'd be in jail with the others, deported back to the old country!"

"Don't be such a damned fool! With my connections, he wouldn't be behind bars longer than twenty-four hours."

"I should never have married you."

"I didn't have to twist your arm."

"But you had to murder Zang."

He mimicked her mercilessly. "*But you had to murder Zang.* Every other day the same singsong shit. I remember you used to whisper in my ear, 'Again, again, Kao, do it again.' "

"I was being polite." She leaned forward. "Kao, I beg you. Let Michael breathe. Let him live a decent life. He must not take up with this cheap baggage he brought back with him."

"She is not cheap baggage!" Kao stormed.

Rhea smiled slowly. "Oh. Of course. The emperor has taken a new concubine to his bed."

"It bothers you?"

"You know I couldn't care less. Kao, tell Michael you no longer want him in the Chi Who."

"You know the only way to quit the gang is by death."

"If anything happens to Michael . . ."

"Yes?"

She glared at him. The hatred was reflected in her eyes like a wall of menacing flames. He pushed his chair back and got up.

"You have one serious flaw, Rhea. You're not a stupid woman. You should have been a stupid woman. Then, like all stupid women, you'd be content." He waved his hand in an arc that encompassed the room. "You'd be grateful for the wealth. The fine furs. The designer clothes and your jewelry. Michael may be your son, but he no longer belongs to you. He's of age. He belongs to himself."

"Not while you're alive."

"And woman, I'm going to be alive for a long, long, *long* time. I know because it's written in the stars." He left her sitting and staring ahead at his empty chair.

Michael may be your son, but he no longer belongs to you. He's of age. He belongs to himself.

If this is so, thought Rhea, then I too am certainly of age. And I too belong to myself. She came to a decision and with a strong look of resolve, began clearing the table while humming some long-forgotten melody taught her by her first husband, Zang.

At the turn of the century, Grand Street had indeed been a grand street. There had been a legitimate theater that boasted each year a fresh edition of a revue known as *The Grand Street Follies,* which saw the start of the careers of many future stars of vaudeville and the musical theater. There were restaurants that boasted fine European cuisine and even finer European wines. There were specialty shops dealing in the finest of men's and women's haberdashery. The saloons too were so elegant they boasted colored sawdust on their floors and the free lunches featured sliced turkey and ham and potato salad and cole slaw rather than tired sliced salami and bologna with sour pickles and half-sour green tomatoes. There were music shops and portrait galleries and several nickelodeons that provided an hour of silent film entertainment for five cents.

The Grand Street that Albert West drove along with Pharoah at his side searching for the building that housed Kao Lee's export-and-import business had fallen on sorry times. There were tenements with boarded-up windows. On their stoops sat the homeless, forlorn and unwanted. Behind many a boarded-up door there was a steady traffic in drugs. Chinese teenagers roamed the street in groups of four or five or more. Cigarettes dangled from their lips and their pockets bulged with money stolen or extorted from local merchants under threat of bodily harm to them and their families. Pharoah called them "The ugly new breed of bandits." He hated them. They hated him. They also hated each other. There was no place in their vocabulary for the word *loyalty*. Few of them could spell it. But they worked superbly together. They had one thing in common: terrorism. They exchanged women like books from a lending library. They sometimes impregnated them and often abandoned them. Love was an alien emotion. They respected little but the arms they carried. They always roamed in a group. Together they bred fear; together they rendered a victim helpless. Singly they were cowards, without exception. A group of four watched the unmarked police car as it tooled along Grand Street in search of Kao Lee's export-and-import house. Pharoah rolled down the window on his side and shouted out, "Hi, guys! Raped your sisters lately?" The four responded with erect middle fingers.

Albert said, "That must be it, up ahead on the left." He read, "Mandarin Exports and Imports."

Pharoah said, "Pull over there. Where it says 'No Parking!'"

When the car was parked and locked, Pharoah led the way into the store. It was cavernous, a huge supermarket designed to house a magnificent variety of goods. There were bolts of cloth of various colors and quality. Pharoah fingered one and said unkindly, "*Shmotta*," the Yiddish word for "rag." There were any number of household appliances on display at bargain prices. There were shoes, hats, rugs, figurines, religious items, exotic groceries from the Far East. There was everything there but peace of mind. Pharoah saw a staircase partially hidden behind a display of electrical supplies. "That must be it," said Pharoah. He headed for the stairs with Albert in his wake. Suddenly their way was blocked by a young man wearing thick-lensed glasses.

"You can't go up there. It's private," he said.

"Is that Kao Lee's office?"

"Yes, it is."

"He expects us." Pharoah flashed his badge. "And we're not chicken inspectors."

"That's good. We haven't any chickens for you to inspect."

Pharoah groaned. "You're too young to know burlesque routines."

"Your names?"

Pharoah told him.

"Wait here, please." He headed up the stairs slowly.

"Come on, Albert," said Pharoah as he followed the man up the stairs. "You know how I can't stand taking orders." The young man turned and glared at them. "Careful, buddy boy," said Pharoah, "or you'll turn into a pillar of salt." The young man opened the door that led into the comfortably furnished outer office, where three young women sat who Pharoah presumed were secretaries. One was busy at a typewriter, another was filing papers and one sat at a desk doing *The New York Times* crossword puzzle.

The young man led them to the woman at the desk. He repeated their names as she looked up. She was, surprisingly, not Asian. "Okay, Francis, they're expected." Francis left them while the secretary offered them seats. "Mr. Lee's on long distance. He should be finished soon." She studied them both intensely. "Either one of you a college graduate?"

Pharoah stuck a thumb toward Albert. "This one. The black sheep."

The woman asked Albert, "What's a surgical instrument that begins with *x*?"

Like a shot Albert responded, "Xyster."

"Will you marry me?" She filled in the word. "They got this new puzzle editor at the *Times*. Very cutesy pie. But I'm addicted, so I continue struggling with them." She stared from one to the other. "Which one is which?"

Pharoah identified himself and Albert.

"I'm Toby Lewis, the token Caucasian."

"Do you feel like a fish out of water?" asked Pharoah.

"No, I feel like a Jew out of Brooklyn. It's very pleasant working here except I'm always hungry."

"You've been with Mr. Lee a long time?"

"About three years. Let me see . . ." She screwed up her face and stared at a spot on the wall. "Yes. A little over three years. A couple of months after my invalid mother passed away, reluctantly releasing me from bondage."

Pharoah said, "You must know a lot of what goes on around here."

"What goes on around here," she said pleasantly, "is importing and exporting."

"I'll bet you could write a book," said Pharoah.

"I haven't got the talent."

"I'll bet you've got the information."

"I know names and addresses that cover the Orient. I'm on long-distance speaking terms with a lot of one-syllable names, some of whom I can understand."

"I'll bet Mr. Lee has been getting a lot of flak about the freighter today."

"Oh, is that what all the fuss is about?"

"Has there been a lot of fuss?"

"More than usual."

"Mr. Lee lost a big shipment."

"He carries a lot of insurance."

"Not for this cargo. I doubt if there was any insurance at all for this cargo."

She returned to the puzzle. "Son of a bitch. Here's another stinker. Does the name Kenny Delmar ring a bell?"

Albert said, "Senator Claghorn."

"Who in God's name is Senator Claghorn?"

"A character on Fred Allen's radio show, *Allen's Alley.*"

"Who the hell was Fred Allen?"

Albert fought an urge to wring her neck.

Pharoah said, "Does he know we're waiting?"

"He'll know in a second. He just got off the phone." She picked up a phone and announced Pharoah and Albert. She replaced the phone and said, "You can go in now."

"Will you be all right without us?" asked Pharoah sweetly.

"Well, if Albert could just give me a hint about 'ballerina Alicia.' "

"Try 'Markova.' If that doesn't work, try 'Alonso.' "

Kao Lee was lighting another of his obscenely long cigars as the detectives came into his office. He was standing at a large desk covered with phones and stacks of papers and a computer and all sorts of accoutrements pertaining, Pharoah supposed, to the export-and-import business. All it lacked, it seemed to Pharoah, was a birdbath. Behind Kao was a large window that afforded an unappetizing view of some abandoned building where a derelict slept on a fire escape wrapped in what were likely torn burlap bags. Kao greeted them surprisingly affably and indicated two chairs that faced the desk.

To Albert's surprise, Pharoah began the conversation diplomatically. "Thanks for not giving us a stall."

"I have no reason to stall. Your request to meet with me was reasonable enough. After all, haven't I been a friend to the police all these years? You are welcome in the Warehouse. You"—he waved his cigar at Albert—"are practically a fixture."

"I like the atmosphere. Very *Shanghai Gesture*."

"How is that? What is *Shanghai Gesture*?"

"A very famous play in the 1920s about a notorious gambling casino in Shanghai run by a notorious half-caste woman called Mother Goddam. In the movie it was changed to Mother Gin Sling."

Pharoah said to Albert, "You are the caretaker of more useless trivia. How do you live with yourself?"

"Quite comfortably."

Kao said to Pharoah, "You've been away." He puffed the cigar. "And I know where. No need to beat around the bush and deny it."

"I don't beat around the bushes, Kao. I'd never admit to a couple of weeks at a Club Med, but the glorious adventure I so recently survived is forever embedded in my memory, like Excalibur in stone." He smiled. "Maybe I can sell it to the movies for Wesley Snipes."

"Denzel Washington is bigger box office. Tell me, are you here to charge me with something or to just ask questions?"

Said Pharoah, "We're not about to charge anybody with anything."

"That's good. I've had enough accusations for one morning. I need a breather." He favored Pharoah. "Michael is very fond of you."

"I'm very fond of Michael. I wouldn't want to marry him, but I'm very fond of him. I would first like to talk about Harry Jen. I don't suppose you care to tell me which one of your gangsters killed him?"

"I see subtlety is not your strong suit."

"No need to beat around the bush. Let's go to the tape. Harry Jen, on his way to Cylla Mourami's after a brief visit to the precinct, was shot in the thigh with a pellet of ricin . . ."

". . . and was taken to an emergency room, where he died," said Kao Lee impatiently.

"You left out a scene. He collapsed in the hallway of Cylla Mourami's stately mansion."

"Oh, good. Thank you. That does complete the jigsaw puzzle. So

Cylla arranged his removal to the hospital. It's nice to know she occasionally does good works."

"We know that you two have agreed to disagree."

"Yes. Professional differences."

"Financial differences, from what she told us."

"Ah! So you *have* met with Cylla."

"I tell you, we are so busy today," said Pharoah, slapping his thigh, "running from base to base and so far no home run. Come on, Kao, be a good guy for once and finger Harry's killer." Kao laughed. "That's such a hearty laugh, Kao. I'd prefer an embarrassed chuckle or even a nonentity of a titter but such a hearty laugh. Do you want to talk about Zang?"

"My brother Zang?"

"Well, he wasn't your sister."

"You killed him, didn't you?" asked Albert bluntly.

Kao asked in mock astonishment, "You saw me kill him?" Pharoah crossed one leg over the other. He wanted to dislike Kao Lee but he couldn't. The man was so delightfully brazen, so completely self-assured, so absolutely taken with himself. If he played the piano and sang he might pass himself off as an Asian Liberace. "Zang died a long time ago. There's the statute of limitations."

"It doesn't apply to murder," said Pharoah.

"Since when?"

"Since always."

"You live and you learn. Did Michael say I killed him?"

"You wanted your sister-in-law that badly."

"Did Michael say I killed him?" Kao repeated.

"Michael said a lot of things that I'm sure if you asked him now he won't remember having said. We became pals right away. We were bosom buddies. Don't be jealous, Albert."

"I'm fighting back tears."

Pharoah snapped to Kao, "Where's Tisa Cheng?"

"She's safe."

"You're harboring a fugitive."

"She's just a teenager."

"Okay, so you're harboring a teenage fugitive."

"Probably keeping her in the hotel," contributed Albert.

"Gentlemen, you are much too clever for me today, much too clever."

Pharoah's hands were outstretched as though he was in danger of dropping to one knee and singing "Mammy." "Kao, we've barely begun! We've got questions about kidnappings and blackmail and extortion and God wot! Shall we go down the list alphabetically or take pot luck?"

Kao was getting angry. "Why aren't you out there rounding up these murderous teenage boys who are threatening and killing at random!"

"They're also playing hookey."

"They don't play hockey!"

"I said *hookey!*" Their eyes locked. "You're in bad trouble, Kao. You may have to close the Warehouse."

"Bullshit."

"Your creditors are closing in on you. There's not enough ricin in the store to take care of all of them." Kao puffed the cigar. "Who do you answer to, Kao? Who's the real boss behind your operation? Who pulls the strings? Who gives the orders? Who's your ventriloquist?"

"You are very insulting."

"I want answers," said Pharoah in a steely tone of voice.

"Have I been subpoenaed? Am I under oath? You phoned and asked to meet to ask questions. I said okay. I didn't stall, did I? I didn't pack a bag and head for the airport, did I?"

"No, you'd have closed a bank account first, if you've still got one to close."

Kao leaned forward, looking vaguely menacing. "I am hardly poverty stricken."

"It's all in your wife's name," Pharoah stated flatly.

Kao Lee collapsed with laughter. Albert looked at Pharoah, who looked back with a silly grin and shrugged. "Oh, that's a good one," gasped Kao. "That's a really good one. All in my wife's name! Oh boy! Do I strike you as being such an idiot? All those holdings belong to her sister. She's the rich one." He stopped laughing.

"Who's her sister?"

"Wilma Joy."

Pharoah raised an eyebrow. "Wilma Joy dresses? Wilma Joy stores? That's your wife's sister?"

"They loathe each other, but politely. That is the way with us Chinese."

"Chinese women are usually thicker than glue. I saw *The Joy Luck Club*."

"This isn't fiction. Wilma was my girlfriend when I brought Zang and his family to Frisco. We were very much in love. But when I laid eyes on Rhea, all that changed. It changed for me. Now I wanted Rhea. I told Wilma because it was the decent thing to do."

"It's nice to know you sometimes do decent things. And Wilma bowed out gracefully."

"Hell no. Wilma has a violent temper and a large and fascinating vocabulary. If it wasn't for her features you'd never believe she was Asian. She went to Zang and told him and tried to beat up Rhea, who fortunately was very quick on her feet. Zang was on his way to confront me when he dropped dead on Delancey Street and lay unidentified in a doorway for so many hours."

"Conveniently dropped dead with a little help from a pellet of ricin. Who did it for you?"

Kao said softly, "I am blameless."

Albert exhaled and said to Pharoah, "Well, this was a nice bonus. You ever in touch with Wilma?"

"To quote Mr. Bernard Shaw, 'Not bloody likely.' "

Pharoah persisted. "Let's get back to Harry Jen."

"Why? He was a very boring person and now he's a very boring corpse. Lena Wing has convinced me that as a former employee it is my business to claim and cremate him."

Albert said to Pharoah, "Lena's a very smart cookie. She's ambitious. She's got big plans for herself. Say! Maybe she's the brains behind the organization. Why not? I like Lena. Sometimes she lets me win at blackjack before winning it all back."

"Put a cork in it, Albert," Pharoah said, and returned his attention to Kao Lee. "It would be easier if you cooperated. Sooner or later we're going to break you. The Feds are at your rear and nipping. They're piling up a big, thick dossier that's going to bring you down. Cooperate and it'll go easier with you. Instead of life you might get fifty years."

From out of nowhere, Kao Lee said, "I'm very impressed with you two."

"Oh, come on, Kao," said the impatient Pharoah, "the weather's too nice for a snow job."

"This is not a snow job," said Kao. "What my organization suffers from is a lack of leaders. I need help. I need two very smart guys to come work for me."

"Why you brazen hussy!" exclaimed Pharoah. "Do you know what the penalty is for attempted bribery?"

"Who's attempting bribery? I'm legitimately offering you jobs. I'll pay you double what you're making now."

"Oh! Oh! Oh!" cried Pharoah, "my knees are turning to jelly! My eyes are glazing over! The room is spinning! Leave the police force? Betray our principles?" He paused. "Double what we're making now?"

They heard gunshots in the outer office followed by hysterical screams.

"Assassins!" shouted Kao as he dived behind his desk.

Pharoah and Albert, guns drawn, positioned themselves on either side of the door. "Albert?"

"What?" hissed Albert.

"Isn't this such a fun day?"

CHAPTER 13

Kao kept an SKS semiautomatic in a bottom drawer of his desk. He retrieved it swiftly and its weight assured him it was fully loaded. Imported from China, it was one of the most dangerous weapons in use on the streets.

His back to the wall, clutching his Glock with both hands, Pharoah said, "Kao, if your hands aren't trembling too much, dial 911 for backup."

"I already have."

"Where do you keep the cash?"

"How much do you need?"

"Kao, you're too old to be cute."

"It's in the safe."

"Where's the safe?"

"Didn't you notice? It's out there with the girls."

"Do any of them know the combo?"

"My secretary. Toby."

They heard a scream.

Kao said, "That must be Toby. She's so sensitive."

Pharoah persisted, "Where does the fire escape lead to?"

"Downstairs. The loading platforms."

"Is there access to the store from there?"

"A door that opens under the stairs that lead up here."

"Albert," ordered Pharoah, "open the window."

"Why? It's not stuffy in here."

"Albert. This is not *Saturday Night Live*. We are under attack by bandits." They heard another scream. "And I don't think Toby has much more scream left in her."

"What makes you think it's Toby?"

"Because it's the only name I know that belongs to anybody out there! Move it, damn it!"

Albert scurried across the floor, opened the window, climbed out onto the fire escape and headed down the one flight to the loading platform. Pharoah moved so fast behind him he almost sent Albert flying face first onto the platform. Behind them came Kao, cigar held tightly between his teeth, the SKS held tightly in his left hand. At the door that led into the store, Pharoah stood quietly with his ear against the wood. He held an index finger to his lips.

"Albert," whispered Pharoah.

"What?"

"Remember, there are innocent civilians in there."

"Don't tell me, tell the bad guys."

"I'm going to open the door very slowly. Back me up aiming your gun into the store. If anybody asks for a discount, shoot."

Cautiously, slowly, Pharoah opened the door. He espied Francis lying on the floor with his hands behind his head. As he opened the door wider, he saw other store employees and customers stretched out on the floor. They hadn't heard gunfire, so all had to be still among the living. Pharoah cautiously edged his body into the store and now saw two slightly built young men with silk stockings over their heads menacing the place with handguns. He had the gut feeling these were two of the four teenagers he had razzed twenty minutes ago on the street. Why the brazen little bastards! We arrived when they were casing the joint for a quick hit! They must have known we were cops but they audaciously went ahead with the heist! He signaled silence and caution to Albert and Kao behind him and then held up two fingers. Albert nodded he understood. Kao mistook the two fingers for an obscene gesture meant for him and wondered how he had offended this outlandish police officer.

Pharoah pushed the door wide. It made a loud, thwacking noise as it hit the wall. "Freeze, you motherfuckers, and drop your weapons!" Amazingly, there was no show of contempt and bravura on their part. They complied instantly. "How many more upstairs?" Pharoah asked Francis, who was on his feet and reaching into a bin for a baseball bat.

"Two," Francis told him.

"Francis," Pharoah pronounced the name with exaggerated patience, "put the bat away. Get some rope and tie the two fuckers up. Kao! Get back out there and cover the fire escape." Kao hurried out. He was a kid again. He was playing cops and robbers and wasn't sure which one he was. "Pharoah," said Albert, "I'm going up."

"Why, for crying out loud? If they can't make it out the fire escape, they'll be coming down the stairs like a pair of show girls." He looked at one of the bandits with his silk-stocking disguise. "You silly bitch, you've got a run."

"It's too quiet up there," said Albert.

"It's too quiet out on the street," said Pharoah. "No sirens. I suppose the ladies aren't back from lunch yet." He started bellowing "Here's to the Ladies Who Lunch" from Sondheim's *Company*.

Albert paled. "You damn fool! They'll hear you! They'll be out here with guns blazing!"

Pharoah took the two store bandits, one by each arm, their hands now tied behind their backs, and walked them to the foot of the stairs while still bellowing.

Upstairs in the office, Toby Lewis, sitting behind her desk with ugly bruises on her face, stared down at her crossword puzzle and, despite her pain, gasped, "Aha! Sondheim!"

The safe was opened. Toby had given them the combination. The two had been clearing out the cash and valuables when Pharoah's serenade attacked their ears. The two other women in the room were huddled together behind Toby, clutching each other as though they were straws in the wind. They heard the sounds of sirens approaching. Toby hoped there was an ambulance with at least one gorgeous, unattached emergency worker.

The bandits were stuffing cash into the pockets of the windbreakers they were wearing. On the backs of the windbreakers was emblazoned the name of their gang, OUT FOR BLOOD. Toby clucked her tongue and thought, Whoever coined the phrase "Damn clever these Chinese" couldn't have had these two dumbbells in mind.

The bandits, guns now drawn again, kicked open the door to Kao Lee's office. One pointed to the open window leading to the fire escape and both made for it. The first one to go out caught a slug from Kao Lee's SKS in his shoulder. He fell back with an indignant look albeit obscured by the stocking he wore. The other boy turned and hightailed it back to the outer office and swiftly past Toby, who muttered, "You forgot to touch second, you son of a bitch."

At the bottom of the stairs stood the two bandits with their hands tied behind their backs. A few feet from them stood Pharoah and Albert, guns aiming up. "Yo, asshole!" greeted Pharoah. The sirens were still wailing as two police cars and an ambulance screeched to a halt in the street. On the opposite side of the street there stood a small but curious audience. It would have been larger in previous years, but the neighborhood had entertained so much police activity that most inhabitants had grown blasé and preferred to wait to read about the action in the morning tabloids.

Each police car ejected four officers who rushed into the store, all eight remembering to draw their guns seemingly bravely oblivious to whatever danger awaited within.

As they arrived, Pharoah shouted to the thug at the top of the stairs to drop his gun, which the young man did with alacrity. Pharoah took the stairs two at a time and, with a cuff to the back of his neck, sent the thug sailing down the stairs, knocking over the two thugs awaiting him there like tenpins in a bowling alley. In the outer office Toby was at a sink attempting to repair her face. "Hurt bad?" asked Pharoah, rushing past her.

"Does it ever hurt good?" she shouted at him, while her two coworkers were on two phones seeking comfort from their mothers.

Pharoah collared the young thug who was slumped on the floor clutching his left arm. "That hurts! Take it easy!" he whined as Pharoah pulled him to his feet.

"You can have a nice long rest on Riker's Island, you little *pisher*."

He shoved him ahead of him into the outer office. As they entered, Toby saw their reflections in the mirror over the sink, turned and whammed the young thug in his face with her handbag. She snarled at Pharoah, "I know! I know! But it gives me satisfaction!" Pharoah laughed and gave the punk a strong shove that sent him sailing out the office and down the stairs. Toby clucked her tongue. "Police brutality. I can never see enough of it." Pharoah literally tapped his way down the stairs and sent one ambulance attendant—the handsomest available—up to see Toby. The other saw to the punk with the wounded shoulder. Kao had come in from the loading platform and was ripping the stockings from the heads of the gang members.

There was no missing the menace in Kao's voice. "I must memorize their faces. I must never forget them."

Pharoah said to the four miscreants, "Haven't you guys ever heard of Kao Lee? This is him. Mr. Chinatown! The Bandit's bandit! You little cockroaches dare shake down Kao Lee?"

Kao Lee was lighting his cigar as he studied the four defiant faces. The two whose hands Francis had tied might have been twins, although it turned out they were only brothers, Tommy and Norton Kim. The one with the slug in his shoulder was Looey Kua, their ringleader. The fourth, when asked by Pharoah, identified himself as Mao Tse Conti. He explained the Conti to a curious Pharoah, "My grandfather owned a pizzeria in the Village."

Albert had helped himself to a chocolate-covered frozen banana on a stick after holstering his gun, and was a picture of contentment. Pharoah said to him, "Albert, that is positively obscene."

"Tough titty. It's delicious and I've had no lunch."

"We haven't finished with Kao."

"Yes you have," said Kao. He had ordered Francis to load a camera and photograph the four hoodlums, which Francis was now doing.

"Christ, they're teenagers! Little *shlimozels!*" Pharoah had learned a colorful vocabulary from his Jewish neighbors in Canarsie. *Shlimozels.* Nobodies. Nothings. "You taking their pictures for your scrapbook, Kao?"

"A very special scrapbook, Pharoah." Pharoah knew what he would do, distribute copies of the photographs to his henchmen with orders to maim them on sight, possibly even kill them. There was no way Pharoah could stop him.

Kao stood in front of Pharoah. "And how will you handle them? If they're under eighteen, you arraign them in juvenile court."

"That's right. I go by the book."

"Your book needs rewriting. Their parents will come to court and weep and wail and tell the judge what good boys they are, sometimes mischievous—after all, boys will be boys. They rob, they kill, they terrorize and beat up women, they extort, they kidnap."

"Such versatility astounds me," remarked Pharoah.

Kao glared at Pharoah. "Don't mock me."

Pharoah snapped, "These punks are just a juvenile replica of you. You rob, you kill, you terrorize and beat up women, you extort, you kidnap, and you smuggle anything and anybody. Kao, you and the rest of your misfits make me sick. The only thing that keeps me from puking is the knowledge you're not going to be around to cause anybody any more trouble any longer."

"Jesus Christ," said Albert, "what awful grammar."

Pharoah wheeled on him. "In an emergency you expect perfection?" He turned back to Kao. "You know something, Kao, I wouldn't be a bit surprised if these kids knew more about you than we did. Where you've got your kidnap victims locked up. Where some bodies are buried." Pharoah's attention was now on the four boys. "Give what I just said to the godfather a lot of thinking over. I might get the judge to go easy on you. Instead of the pen, maybe the girls' dormitory at Barnard."

"Oh, yummy," said Mao Tse Conti.

"Putz." Pharoah spat the word at them. He went to the stairs and shouted up, "How she doing up there?" Toby Lewis herself appeared in the doorway, two neat squares of white bandage on her left cheek and left forehead.

Hands on hips, she asked, "Do you think this could be the start of a fad?"

"Toby Lewis, you're real cute. You ought to think about becoming a cop."

"Maybe not a bad idea."

"I'm at the Fifth, if you need some help."

"How about your partner?"

"Of course he's there too."

"My mouth is watering." She winked and returned to the room. Kao walked past Pharoah up the stairs.

"Sorry," said Pharoah.

Kao stopped in his tracks, turned to the detective and asked, "Sorry for what?"

"I thought I was crowding you."

Kao didn't respond. He just glared and continued up the stairs while Francis hurried to the back of the emporium with the camera. The police herded the punks into the street as a paddy wagon arrived.

Pharoah and Albert exchanged a few words with some of the police officers and then got into their car. As Albert revved the motor, Pharoah slumped in his seat dejectedly.

"What's wrong?" asked Albert.

"These extracurricular activities depress me. These perps have ruined my day."

The motor stopped. Albert turned and stared at Pharoah. "I thought you said variety was the spice of life."

"Those kids are just *kids*. What's worse is each and every one of them's a killer. A life means nothing to them. That punk could have murdered Toby. Look at the way he hurt her face. Was there any reason for that violence?"

"Maybe she sassed him. She's a strong lady," Albert stated with admiration.

"Punks. Stinking little punks. I'll bet each and every one of them was born here. Learned it all on the street. And now we've got *them* to worry about."

"Why?" Albert was back to revving the motor.

"You think Mao Tse Conti and his all-boy Cantonese band are going to forget us? Once they're on the loose again they'll be on the prowl for us. They'll be thinking about it and lusting for it while serving their sentences."

"You're so sure they'll be serving sentences?" Albert asked.

"Oh God. There's that too. The bleeding hearts will come running to their defense." He mimicked savagely, "These poor underprivileged youngsters. Brought up in the slums. Living with rats and mice and lice. Their mothers are whores and their fathers are alcoholics."

Albert corrected, "Their mothers are seamstresses in a sweatshop and their fathers iron shirts in a basement laundry that's twenty degrees hotter than hell. These peasants came to America looking for a better life, look what they got. The hell with those kids. Let them come after us. We are brave, fearless police officers who have stared down death on many an occasion."

"Albert, you're watching too much public television. Where we headed?"

"Back to the station to file our report. Then we try playing pin the donkey with Tisa Cheng. I'm sure Kao has her stashed in the hotel behind the Warehouse." He paused. "He's probably put dibs on her by now, which leaves poor Michael staggering against the ropes."

"Poor Michael, let me assure you, doesn't give a crap. He'd had it with Tisa by the third week at sea. Hey! Pull over. Let's get lunch. Over there. The Leaning Tower of Pizza."

"Of course," said Albert, "we're in SoHo."

In the restaurant, Pharoah was enjoying making a big display of ordering a certain mixture of pizza. The waiter was young and when asked if he was a moonlighting actor his eyes and cheeks brightened but his brain remained as sluggish as always. "Had any callbacks lately?" asked Pharoah as he perused the menu and Albert sat with his arms folded waiting for Pharoah to return to a semblance of sanity.

"Yeah. I sure did. The road company of *Grease*."

"Does it look good?"

The young man said frankly, "It would look better if I slept with one of the producers."

"So what have you got to lose?"

"I'm not sleepy."

Albert liked that and smiled. Pharoah nudged his leg under the table.

"Are you ready to order or do you want a few minutes?"

Pharoah asked, "Albert?"

"Let's order. We haven't got that much time. No anchovies."

"Right." He rattled off to the waiter, "Pepperoni, mozzarella, peppers, black olives, sliced onions and some Maalox."

Albert added, "Two light beers. The brand doesn't matter as long as they're light."

The boy nodded and walked away while still meticulously jotting down their order.

Albert resumed the conversation they were in the midst of in the car. "Poor Michael doesn't give a crap. What does poor Michael give?"

"Meaning?"

"You really think he's hanging in there just in the hopes of cashing in if and when Kao Lee goes?"

"In his place, I suppose I would. He's got at best a chancy future without stepfather/uncle's patronage."

"You're sure that under that much-too-placid exterior there does not boil a seething volcano ready to erupt and wreak havoc?"

"Cut the melodramatics and get to the point if there's a point to get to."

"Revenge, Pharoah. Satisfaction. Kao murdered Michael's father and defiled and corrupted his mother."

"Mother strikes me as having been a very willing victim."

"Mother steals sister Wilma's boyfriend. There's that to consider."

"We only have Kao's word for that."

"You think he's made it all up?"

"Albert," he said as the waiter plopped their beers and two glasses on the table, "Kao is a professional bullshit artist. All these thieves are. They've got more twists and turns in them than the Grand Corniche." He paused as he thought. "We should have a talk with Mama. And Kao mustn't know about it. Rhea must know plenty about what's been going on behind the scenes. Rhea and Lena Wing."

"They're both within easy accessibility," said Albert as he poured his beer. "What are you thinking about now?"

"I'm thinking about Michael and his mother and Lena Wing and maybe Tisa Cheng. I'm wondering which one of them is going to unite Kao with his ancestors."

"Do you think it's worrying Kao?"

"Albert, behind his phony brave facade, there trembles a very frightened man. I mean when the excitement broke out at the store, did you see that dive he took behind his desk? I think he's been practicing a lot of diving."

CHAPTER 14

Rhea Lee sat at the counter of a coffee shop on Madison Avenue in the Sixties, toying with a small Caesar salad and sipping black coffee. Through the window she could see across the street her sister's most famous dress shop, this one, the New York flagship. It was a shrine to Wilma Joy's exquisite taste and showmanship. The Wilma Joy look was world famous. She ranked with Bill Blass and Oscar de la Renta as a leader in the field of fashion. On the second floor in the front were the firm's offices, and in the back, Wilma's small theater, designed by herself, where four times a year she previewed the coming season's fashions. Tickets to these shows were always at a premium. Fashion arbiters flew in from all over the world and fought, pleaded and bribed for a ticket to the epiphany. The fortunate ones took great pleasure in lording it over the less favored, many of whom were ingenious enough to have themselves called out of town or booked into private sanitariums by way of feeble explanation as to why they were not at Wilma Joy's showing.

When one season Wilma announced in the gossip columns and trade papers that her next showing would feature world-class celebrities as her runway models, Wilma was besieged with stars offering themselves for participation, like sacrificial offerings to a bellicose god. Wilma treated all this with great good humor, which disguised her basic contempt. It was an open secret that Wilma did not design all her clothes. Promising young designers fresh out of school fought for the opportunity to give Wilma a first look at their work, and Wilma cannily made some very sound selections.

Although in her late fifties—some cattily said early sixties—Wilma was ageless. Her clear and unlined skin was porcelain white. She wore just a trace of makeup, a blush of rouge for her cheeks, a hint of carmine for her lips, a light application of mascara for her eyelashes.

In her private office overlooking the hustle and bustle of Madison Avenue, Wilma's floor was covered with numerous designs by young hopefuls. Seated at her desk, Wilma was finishing an exotic lunch of hot potato knish and cold borscht with a boiled potato. Later, there would be champagne from her vineyards in France sent to her by special Concorde. Although her office door was closed, Wilma could hear the steady rush of activity in the other offices: typewriters, fax machine, computers, models cursing fitters, fitters cursing models, lots of dashing about and the slamming of doors. Frequently one of the numerous phones on Wilma's desk would ring and the store manager would apprise her of the arrival of a celebrity or a politician's wife or somebody's mistress. Occasionally somebody's mistress and somebody's wife would strike up a conversation unaware of each other's true identity while the manager would eavesdrop, ready to politically intervene should the cat be about to escape from the bag. It was not unusual for a gentleman to enter with his latest escapade only to find some object sailing past his head flung by the recent discard. The manager tried to keep the breakage of decorative bric-a-brac to a minimum, which required some fancy footwork and a boardinghouse reach.

Wilma relied completely and heavily on her assistant, Chana Ritch, who had been with her for over a quarter of a century. Chana had been a Radio City Music Hall Rockette forced into an early retirement by varicose veins and fallen arches. She had a great sense of fashion and a wonderful eye for style, and Wilma was at the time beginning to create what was to become a monster of an empire. Rumors circulated about Wilma and Chana early in their relationship, they were so constantly together both at work and outside of it. But Kao Lee was also in occasional attendance during that time. His then sister-in-law Rhea, being Wilma's sister, had introduced Wilma to Kao. The handsome, wiry, sometimes too clever Kao amused Wilma when he dated her, but secretly Kao's sights were set on the more delectable Rhea. Chana bore the interlaced relationships with forbearance unusual for an ambitious Hungarian. In time she learned to take anything that befell Wilma in stride. It was soon clear Wilma cared more for Chana than she did for either Kao or Zang's wife, Rhea. Soon Zang would be dead and Rhea would marry Kao and Wilma wouldn't see too much of either of them, especially now that her empire was beginning to expand across the country and across oceans into Europe, Africa and Asia. She was listed in *Forbes* magazine as the wealthiest woman in the world but she was never quick with a handout.

So now Wilma sat in her office, having finished her lunch, willing herself to her feet to examine the costume designs on the floor where Chana laid them, while across the street in the coffee shop, her younger sister, unbeknownst to Wilma, toyed with a Caesar salad. Chana entered the office carrying a pad and pen and chomping on a

McIntosh apple. Her mass of hennaed hair was artfully piled atop her head like a display in Bergdorf's window. Her Wilma original from neck to a few inches above her knees tightly encased her, so that she was forced to walk in short, mincing steps. Around her neck were several strings of faux multicolored pearls, the work of a jeweler in Singapore who it was whispered planned to overthrow the government with the help of the Chinese communists, despite a shrewish wife who wanted to live in Paris. Chana sported several diamond-and-emerald bracelets, and a cocktail wristwatch (of sentimental value as Wilma's first gift to Chana, and worth a small fortune despite its age) decorated her left wrist. On a finger of that hand she sported a star sapphire that was almost blinding with its brilliance.

"Oh, good. You finished your lunch," said Chana. She pressed a buzzer on Wilma's desk and soon a young secretary arrived to whisk the lunch dishes away on a tray but not before Chana further ladened her with the remains of her apple.

"What time is it?" asked Wilma.

Chana referred to her wristwatch and told Wilma, "It's three rubies past an emerald." She watched Wilma step out of her shoes and commence a slow walk among the dress designs. "Cylla Mourami's here. She's in sportswear."

"I wish she was in a coma."

"Oh, now," said Chana, who was impressed by Cylla's style, "she's not all that bad."

"She's not all that good. I don't want to see her."

"She hasn't asked to see you."

"She might. If she does, tell her I was cremated this morning."

Chana slipped out of her shoes and examined the drawings on the floor, taking a different path than Wilma's. "What's with this morbid mood all of a sudden? This morning you were all Elsie Dinsmore shouting 'Good morning, world,' 'Good morning, sun,' 'Good morning, bathroom,' 'Good morning, toilet paper' . . ."

"I never said that," snapped Wilma. She indicated a drawing at her feet. "I like this. I like it very much." Chana joined her for a look.

Chana said sternly, "That trimming is monkey fur. You said no more animal furs. No more animal skins."

"We can have ersatz made. Not to worry." She picked up the drawing and carried it to a table where reposed other drawings she had selected earlier in the day as possibilities. She added matter-of-factly, "I may be leaving on a trip soon."

"You just got back from one. Where to this time?"

"Hong Kong, Singapore, Beijing. Meetings, conferences, you know the routine."

"You need a rest."

"We both need a rest." She was crisscrossing the drawings again. "I need to retire."

"Ha!"

"Go ahead. Laugh. I'm serious."

Chana laid the pad and pen on the desk and leaned against the desk with her arms folded against her ample bosom. "You know, I think you mean it this time. Well, we could let the word sneak out that you're interested in a suitor. You'll be besieged."

"*Sounds* easy, doesn't it? It will take years before I can shake myself loose from this business." She knelt beside a painting. "Now this one's really a knockout." Chana joined her.

Chana said, "Didn't you do a similar number a couple of years ago? You know, the red thing that crooked couturier tried duplicating until you got your lawyers after him."

"Well, he claimed it was just a coincidence. And I like this. Here"— she handed Chana the drawing—"put it with the others."

"Don't you plan to do any new designs of your own?"

"Of course I do." Then, "I wish I didn't." There was a buzz, followed by a disembodied voice coming from a square box on the desk.

"Miss Wilma," said the voice, "your sister's here to see you."

Wilma and Chana exchanged glances. "Thank you," said Wilma. "I won't be a minute."

"I smell trouble," said Chana.

"You always smell trouble."

"She rarely comes to see you. Not here. She usually makes a date for lunch."

Both women had put their shoes back on. Chana retrieved the pad and pen from the desk. Wilma crossed to a miniature refrigerator and found a bottle of champagne, which she handed to Chana. "Make yourself useful while I get the glasses." Chana was soon working the cork with her very strong thumbs while Wilma took two glasses from a cabinet. She heard the cork pop as she crossed to the desk.

Chana stared at the two glasses as Wilma passed her. "Aren't I joining you?"

"No, sweetheart. This is going to be sister talk and we don't need any editorializing. Go keep Cylla company if she's still here. But, I repeat, keep her away from me."

Chana plopped the champagne bottle on the desk and, with an undisguised look of annoyance for Wilma, left the room. Wilma poured herself a glass, tasted, shrugged, then said to herself, "Family champagne."

The secretary seated outside Wilma's office smiled at Rhea as Chana emerged. Seated on a settee, Rhea arose at the sight of Chana, who managed a friendly smile. "Why, Rhea, it's been so long. Love your dress. Not one of ours, is it?"

"Saks. Off the rack. There was a sale. I can't resist sales."

Chana said, "Go right on in. Wilma's waiting."

Wilma was headed for the door to see what was keeping her sister, when Rhea entered.

"Why didn't you phone me? We could have had lunch." She led Rhea to a corner of the office arranged as a small sitting room. She carried the bottle of champagne and her glass. She deposited them on a coffee table and said, "I'll get your glass."

"No, no, none for me," begged off Rhea. "Nothing for me." She sat on an Eames chair and Wilma sat on the chaise opposite her.

"What's the trouble?" asked Wilma. "You didn't just come to visit."

Rhea leaned forward. "I need your help, Sister."

Sister? Not Wilma? "What's wrong? Are you ill?"

"Is one ill when one is sick at heart? There's no place for me anymore. Kao has found himself a new mistress. Michael is no longer a part of me." She quickly filled in the previous twenty-four hours for Wilma, from the grounding of the *Green Empress* to Michael and Tisa Cheng's arrival, through the unpleasant breakfast with Kao and, after much agonizing soul searching, her decision to leave her son and husband forever.

"I warned you against marrying him."

"I thought then you were jealous."

"Of you? You with Kao? Good God, never. So why don't you just up and go? Pack and take a powder."

"You know he won't let me. Even if I make good my escape, he'll track me down and bring me back. Wilma, contrary to what you and everyone else thinks, I have very little money."

"Kao has given you no money? No furs? No jewels?"

"No nothing. And now Kao's in trouble. This time it's real bad. Not just money, but the FBI are closing in on him. They had a spy on the freighter. Pharoah Love. A New York City detective they borrowed from the Fifth Precinct."

"Didn't they have a man of their own they could use?"

"They say this man Love is something unique. Kao knows him. Michael admires him." She told Wilma about the closeness that evolved between Pharoah and Michael on the trip. "Wilma, help me to settle in Switzerland."

"Switzerland? Why Switzerland? It's so sterile. There's nothing there but cheese, chocolate and avalanches."

"I have always dreamt of settling in Gstaad. Where the movie stars go."

"The movie stars are gone," she said impatiently. "Come down to earth, Rhea. You're walking in your sleep. You're in cloud-cuckoo-land."

"I don't think so. Switzerland is safe. It's been a refuge for people for centuries. I was thinking I might go back to making ceramics. Don't you remember? I did some very good ones when we were young girls."

"Were we once young girls?"

"We were so close."

"I remember."

"I'm glad you do. Wilma," she pleaded, "let's try to be close again."

"I think that's an undertaking much too big for either one of us."

Rhea stared across the room at the window overlooking Madison Avenue as though it were a movie screen and some special film created only for her was being projected there. "Chinese women in America have come a long way. There's you. There's Maxine Hong Kingston and Amy Tan and the other successful writers. I could be a writer too. Perhaps you don't remember, but I wrote lovely essays when I was in school," she said slyly as she looked upon her sister again.

Wilma sipped some champagne. "What would you write about now?"

"Myself."

Wilma smiled. "Do you think there are so many out there who would be interested in reading about you?"

"Oh, I think so. How Kao brought Zang and me and Michael to San Francisco. And then transported us to New York and got a foothold in the rackets. The killings, the extortions, the kidnappings.

Zang's murder. Everything right up to the present. Doesn't that sound exciting to you?"

The door flew open and Chana bolted in and said, "Sorry to interrupt, but it just came over the radio in the workroom. There was trouble at Kao's export-import place."

"What happened?" cried Rhea.

"Attempted robbery by four teenage bandits."

Rhea cried eagerly, "Is Kao dead?"

Chana cast a fast glance at Wilma. "Nobody's dead. One of the kids caught a slug in his shoulder and Kao's secretary got banged around a little. There were a couple of detectives talking to Kao at the time and they managed to handle things."

"Thank you, Chana," said Wilma. "We'll be finished soon." Chana winked an eye and left. "Speaking of the devil, right, Rhea?"

"It seems as though the stars are against Kao, although perhaps not as much as one could wish," said Rhea thoughtfully. "He consults the famous Madame Khan."

"It sounds like Madame Khan's got a slightly clouded crystal ball."

"There's so much working against Kao. The freighter. The murder of Harry Jen. Did you see that in the papers this morning?"

"Yes. Was he connected to Kao?"

"Of course. It even said so in the articles. He was a pit boss in the Warehouse. He was also a spy for the police and for Cylla Mourami. I'm sure she shops here."

"She browses. Well, what do I do with you?"

"You have powerful friends. Much more powerful than Kao. They could arrange Swiss papers for me. I could become a citizen. I promise you, once I'm away, I will never be a bother to you again."

"This will take a little time, Rhea. This is complicated."

"I will be patient, the way we were taught to be patient."

After Rhea left, Chana returned to the office, where Wilma had just hung up the phone. "Rhea was all aglow. What did you promise her?"

"Chana, when she and I were kids, we were inseparable. She tagged after me wherever I went. She was my shadow. It gave me a feeling of superiority and it took her off my mother's hands."

"What does she want now?"

"She wants me to stop the world so she can get off."

Downstairs in the store, Rhea Lee paused when she reached the bottom of the staircase. She saw Lena Wing and Tisa Cheng being shown some of the more expensive Wilma dresses by a pair of anorexic models. Rhea studied Tisa, her hair now washed and becomingly set, dressed in slacks, shirt and a sweater. Rhea couldn't hear what she was saying, but in dumb show she was waxing eloquent over the quality of Wilma's clothing.

There was a bit of a bitch in Rhea always struggling to get out, and she decided there was no time like the present. She crossed to Lena and Tisa and presented herself. Lena unleashed her own inner bitch and asked smoothly, "Doesn't Tisa look lovely?"

"Yes," said Rhea, "it's remarkable what soap and water can do for a girl." She said to Tisa, "Perhaps Lena told you this is one of my sister's stores."

"Yes, she has. How lucky you are to have such a well-stocked sister."

Rhea ignored this and asked Lena, "Did you know there was an attempted robbery at Kao's store? Kao was right in the middle of it."

"He's not hurt?" gasped Tisa.

"No, he was being questioned by some detectives, luckily for him. They caught the robbers, or something like that. Well, how nice it's been to run into you both." She asked Tisa, "You're living at the hotel?"

"Oh yes," enthused Tisa, "it's so lovely!"

"Yes." Then she added, "For a whorehouse. I'm sure you'll feel at home there." She walked away, now thinking of escape, of Switzerland, of freedom, of how kind and generous Wilma was again after all these years.

Tisa was now alone looking at dresses, Lena having excused herself and gone to phone Kao. She reached him at his office in the store.

"I'm fine," he reassured her and then spoke some choice words reserved for Pharoah and Albert.

"We just ran into Rhea. She was here visiting Wilma." There was silence. "Kao, did you hear me?"

"Lena, do you suppose my astrologer is full of crap?"

CHAPTER 15

The conference room was used mostly as the place where lawyers met with their clients in privacy, or where the brown baggers gathered to eat lunch or dinner. This afternoon, Christy Lombardo was conducting a meeting with a group of Chinatown's leading merchants. Pharoah recognized a restaurant owner, a bank official and the owner of several of the neighborhood's better men's stores. Returning to the precinct to file their report on the attempted robbery, Hutch told them about the meeting called by Christy. Pharoah, anxious to participate in the proceedings, convinced Albert that he was the literary one and better equipped to write the report. While Albert reluctantly repaired to his office, Pharoah made a hasty visit to the men's room, where he combed his ponytail and did some eye exercises, which consisted of touching his nose with the right index finger, then extending the hand as far as possible, and then index finger back to tip of nose until boredom or improved eyesight set in.

He entered the conference room as Christy was being scolded by the restaurant owner, Gai Kiong. "You say not enough Chinese youths make application to join the police force? Is that what you say? You say it would be more powerful to see Asian young men enforcing the law in Chinatown. I agree with you! You hear that? I agree with you. But how many of our sons are being held prisoners, held to ransom under threat of death! How many? *Dozens!* Is there anyone here in this room not suffering the loss of a loved one? So, tell me, Mr. Lombardo, instead of inviting us here for a lecture on good citizenship, why not instead produce the missing?" There were murmurs of assent, and Christy Lombardo wished he could wipe the smirk off Pharoah's mouth.

Kiong continued, "My son has been missing now for three months. Three months! You police have forgotten him! You have filed him away in your dead-letter office. And my cousin! His wife mourns him as though he is dead, but if he is dead, where is his body? These kidnappers and extortionists have hideaways all over the city and in the suburbs. You know many of these locations! Why you don't raid them?"

"Mr. Kiong," began Christy, a bit groggy from the verbal strafing he'd been receiving, "we raid these hideaways as a matter of routine. Somehow they know we're coming. The places are empty."

Tai Liang, the banker, commanded attention. "But many of us *are* paying the ransoms—and still these poor souls are not returned to their families. Where, then, is this money going?"

"Into Kao Lee's Warehouse," piped up Willie Lau, the men's stores tycoon. He stood with hands on hips, causing Pharoah to reflect that a man who hawked men's clothing should appear in public with a better fitting suit than the one he was wearing now. "Why do you not bring down Kao Lee? He operates illegally. Yet you avert your eyes because he is presumably valuable to you. We are worldly men. We know it is frequently necessary for the police to entertain strange bedfellows. But—"

Christy interrupted him, "We've destroyed the Fuk Ching."

"Which is appreciated," acknowledged Willie Lau, "but other established gangs are turning to the Fujianese to reinvent themselves with fresh blood. Shall I tell you why no one has stepped forward to speak for the illegals you have under lock and key? Because they do not dare. Mr. Lombardo, hasn't it occurred to you that the male illegals on the *Green Empress* were possibly imported to join gangs?"

Pharoah and Christy exchanged glances as Albert edged his way into the room, followed by Hutch Casey.

Willie Lau continued, "I myself am of Fujian origin and have recognized other Fujians who I suspect are affiliated with these gangs. I have three daughters. They do not go out in public without bodyguards. They do not have suitors because suitors wish to date a girl, not a girl with a bodyguard." He shook his head from side to side and sighed. "Although we are Chinese, this is a Mexican standoff. You see, Mr. Lombardo, you are expending so much energy which you should be husbanding to bring down Kao Lee and his Chi Who. There's the cancer desperately in need of surgery. I am always willing to cooperate with the police. I contribute to their charities and I always subscribe to your annual Christmas ball."

"*What* annual Christmas ball?" growled Christy.

"The one I shall now cease to subscribe to," said Willie Lau smoothly as his fellow former subscribers exchanged embarrassed glances. "Mr. Lombardo, I have a suggestion to make," Willie Lau offered.

"I'm listening." Christy was also bristling. Annual Christmas ball. Damn those rogue cops!

"These illegal men you hold in custody. Why not offer freedom to those who enroll for police training and successfully complete the course?" His sarcasm was lapping at Lombardo's feet.

"Great idea!" spoke up Pharoah, "and Mr. Lau, you'll certainly do us the honor of addressing the graduating class." Lau's stare at Pharoah was cold enough to freeze the building's pipes. Pharoah flashed teeth in return and soon the room emptied of all but the law officers.

"Well, that went over like a lead balloon," said Christy. "We've known for years the gangs have been smuggling in new recruits but can any one of you tell me that you can go to the holding rooms and point out which of those illegals are gang members?"

"I for one would begin with the ones who were doing the raping. But I have the advantage. I've been privileged to witness the iniquities suffered by women on the voyage. Hutch?"

Pharoah had roused Hutch Casey from a reverie. "Yeah? What?"

"Where they holding the four *momsers* who pulled the heist on Kao?"

"They're upstairs. Separate cells."

"I want to talk to one of them."

Hutch said sarcastically, "You can pick one from column A or one from column B."

"Racist. Albert, who was the kid with the Italian father?"

Albert looked at the report he had typed and was about to give to Christy. "Mao Tse Conti."

"Come on, Albert," said Pharoah. "I've got a hunch, and for a change, maybe I'm right."

A few minutes later, Pharoah and Albert were sitting with Mao Tse Conti in his tiny cell, which had a toilet facility, a sink, a plastic stool and three bunks stacked above each other, so close together that Albert always wondered how an obese prisoner managed to turn over in his sleep. Pharoah sat on the stool, Albert sat very uncomfortably on the bottom bunk and Mao Tse Conti sat on the toilet puffing an unfiltered cigarette.

"I ain't confessing to nothing," said the boy, although he'd been caught red-handed.

"If we wanted a confession," said Pharoah, "you'd be down in the basement sitting under a glaring light while Albert and I took turns hitting you with a rubber hose."

Pharoah paused and considered the delinquent on his perch. "Who sent you to rob Kao's safe?"

"Nobody sent us. We got the idea from watching television. Television is ruining the youth of America, you know that?"

Pharoah said to Albert, "A moralist, yet."

"We got the idea of stockings over our heads from a cable TV station."

"That's old hat," said Albert.

"That's old stocking," said Pharoah. "How old are you, Mao Tse?"

"I'm not sure. I was very little when I was born."

"If you're over eighteen, we can throw the book at you. You're kind of small, though."

"I'm big where it counts."

"Oh? Yours can count?" Swiftly, "Who sent you to rob the safe?"

"I won't talk without my lawyer."

"You were pretty desperate to get into that safe. If not, you're four idiots who need your heads examined. You recognized us. You saw us going into the place. You could have waited until we left."

Mao Tse lifted himself slightly and tossed the cigarette butt into the toilet. "You could have phoned an alert from the store warning the precinct there were four guys casing the joint. It's been robbed before. There's plenty of cash in the registers at the checkouts."

"Thanks for reminding us of that small detail. But you wanted what was in the safe upstairs. That's what you were sent to collect by someone who knew where the article in demand could be found."

"Nah!" he said, waving a hand disdainfully.

Pharoah scratched his chin while he stared at Albert, whose eyes never left the boy's face. "You were after a little book."

"Nah!" Another disdainful wave of the hand.

"A big book?" Mao Tse stifled a yawn. "Some kind of book?"

"You ain't even warm. What do I want with books? I want a book I can rob a library. Anyway, I don't read books unless they got a lot of dirty pictures and there ain't none like those in the library." He added as an afterthought, "Though there's a couple of cute kids working there I wouldn't mind humping." Albert suppressed a shudder.

"Maybe a ledger?" suggested Pharoah. Mao Tse stared at him with dead eyes. Pharoah tugged at an earlobe. "Sounds like?"

"You ain't funny."

"The person who sent you to rob Kao, maybe it's someone associated with Kao?"

"Hey! Hey! I just thought of something funny! Maybe you think this is Kaogate?" He had a singsong laugh that was almost like the sound of a chicken cackling; it was the kind of laugh that suggested a mental aberration. Pharoah remembered hearing one like it at a publishing party. A publisher's girlfriend squawked like that and someone snapped, "For God's sake, drop the egg already!"

The boy stopped laughing and said snippily. "You know, guys, when I get bored with a life of crime, I'm going to pursue a career as a stand-up comic." Definitely insane, decided Albert, and a danger to himself and to the community. "You know what's a Castro convertible?" His delivery, Pharoah had to admit, was pretty good. "A Cuban bisexual! Yah! Yah! Yah! How's that? Ain't it a good one?"

Pharoah said, "I'll laugh if you tell me who set up the robbery."

The boy got to his feet and feigned irritation. "Gee whiz, Mr. Detectives, can't you let a guy take some credit for his own ideas? I mean it ain't easy being a criminal mastermind."

Pharoah persisted, "Whatever you were promised, we'll pay you double."

The boy whispered as he looked at the ceiling, "Get thee behind me, Satan."

"Am I tempting you?" asked Pharoah seductively.

"You know, there used to be a kid on Mott Street who pranced around in duds like yours. Began to get on everybody's nerves. Found him one morning in an alley clubbed to death." Mao Tse yawned elaborately and stretched. "I've had a very busy day. I've got to take a nap. You guys going to join me?"

Slowly walking back to Pharoah's office, Albert asked him, "What makes you think Kao's the victim of another double cross?"

"You know why Kao's going under? He's old-time. Old hat. The godfather. Godfathers are on their way out. Even the Mafia's reinventing themselves. Respected businessmen. From what I've learned from Michael and from what I've seen firsthand, Kao is a throwback. He's gotten so far but no further. Michael makes small noises about one day occupying Kao's throne, but I think even he is finally seeing the handwriting on the wall."

"Maybe he's the one who's writing it?"

"Maybe Lena Wing. Maybe that henchman of his . . ."

"Nick Wenji?"

"That's him. Maybe even his wife. But none of them strikes me as being clever enough to be choreographing the big picture." They passed the office of the precinct captain, Oswald Schmidt. They heard him explode, "Christmas balls! I'll give them balls! I'll *kick* them in their balls, the sons of bitches. . . ."

Pharoah hustled Albert down the hallway. "What awful language that silly bitch is using! I should go back there with a bar of laundry soap and scrub his mouth until his upper plate shatters. Christmas balls indeed! Ugh!"

They entered Pharoah's office and Albert slumped into a chair. Pharoah picked up the phone and was connected to the sergeant's desk. He began shouting, "There are no messages here! I've been away for hours! I even participated in a heroic collar. Where are my messages?" He paused "Not one *farshtunkener* phone call?" He mock-snarled, "Young man, you are one of life's major disappointments." He slammed the phone down. "Where were we?"

"Rhea Lee."

"She must be fed up to the teeth with him."

"That rumor has been corroborated?"

"Hey. We're forgetting Cylla Mourami."

"How would she get to those four bandits?"

"Harry Jen could have told her about them," said Pharoah, finding this thought a very likely possibility. He stared out his filthy window into a filthier alleyway filled with garbage and a variety of corpses, from dead mice to dead dogs. He muttered something mean about the mayor being an inept and incompetent housekeeper and made a mental note to have that alley rehabilitated or demand an office on the street side of the building. At least the vermin he would see from a window there would be ambulatory.

"Pharoah. Come away from the window. It will only depress you."

"Too late. I'm a basket case." He sat at his desk. "Cylla Mourami and Mao Tse Conti." He shook his head. "Somehow, I can't see Cylla playing hostess to these kids, not in her elegant town house I don't."

Albert said, "I see her maybe sending Hiram Wiggs or maybe even her butler down here to sniff them out. Have you any idea as to what they might have been after?"

"Yeah. Like I said in Mao Tse's cell, a book of a certain size."

"Okay, so what's in the book?"

"Names, darling, names, and next to each name, the sum of money owed for their passage to America."

"Aha!" cried Albert as an invisible light bulb incandesced over his head. "Came the dawn! Kao's private file. Of course. When do we go back to burgle the joint?"

"You're such a turtle, you silly thing. He's undoubtedly moved it elsewhere by now." He thought for a moment. "Or he's planning to move it elsewhere." He added facetiously, "Or he's selling it to the highest bidder. I'll bet Kao is beginning to wish he was anybody but Kao Lee."

"Has it occurred to you that Kao in his egomaniacal smugness is convinced that like the Phoenix he'll emerge remarkably well preserved from the ashes?" Albert's head was cocked to one side, inquisitively.

"But first, Albert, let's give me his ashes from which he might possibly reemerge. I want to see Christy. Maybe he's through kicking those balls around."

They found Christy in his office staring into a mug of lukewarm coffee. Christy heard them coming in. He looked up. "My mother begged me to be a priest. 'Christopher, study hard and one day you'll be Pope! She pronounced it 'poop.' My father was the practical one. My brothers were already on their way professionally. One's a teacher, one's an accountant, one's a ticket scalper. . . ."

"Who of course never gets investigated," said Pharoah.

"He better not be. That's how I get to see all the shows in town. And my kid brother's part of a rock group. They're on the road now."

"And that leaves you, a schlemiel of a law officer," said Pharoah.

"My father said, 'My boy, open a pizzeria. People always have to eat.' It's not too late, damn it. I know lots of real estate people in Little Italy. They'd be glad to find me a good location. Why shouldn't they? I did all of them lots of favors. Fixed their parking tickets, got them gun permits . . ." He looked out his window, which afforded him a view of several forlorn restaurants that just about eked out a bare living for their hapless proprietors, and reconsidered. "What the hell do I want with a pizzeria? What do I know about restaurants? Who wants to get up at four in the morning to go to the market to buy fresh produce? Who wants to stand guard at the cash register to make sure the bartender isn't helping himself to some of the receipts?" Christy walked to the window and yanked down the blinds to hide this dismal—albeit hypothetical—future. Turning to the detectives, he growled, "Well, what the hell do you two want?"

"Not until you ask us to sit," said Pharoah. "My feet will soon be killing me. And you might at least congratulate us for collaring those four snotnoses at Kao's store." Christy continued glaring at them. "Albert, let's sit. He's in no mood for frivolity, and here we think we can solve the Kao Lee predicament, which has, in my not very humble opinion, just about run its course." He told Christy his theory of what the Chinese boys were sent to steal. "That would be strong evidence against Kao, get it?"

"Sure, I get it. But how would they use it against Kao? If *Kao* is having trouble collecting what he thinks is owed him, how does *this* person expect to collect?"

"This person doesn't expect to collect or certainly doesn't want to. This person is going to sell the evidence for a very high bid. This book has names, money owed, places where the victims have been warehoused. I mean, after all, Christy, there are all sorts of statutes to cover these foul deeds and help incarcerate Kao forever"—he fluttered the fingers of his right hand gracefully up and down—"and it's bye'sy-wye'sy to the Chi Who."

"Who do you think will pay?"

"Most obviously," said Pharoah, "there's Cylla Mourami. She and Kao have this in common, they now hate each other. That source of income has dried up for Cylla, so she may just as well cut her losses and at the same time cut Kao's throat."

"Now who do we cast in the part of the sneaky go-between?"

Pharoah folded his arms. "A two-headed spy. Someone who works for Kao and who also works for us."

"That was Harry Jen. He's dead."

"There wasn't just Harry Jen. His was a supporting role. There is somebody else, somebody much closer to Kao."

"Not his wife!"

"Oh heavens, no, Christy. I don't think they've been close in any way for years. And certainly not Michael, because to openly betray Kao is to openly betray his mother, and the Chinese are taught to respect their parents whether they like them or not. Maybe Nick Wenji?"

"No, Nick's my candidate as the ricin shooter. He's Kao's hatchet man, and I'll get the goods on him before I retire, I've promised myself."

"And so that leaves, last but not least, and if I'm wrong, I'll hurl myself against the wall and scream the precinct down."

Albert piped up, "That leaves Lena Wing."

Pharoah glared at him. "Spoilsport!"

CHAPTER 16

After Rhea Lee left her sister's establishment, she stood examining Wilma's windows. The displays were often original, frequently bizarre, always talked about. One display featured some exquisite dirndls, undoubtedly Swiss inspired, perhaps a prophecy that in Switzerland Rhea would at last find peace and sanctuary. She was once a religious person, but after her marriages to the Lee brothers, her faith slowly drained away. Kao was the final straw. He had robbed her of all belief in Buddha. She briefly entertained the thought of converting to Catholicism, maybe becoming a nun, but that would be too restrictive, too inhibiting. She didn't relish the thought of isolating herself from men. She was only in her fifties, younger than her sister

Wilma; men still found her attractive and she still enjoyed occasional casual flirtations.

Of course, there had been much more than a casual flirtation recently right under Kao's unsuspecting nose. Nick Wenji wasn't a model of Chinese manhood, but he had a way with him. He knew how to satisfy a woman. At least he satisfied Rhea, who in her innocence did not know that had she willed him to he could have literally sent her rocketing to the moon. She shook off the brief reverie and returned to examining the dirndls. She smiled as she imagined herself in the future standing on a balcony of her multigabled chalet, drinking heavily of the crisp, clear smogless air, overpowered by the majesty of the Alps, in the distance hearing a young shepherd yodeling to his love. Perhaps Rhea would be his love. Then the jangling of cowbells, the beauty of the edelweiss in the fields, on a snow-covered slope not too far away skiers schussing and slaloming their way downhill, one or more who would break a leg or an arm and display the multiautographed plaster cast like a medal of honor.

"*Ouch!*"

She'd been stung in her left calf. Stinging insects on Madison Avenue? Impossible. She tried to rub the pain away but it persisted. As she limped into a doorway, she caught a glimpse of a man getting into a taxi carrying a green umbrella. It looked like Nick. Why would Nick be uptown? An errand for Kao? Why the umbrella? There was no forecast of rain.

Sting. Umbrella. Beads of perspiration were forming on her forehead and her upper lip. Sting. Umbrella. Oh God. Oh God. What God? Zang. Sting. Ricin. *Ricin.* Zang dead on Delancey Street. Not nearly as chic as Madison Avenue. She heard someone giggling, never realizing it was herself. Pins and needles in her fingers. In her toes. *Help me. Somebody help me.* She held out a hand, palm up. A passerby slipped her a coin. She stared at the coin. She heard more giggling. She was leaning against a storefront. It was an art gallery. She stared at the window display with hazy eyes. Abstract. Impressionist. She knew which was which. She wasn't stupid. She was better educated than most Chinese women. She was a skilled ceramist. She had a marvelous eye for color and composition.

Slowly she slid to the pavement. She stared almost sightlessly ahead. Buses and automobiles were bumper to bumper. She heard someone say, "Can I help you. Do you feel ill?" There it was again. That stupid giggle. "Please call 911. Hurry. This woman needs help. Hurry!"

Lena Wing and Tisa Cheng left Wilma's establishment. Tisa was the first to see the small crowd on the sidewalk a few hundred yards up the street. "Look, Lena. An accident."

Lena gave a perfunctory glance in the direction Tisa indicated with her head but was more concerned with hailing a cab. They were each laden with packages. Kao had told Lena to spare no expense in outfitting Tisa, and Lena was adept at carrying out orders. Lena wondered what had become of the doorman, probably up the street exercising his curiosity. If Wilma knew, she'd have Chana give him hell. Luck was with them, and a taxi pulled up ejecting two smartly attired women jabbering away in French. One paid the driver while the other, her motor mouth purring away, continued on to the store.

"Get in," said Lena, and Tisa slid into the backseat. Lena followed her and gave the driver the address on Catherine Slip. The driver nodded more to himself than them. Just as he had suspected, they were Chink hookers. But definitely upscale ones.

Tisa asked Lena, "Kao will not be angry?"

"About what?"

"All the money you have spent."

"He told me to spend it. Why should he be angry? You're his number one now."

"What is number one?"

"The sheriff's gal."

"I am confused."

Lena told the hoary joke that gave birth to the expression. A traveling salesman over a century ago arrives at a town in the outback singularly devoid of women. After three days and no sex, he asks a bartender what they do about sex. The bartender directs him to a herd of sheep on the outskirts. Reluctantly, the salesman goes in search of the sheep. At a crossroads, he comes to a house. On the porch rocking herself slowly back and forth sits a pink pig with a ribbon in her hair. "Oink," she oinks seductively, then again "Oink," and the salesman succumbs. Back in town, he shyly tells the bartender of his conquest. "You mean the pink pig in the rocking chair at the crossroads, a ribbon in her hair?" "Yup. That's the one." "Son, you better hightail it out of town real fast. That's the sheriff's gal!"

"A very sweet story," said Tisa.

Under her breath to herself Lena said, "Oh boy."

"Lena?"

"Yes?"

"Do you know what Kao intends to do with me?"

"He's already done it."

"Does it mean I am now his one and only?"

Lena said dryly, "Until the real thing comes along."

"What do you mean by real thing?"

"A man you'll genuinely fall in love with. Unless you're in love with Kao."

"Is it required that I be in love with him?"

"Hell, no. Just close your eyes and think of China."

Tisa blinked her eyes. "You say such strange things."

"We live in very strange times."

Tisa still had the robbery on her mind. "It takes great bravery to attempt to rob Kao Lee in broad daylight, doesn't it?"

"Not if you're four lichee brains encased in bamboo."

Tisa was intrigued. "You know them?"

Lena said, "Just your everyday off-the-rack, ready-to-wear young Chinatown hoodlums. High on crack and low on brains."

"Does Kao know them?"

"He knows them now. He's probably had them photographed by the store manager and the pictures tacked to the wall of the store-room. He's got quite a gallery."

"You have known Kao a long time?"

"Long enough."

"He trusts you?"

"As much as he trusts anybody. Maybe more. Kao has one sterotyp-ical Asian trait. He's very inscrutable."

"What does that mean?"

"You can't read his mind."

She screwed up her face in disbelief. "You are a mind reader?"

"Tisa, I try to be. I find little scope for my talents in my present life."

"I have a feeling you do not intend to be with Kao Lee much longer."

"All not-so-good things must come to an end." Lena was staring out the window at the garment district factories.

"May I ask what you plan for yourself?"

"I've had the plan ever since I went to work for Kao. A restaurant. My own restaurant. Very elegant. A restaurant that will be to din-ing"—her eyes were aglow with the fervor of her ambition—"what Wilma Joy is to fashion."

"That will be lovely. Perhaps if we become friends, there will be a place for me in your establishment."

"I thought you wanted to be a big movie star."

"Whatever befalls me first. Surely you have heard what Confucius said about a bird in the hand."

Lena sighed. "When did they hang that one on him?"

•   •   •

Nick Wenji directed his cab to the rear alley behind the Warehouse. He paid the driver off and watched as the car threaded its way cautiously, trying to avoid the garbage cans that were lined up in a row. The umbrella under his left arm, Nick let himself in the back door with his master key. The pungent smell of food enticed him as he strolled through the none-too-sanitary kitchen. Health inspectors were paid a fancy stipend for giving the place a clean bill and it has been said in the past that more than one case of hepatitis could be traced to some of the Warehouse's kitchen help. He nodded to two chefs who ruled their domain like satraps. One was reading a racing form and the other was stirring a huge pot of soup into which his perspiration dripped. There was a man mincing scallions and another shredding cabbage, and a third was making wontons, stopping occasionally to brush a brazen roach from the dough.

Leaving the kitchen, Nick was in the room that housed the baccarat and poker tables. The tables were sparsely populated. Nick recognized one of Chinatown's wealthiest madams at a poker table playing against what he suspected were two of her more affluent clients. They were from out of town and dealt in notions, most of them unsavory. From the next room Nick could hear the spin of a roulette wheel, and when he entered the room he frowned at the three waitresses near the bar deep in conversation about nothing terribly important. He snapped his fingers at them. The girls drifted to other parts of the room. Nick went through the lounge, where the bartender was hunched over the bar reading a copy of *Popular Mechanics*. There were no patrons for him to serve. Sensing Nick's presence, he looked up and made a very Gallic shrug, eloquent in its feeling of hopelessness and abandonment.

He said to Nick, "I thought they said the recession was over."

Nick responded, "Chinatown is always the last to know." He took a handful of pretzels from a crystal bowl on the bar while asking, "Is the lord high executioner up there?"

"He just got back. He's not himself I don't think."

"Who is he?"

"You heard some punks tried to pull a heist at the store?"

"Yeah. I heard Kao was saved by the marines. Has Michael Lee been around?"

"He's upstairs with the old man," said the bartender, wishing he was in his garage behind his house in Brooklyn where he enjoyed puttering with electrical appliances.

Nick picked up a phone from a row of them suspended on the wall. He pressed a button. He listened, and after hearing Kao Lee's voice, said, "It's me. I'm back. It's done." He hung up the phone. "Give me a Bud Light. I'm feeling morose."

Now his thoughts returned to Rhea. A fluttering little butterfly who had been more like a moth attracted to a very dangerous flame. He wasn't often attracted to older women, but Rhea was something special. She was dainty and delicate, like the ceramics displayed on shelves in her living room. There was no need to fear Kao surprising them in what could be an embarrassing situation. He never came home during the day and, often, not at night either, Rhea had shyly told him.

Rhea had confided that she rather enjoyed her husband's neglect. There was all that time to dream and to plot, all that time to fantasize the future and life without Kao. How she had often contemplated killing him. So often, she would blush at the thought of it. Nice girls don't murder their husbands, though her friends back in China were always gossiping about rumors of such fiendish occurrences. She had thought that if her sister Wilma had ever married she would long ago have rid herself of the encumbrance by doctoring some rice wine or sprinkling rat poison in hot and sour soup.

Rhea would also often speak of her sister's cleverness and great success. Yet, how did Wilma get her start? Who was her benefactor?

There *had* to be one; why, it seemed as though in no time at all she was the mistress of her vast empire.

Wilma had all the luck. Men flocked to Rhea, but opportunity flocked to Wilma. All this she had confided to Nick. He had once boasted of knowing at least twelve different sexual positions. Rhea had laughed and said, "Let's see. First there's the most common one. A man mounts a woman."

"Thirteen," Nick had said.

Now, dwelling on the woman he had murdered, he remembered the hearty, raucous laugh that emerged from Rhea's delicate, flower-petal lips. The bartender had poured his beer but it rested in front of Nick, untouched.

Upstairs in Kao Lee's office, two other men were also thinking of Rhea—albeit less quietly. Kao Lee was astonished by the vituperation that poured from Michael's mouth, and he was grateful that he had had the sense to soundproof his office. "My mother! Your wife! You once loved her very dearly! That counted for nothing?"

"Your mother posed a serious threat to the organization."

"You son of a bitch, she would have been content to idle away the rest of her life in Gstaad. She'd have found herself a boyfriend—"

"And boyfriends are very inquisitive!" interrupted Kao Lee harshly. "Do you know the kind of men who prey on single women, especially single middle-aged women, in those phony resort towns?" He pounded the desk. "Rhea succumbs very easily to the importunings of a lover. As I know firsthand. I was there. That's right. I was there. You think it was *my* idea to steal her from your father?" He snapped his fingers. "Like hell! Sure, I was attracted to her when I first met her that day in San Francisco. She was beautiful and alluring. It was hard to believe she and Wilma were of the same flesh and blood. Wilma is bloodless. Heartless. But that first time Rhea even bowed three times before me, insisting in true old-fashioned Chinese tradition that she was unworthy of me and of my protection. Take it from me, the minute your father told her I was bringing you three to San Francisco, she planned to hook me."

Michael was trembling. "I don't believe it."

"It's the truth. She told me so herself. When Zang was found dead, she told me not to blame myself. It was the will of the gods and a lot more of that crappy ancient mythology. It was the will of Rhea! She convinced me to kill him."

"You make me sick!"

"Your mother was a very shrewd lady. It wasn't me she was after, it was my money. She wanted position and power. Did you know Rhea tried for a political position in China with the Gang of Four before they were overthrown? She tried to ingratiate herself with Mao and his wife but someone threw a wrench in the works. So she settled for next best. My brother. Zang. And then she set her sights on me. It's the truth, Michael, I swear to God . . . take your choice . . . Christ or Buddha . . . all of it is the truth."

He reached for a cigar while Michael stared at the floor, thinking, This is not my mother he is telling me about. He is a liar.

Kao took his time lighting up, then continued more calmly, "Rhea knew too much. I couldn't take the gamble. When Lena phoned from Wilma's shop and said Rhea was there, I knew the time was now. I sent Nick and he did the job. He's downstairs in the bar. Now it's just a matter of time before the police call." Michael looked into Kao Lee's face.

"Before the police call?"

"To tell me my wife is dead . . . or perhaps still dying." His voice became stern. "Michael! Pull yourself together. There is much to be done. We're far from out of the woods. Pharoah Love had a long closed meeting this morning with two men who were Feds. They're piling up evidence against me, and soon they'll be in a position to strike."

Kao now felt master enough of the situation to begin bullying his nephew. "Pharoah Love! Archie Lang! How you couldn't see through him I don't understand!"

Michael slumped in his chair, didn't even look up. A marionette without strings. Little boy lost.

Kao Lee lifted a phone and pressed a button. "Send Nick up. Tell him chop chop."

Nick downed the last of the beer and took the stairs to Kao Lee's office two at a time, entering the office and not liking the picture of dejection Michael presented. He gave Kao Lee a questioning look, and Kao Lee winked with reassurance. Nick put the green umbrella in the umbrella stand and Kao cold-bloodedly asked him where he found Rhea. "Well, like you said, it was lucky she likes to window-shop a lot. She was in front of an art gallery. A couple of yards up from Wilma's place. It wasn't easy. The street was crowded. I was afraid she'd turn and see me. But it was as smooth and easy as talcum-powdering a baby."

With an animal cry, Michael suddenly came off his chair, lunging at his mother's murderer, blood in his eye, murder in his heart. Nick was too quick for him. He decked him with a hard uppercut to his jaw. Michael's legs folded beneath him. Nick caught him under the armpits and pushed him back onto the chair he'd been occupying. There was a quick tap at the door. Lena entered without waiting for Kao's permission. She never did. She stared at Michael.

"What happened to him?" she asked.

Said Kao Lee, "He fainted. You got any smelling salts?"

"I'm fresh out. What happened?"

"Rhea's dead."

Lena was stunned. She managed to ask, "Does Wilma know?"

"I'll phone her as soon as I hear from the police. I must say, they're a long time in identifying her. Nick, wasn't she carrying her handbag?"

"Sure she was."

Kao was irritated. "Don't the cops open a handbag anymore for some identification? Where's Tisa?"

"I dropped her at the hotel, where she's undoubtedly trying on all her new Wilma Joy goodies." She stared at Nick. Then at the umbrella in the stand. And then at Kao Lee. "Was killing Rhea all that necessary?"

"She was leaving me. She could not be trusted," answered Kao flatly. A buzzer rang and he picked up a phone. "Yes?"

In his office with Albert West and Hutch Casey polishing off some impudent and unappetizing bologna sandwiches, Pharoah Love said into the phone, "Hi, honey. It's Pharoah here. Lenox Hill Hospital's got your wife. She collapsed on Madison Avenue outside a gallery near your sister-in-law's shmottery. I'm awfully sorry, Kao," Pharoah added generously. "Are you?"

CHAPTER 17

"Humor is uncalled for," snapped Kao. "Do you know how she died?"

"Kao, don't be so anxious to give her the big send-off. She's in intensive care. And it's very intensive."

"What happened to her?" He was staring at Michael, who was beginning to revive. Lena had been rubbing one of his wrists. Now she was more interested in Kao's conversation. *Do you know how she died?* Fool. So positive the dose was fatal. So many slipups lately, Kao. The cops make note of them, then when the time is right, they add them up. That's when they pull you in and measure your neck for a noose.

Kao heard Pharoah telling him, "She collapsed on the street. Madison Avenue. Just a short way from your sister-in-law's take-out place."

"Was it her heart?"

"Nothing so commonplace. The doctor examining her was a little perplexed until I gave him a hint. I suggested he look for traces of ricin. He found ricin in her left calf. Now I'm a hero. You've heard of ricin, Kao. Your brother got some. Harry Jen got some. The blessed Lord knows how many others. What we haven't been able to figure out is how the killer gets to inject the stuff in broad daylight among crowds. But we'll get there. Kao? Is Lena around?"

"What do you want with Lena?"

"I've got some socks that need mending. I've heard she's a fine seamstress. She really gives a darn." Even Pharoah hated himself for that one but couldn't resist. "Do me a favor. Tell her to call me at the precinct. And call your sister-in-law in case you've forgotten due to the shock. You *are* shocked, aren't you, Kao?" Kao slammed the phone down.

With mock rage, Pharoah snarled into his phone, "Kao Lee, that's the last time you do my laundry." He hung up the phone and leaned back in his swivel chair. He said to Hutch Casey, "Is Christy up to date on what's going on?"

"He knows about Rhea Lee. All he's missing is your phone call to Kao Lee."

"He's not missing much. Kao's getting real antsy. If he orders his wife offed, he's real antsy."

"That's *if* he gave the order," said Albert.

Pharoah mused aloud. "Now why have her killed? The new girl in town? Tisa Cheng? Kao's had a long procession of obliging dolls prior to her, but Rhea never gave Kao much trouble about them."

"At first she did," said Hutch Casey.

"How do you know?" asked Pharoah.

"A lot of idle chatting goes on at the Warehouse. The bartenders.

The waitresses. The busboys. When there's a fight the hired help, among others, hears about it and the word is passed and I eventually get to hear about it."

"Since you know so much, when did the wife no longer give a damn?"

"When she had a thing going with Nick Wenji."

"Don't hand me that!" scoffed Pharoah. "She's old enough to be his mother!"

"So what?" asked Albert West. "Didn't Oedipus bang his mother?"

Pharoah remained incredulous. "Rhea and Nick Wenji? For real?"

"For a couple of very passionate months."

"And Kao never cottoned?"

"Nick still works for him. It's Rhea who's dying."

The phone rang and Pharoah picked it up. "Pharoah Love." He heard Lena Wing say Kao told her to call. "Yeah, Lena. I got an important matter to discuss with you." He listened. "Get over here as soon as you can. Has Kao left for the hospital?" He listened. "What's he waiting for? A police escort?" Pause. "Okay, Lena. Just get here."

Lena had phoned Pharoah from the bar in the Warehouse. As she hung up, Michael came hurtling down the stairs from Kao's office. "Where are you going?" she cried.

"My mother. She's still alive!" He tore past her and out the front. At the head of the stairs stood Nick Wenji staring after Michael. Lena took her handbag from atop the bar, opened it and fished for a hand mirror. She examined herself and, satisfied with what she saw, placed the mirror back in the purse, snapped the purse shut, and without a backward glance to see if her departure was also being monitored by Wenji, headed for the exit.

In Wilma's office at the Madison Avenue store, Chana Ritch was alone and speaking into the phone to Kao Lee. She asked him anxiously, "Do you want to tell Wilma yourself? I can fetch her. She's in a fitting room. I won't be but a minute." She paused. She was listening to wind squeezing out of a paper bag. She detested Kao Lee. She had met him at several of Wilma's socials and was quite vocal in wondering why Wilma bothered inviting him.

In the time that Kao kept Chana on the phone, she could have fetched Wilma. Dear God, his wife wasn't even dead yet and he was busy instructing Chana to tell Wilma that he'd chosen the Pagoda of Heaven funeral parlor in Chinatown as Rhea's point of final departure. He was ordering a traditional procession to the Buddhist temple complete with firecrackers and much banging of drums and tootling of whistles to frighten away the evil spirits that might try to capture Rhea's soul, Kao said piously. Chana cynically thought that professional mourners would have to be hired as, between them, Kao and Michael couldn't scare up an impressive array of friends or relatives to attend the services. Then again, there was always the probability of flushing out some by announcing a splendid buffet to be served after the burial.

Wilma returned to the office, and Chana immediately spotted several loose threads clinging to her dress as she explained the phone in her hand. "It's Kao. Rhea is dying."

"She wants to go to Switzerland," Wilma heard herself saying and then took the phone. For some inexplicable reason after so many years of speaking English exclusively, Wilma broke into the native dialect she and Kao had grown up speaking. It was a singsong language that Chana had never mastered. As she once explained to a friend, "It's all Greek to me."

When Kao finally released her to follow Michael to the hospital, Wilma sat at the desk hearing Chana's condolences but not acknowledging them. Finally she said, "So unnecessary. All so unnecessary."

Chana asked, "Are you going to the hospital?"

"I'm her sister. Mrs. Richmond is in fitting room C. Overcharge her accordingly."

• • •

Kao Lee walked slowly down the stairs from his office, another of his obscenely long cigars protruding from his mouth. Nick Wenji followed him, not daring to ask if he was expected to accompany Kao to the hospital. Kao was looking around the room with narrowed, searching eyes. He asked the bartender, "Where's Lena?"

"She went out."

"Did she say where?"

"No sir. She just made a phone call, grabbed her purse and went."

Kao gave the information some thought. Then he said over his shoulder to Nick Wenji, "Get the Cadillac out of the garage. You're driving me to Lenox Hill." As Nick Wenji left to carry out the order, Tisa Cheng emerged from the long narrow hallway that connected the Warehouse to the hotel in the rear.

"Kao!" she exclaimed. "I was just coming to look for you. Look at me!" Her arms were outstretched as she modeled one of the newly acquired possessions that exquisitely showed her off in all the right places. The bartender held a cold bottle of beer to his left temple to soothe its sudden throbbing while Kao resisted the urged to pounce on and ravish her. "Don't you just love this?" asked Tisa with a sultry smile.

"Exquisite," gasped Kao.

"Where is Lena? I want to show her too."

Kao explained he thought she might have gone to the hospital to see Rhea and of course had to tell her about Rhea's misfortune.

"Oh how terrible! Awful! Shall I go with you to the hospital?"

"No," demurred Kao, "it would be inappropriate. Go back to your suite and watch television. When I get back, I'll take you to dinner uptown, someplace very chic where I shall be the envy of every man in the room."

The bartender wondered if after Kao's departure he dare make a pass at Tisa, while Tisa wondered if the bartender might possibly make a sexual overture. There would be plenty of time before Kao returned, if they got right to it and didn't dawdle.

Lena Wing knew the location of Pharoah Love's office as she knew the location of everybody else's. The desk sergeant had been alerted by Pharoah to send her in the minute she arrived, and Lena jauntily made her way to him. Although his door was wide open, she tapped on it as she stood in the doorway. Pharoah looked up and winked. "Come on in. Shut the door." He indicated the chair opposite the desk. "Park it there."

As she walked to the chair she said, "If this is a complaint about the Warehouse, I could have taken it over the phone."

"No, beloved, this is a complaint about those four snotnoses you sent to rob Kao Lee."

"What four snotnoses?" She had put her handbag on the desk before sitting. Now she crossed her legs and waited for Pharoah's answer. He told her their names.

"They said I put them up to the heist?"

He tapped one side of his head with an index finger. "Deductions, beautiful, deductions."

She sniffed. "You do better deductions on your income tax."

"Kao kept what I call his kidnap book at the store. Don't give me such a dumb look. You know what I'm talking about. His list of who he's holding for ransom, where they're being held, and how much is owed on them. He kept that book in the safe in his office upstairs. Toby Lewis's domain."

"Nice lady, Toby."

"She wasn't looking all that nice when I last saw her. She'd been roughed up a bit by your putz Mao Tse Conti."

"Was she hurt badly?"

"Why? You're going to slap his fingers?"

"How'd you enjoy your trip to China?"

"Don't you try to derail me, Lena. I'm going to take these kids, these slimeballs, off the street and that goes for the dozens of others just like them." He was working himself up. "It's a battlefield out there! Chinatown's a battlefield! What's happening around here, for Crissakes? You send them to pull a heist on Kao Lee in broad daylight. Heisting Kao Lee is bad enough but in broad daylight, in his own store, and after they see Albert West and me going into the joint. I mean talk about chutzpah! Who you stealing the stuff for?"

"Me."

"Just like that you're fessing up?"

"I wanted the book to hold over Kao's head. Cylla Mourami's going to be awfully disappointed. She wanted to buy it for herself to hold over Kao's head. He owes her hundreds of thousands."

Pharoah sat back in the swivel chair. "What did Kao do with all the money?"

"He's been losing his shirt at the Warehouse for a long time. Even Atlantic City and Vegas are hurting now that they've got big casinos on Indian reservations."

"You mean the locals are schlepping out to Connecticut and up-state New York. . . ."

"And to the riverboats in the Midwest. And getting back to Kao, there are too many rollers into him at the Warehouse because he's 'Jes' a gal what cain't say no.' You want the names of some big stars who owe him some big money and he doesn't know how to collect?"

"He could shoot them with ricin."

"I think Kao realizes his days are numbered. The FBI is closing in. There's a lot of wealth that extends from Chinatown to Asia. Kao's stepped on a lot of important toes."

"Who gives him the orders?"

"What are you talking about?"

"Don't snow me, honey, or I'll burst into tears. Kao's just a front, which means he's going to be the sacrificial lamb. Who is it, Lena?

Cylla? Her lawyer? X the Unknown? Who? I mean once they finally nail Kao, he won't have enough years left to him to satisfy the sentences." He sounded very serious. "That goes for you too, Lena."

"Says who?"

"Says me. Accessory. Accessory to illegal gambling. Accessory to the whorehouse. I guess that's still doing big business."

"Not as big as it used to be or ought to be. AIDS, you know."

"AIDS I don't know and never want to know. Play cards with me, Lena, and you'll come up smelling of roses. You don't, and that restaurant you're dying to own will be located behind bars. What kind of cuisine you planning on?"

"Very elegant. Very European."

"What you going to call it?"

"Lena."

"Why not?" Then he said swiftly, "Where's the book?"

"In the Warehouse."

"Where in the Warehouse?"

"Where only Kao knows it's hidden."

"I thought you knew everything there is to know about the place!" He was on his feet walking back and forth, hands plunged in his windbreaker pockets, looking to Lena like an amusement park Kewpie doll about to run amok. "What kind of hiding places has he got?"

"Pharoah," she said, feigning weariness, "the Warehouse was once really a warehouse. There are all sorts of hidden tunnels below ground level and above ground level. There are wall safes all over the place. There are secret rooms that date back to the Prohibition era. And if you start digging around and tearing up the place, don't be surprised to find some skeletons. Real skeletons."

"Good heavens," gasped Pharoah, "do you suppose the premises are haunted?"

"Possibly the kitchen. All those ptomaine victims."

Pharoah was now hovering over Lena, his back to the desk and

leaning against it, his arms folded. "Was Rhea Lee's murder necessary?"

"All I know about that—and it's God's honest truth—is that she
wanted to leave Kao, go abroad to live, and he thought she'd be rat-
ting on him. After all, she undoubtedly knows a lot more that would
incriminate him than any of us."

"Does he talk in his sleep?"

"Don't ask me. I never slept with him."

"What, never?"

"No, never!"

"Have you ever slept with Nick Wenji?"

She burst out laughing. And then as her laughter subsided, she
cocked her head to one side and said, "Pharoah, you can't be all that
innocent."

"What am I missing?"

"Me, baby, you're missing me. I'm gay, sweetheart. To be perfectly
archaic, I'm one of Sappho's daughters."

Pharoah crossed around the desk to his swivel chair and sat.
"Why," he asked, "am I always the last to know?"

"Nobody knows. Most of them think I'm one of Kao's girls. I don't
deny it."

"So you're a dyke."

"That's right."

"And nobody knows."

She literally sang her response. "Tha . . . at's rii . . . ight . . . !"

"And nobody knows." He leaned forward, his eyes twinkling. "You
find that book for me and you tell me everything I want to know or
I'm going to spread the word about you, *capisce?*"

She favored him with the middle finger of her right hand.

CHAPTER 18

Michael Lee stared at his mother lying on her bed, curtained off on three sides from the rest of the ward. Her body was a patchwork of tubes connected to a series of medical gadgets that meant little to Michael, but told him much. The doctor attending her was a young East Indian, Singh Bebbisingh, who bubbled and thrived on delivering bad news. His voice rose and fell like tiny ripples on a lake, and it was obvious to anyone of any intelligence, which excluded Michael, that the young doctor loved the sound of his own voice.

"There is no hope at all that she will recover," said Dr. Bebbisingh, the bad news making his eyes flash with something that could pass for sexual ecstasy. "Her nerves and her muscles are almost totally paralyzed." His smile was one of his most appealing features, the enchantment of which totally escaped Michael. "That she has survived this long is a medical miracle. There has been so much of this ricin pumped into her body. Such a small, frail body. Look how she struggles for breath even with the help of the oxygen tubes. It is so dramatic." Rhea's lips were moving but no sounds emerged from her mouth. "See how she's trying to speak? I think she's trying to scold someone." He favored Michael with another assortment of smiles. "Is it you? Have you been a naughty boy?"

Michael exploded, "Do something! Help her!"

The doctor urged Michael to lower the volume of his voice. "You will frighten the other patients. This is intensive care. You must never be intense in intensive care."

"She should have a private room and private nurses!" raged Michael.

"Oh no, that is easy enough for you to request. But there are no private intensive care units. And besides, like your best hotels over the Christmas holidays," he added with a really wonderful, glowing smile, "we are full up! Your mother is lucky to have this bed. A burn victim expired just as your mother was brought in. Quite a stroke of good luck for her. The patient she replaced was only thirty years old. She smoked in bed watching a late-night talk show. The host was obviously a bore, and she fell asleep."

Rhea's eyes were open and trying to focus. Her eyes darted from the doctor to Michael and then back again, a process repeated for several seconds until she realized one of the two men was her son. She whispered his name. Michael knelt at her side as he heard the doctor say, "Unbelievable. She should be playing mah-jongg with her ancestors."

Michael held Rhea's hand. "You're going to be fine, Mom. You're going to be okay. The doctor says so."

"Oh, Mr. Lee, you must not perjure yourself," said the doctor, "she hasn't a hope in hell of pulling through." This smile was dazzling. Michael shot him a filthy look.

"My jewels," whispered Rhea, barely audible. She mentioned a bank and a safety box number. Michael lowered his ear to her mouth. She wanted her handbag. There was something she wanted. He opened the bag and held up her key chain. She blinked her eyes "Yes." Then he held up her wallet and her change purse. It was obvious she wanted him to pocket everything, which he did, as his long trip from Fujian had left him a bit short of the green stuff. He'd get more from Kao Lee. Then he noticed Rhea's eyes narrowing as she stared past him. He turned and saw his Aunt Wilma.

Michael acknowledged her. "Aunt Wilma. Do you know a specialist?"

"Specializing in what?"

"Deteriorating nerves and muscles."

"Offhand, no."

Kao came hurrying into the ward. "Oh, dear me," murmured Dr. Bebbisingh through another intriguing smile, "this is much too many visitors, someone will have to go."

Kao favored him with a ferocious snarl. "I am her husband. And this is my sister-in-law. And this is our son, who is also my nephew." The doctor's head was reeling. "We are all the family she has. We have every right to be here together. It is our first family reunion in months." The doctor was too busy trying to figure out how Kao's son could also be his nephew and wondered if there was some sort of sneaky plot afoot at the hospital to drive him insane. He wasn't too popular with the staff because of his extensive efforts to please everyone. The patients in the intensive care unit loathed him for his constant good humor and perennial greeting of "Still with us?"

Rhea and Wilma had locked eyes. Wilma was distinctly uncomfortable. In the taxi on her way to the hospital, she prayed Rhea would be dead before she arrived. Like so many other people, Wilma was uncomfortable with death. She looked away from Rhea to Kao. He was standing next to the kneeling Michael, wondering if he dare be hypocritical enough to cross to the other side of the bed and avail himself of Rhea's other hand. If she was still alive, there couldn't be all that much ricin in her. Nick Wenji had bungled, and he had never bungled before. Nick's victims had always been swiftly dispatched before; nobody lingered.

Rhea gasped. From the depths of her throat they heard what Kao thought was a Bronx cheer. It was the death rattle. Dr. Bebbisingh clapped his hands together, and though his voice was mournful, his new smile seemed to speak of a happy afterlife. "She has left us." He pulled the blanket over Rhea's face with difficulty due to the placement of some of the tubes.

Kao said firmly to the doctor, "I will not authorize an autopsy."

"Oh, there is no need to," said Dr. Bebbisingh quite jovially. "We know she was murdered with an injection of a ricin pellet. A very clever detective who I believe goes by the name of Pharoah Love, though he does not spell Pharoah correctly, suggested we look for traces of ricin and, by golly, thanks to his remarkable suggestion, we did indeed find traces of ricin in Mrs. Lee's body." He made a swift bow. "I shall of course share my knowledge with the police coroner. Now I must excuse myself. There's a gentleman in the men's intensive unit whose departure is long overdue and I must see what is delaying him." Bobbing his head toward the three of them, the doctor made his exit with some nimble footwork that gave Wilma the impression he was hopping over invisible puddles.

Kao spoke to Michael. "Please inform the hospital's main office your mother's body is to be taken to the Pagoda of Heaven mortuary on Grand Street. I will speak to the police and journalists in the hallway. Michael? Did you hear what I said?" Michael stared at Kao with undisguised loathing.

Wilma spoke up. "I'll instruct the main office."

Kao said to her, "Please don't leave. I must talk to you."

"I'll wait in the office," said Wilma. "Michael, you can't remain here. It's not good for you."

Michael said, "My mother won't hurt me. My mother loved me."

"Of course she did," said Wilma. "Now come with me." Kao followed Michael and Wilma out of the room. In the hallway, he stood patiently while two photographers snapped pictures, answering questions and sidestepping any queries about the smuggling of illegal aliens. He saw Wilma and Michael enter an elevator and recognized Hutch Casey among the plainclothesmen in attendance. Their eyes met for an instant, and then Kao asked a reporter to repeat a question he hadn't heard.

In the hospital's general office, while arranging for the disposal of Rhea's body, Wilma studied the nurses and wished someone would ask her to redesign their uniform. White was so starchy and stodgy. Patients needed cheering up. Wilma thought it would be rather amusing to design graffiti for the white uniforms to liven them up a bit. Nothing racy, of course, but some of the cuter phrases she saw sprayed on the walls of derelict buildings. Michael sat in a chair watching and listening. Wilma was in charge. Wilma was issuing directives. Wilma knew what she was doing. She told Michael she would later go to the Pagoda of Heaven and get *them* straightened out. In death, Rhea was getting the sort of attention she had craved but rarely received in life.

He remembered as a small boy asking her why his father had to die.

"He was meant to die," she replied.

"But why now?" Michael had persisted.

"Because he had come to the end of his cycle."

"I don't understand."

Rhea took a book from a shelf, a very old book with yellowed pages. "This was my grandfather's book. The father of my father."

Michael read the title aloud, *"The Wisdom of Moncius."* He looked up at his mother. "Who was Moncius?"

"He was China's second greatest philosopher. Confucius, of course, was the greatest. It was the theory of Moncius that we die when we are supposed to die. Our life cycle is preordained. Some live to be very, very old. Some only live a few days, a few hours. It is Buddha's will."

Michael listened to Wilma as she gave the nurse taking down the information her office address and phone number. Then the nurse got the Pagoda of Heaven number from Information and dialed. No push-button telephone. A little behind the times. He could have sworn he'd seen some on the intensive care floor. The nurse informed someone at the downtown mortuary that they could expect the body of Mrs. Rhea Lee to be delivered within a few hours. Wilma gestured for the phone, and when she got it, introduced herself and made it quite clear to the gentleman she had at the other end that Rhea Lee was Mrs. *Kao* Lee and assumed he was suitably impressed.

At the other end, David Waha, the funeral director at the Pagoda of Heaven, refrained from asking if she'd like to book the Imperial Suite for Mrs. Lee and serve a light repast to celebrate the deceased's passing. He had been treating his fingernails to a buffing when the call came from the hospital and resumed when Wilma said good-bye and hung up.

"Mrs. *Kao* Lee," he mimicked viciously. "Well, now I can get back some of that hard-earned cash I dropped at his roulette tables."

In Christy Lombardo's office, Pharoah was telling his chief and Albert West about his talk with Lena Wing. Christy knew Lena and was fond of her.

"She's a straight shooter," said Christy. "She's been very good to us."

"Good to us? In what way?" asked Pharoah in surprise.

"She's been one of our informers for a long time."

"You're kidding!" said Pharoah. "She didn't say a thing about that to me."

"That's why she's a straight shooter. She figures probably you're not supposed to know she's a faux Mata Hari, so she kept quiet about it."

"I don't get it. Where did Harry Jen fit in?"

"Pharoah, *you* know a cop can never have enough informers. We'd get next to nowhere without them. There was very little crossover information from Lena and Harry. Lena's is strictly Kao Lee and his little exclusive world, and Harry was there to feed us everything he could find out about the many forms of smuggling that kept Kao on the go. Now how do we get our hands on that little book of Kao's? Let's play a game. I used to play it with my father and mother when I was a kid." He was on his feet and boyishly enthusiastic. "Say I've lost my house keys, which I did frequently. Now my dad would ask, 'If I was the house keys, where would I be?'"

"Hot damn!" cried Pharoah, delighted with this game. "Where would you be, Mr. House Keys?"

"You're not taking this seriously," Christy said accusingly.

"Yes I am. So's Albert. Albert, you are house keys. Where are you?"

"Asking for a transfer to another precinct." Albert slumped in his chair. He was tired of Chinatown. He was tired of Kao Lee and murderous teenagers and of dim sum and wonton soup and he wanted to be transferred back to his old precinct with good French restaurants and Jewish delicatessens.

"Perk up, Albert," said Pharoah cheerily, recognizing Albert's mood, having experienced it before too often. "We'll soon be going home."

Christy was offended, although he tried to mask it. "Don't you like it down here, Albert? I thought you'd be tickled pink for the change of pace. I mean what were you getting uptown? Mafia guys? They're tired stuff. Boys in the hood? More tired stuff. Down here it's exotic! It's the Arabian nights! Where else would you get ricin pellets in the leg? Where else do you find smuggled illegal coolies and clandestine gambling houses and disease-ridden whorehouses? Didn't you like helping collar four embryo killers? The Kim brothers! Looey Kua! Mao Tse Conti! Now there's a beauty for you. You think he'll live to see thirty?"

"You think he'll live to see twenty?" asked Pharoah.

Christy rolled on. "And you met Cylla Mourami! You rubbed shoulders with billions! The celebrated Greek heiress whose lawyer should use a bit more discretion in lining up her business partners."

Said Pharoah, "Another one of those legal slobs who charge five hundred bucks every fifteen minutes and if you sneeze in their offices that's another hundred and you better have your own tissue paper or you'll be on the verge of bankruptcy." The phone rang. Without waiting to be asked, Pharoah picked it up. "Yeah?" It was Hutch Casey at the other end informing them of Rhea's death. Pharoah passed the news on to the others. Christy crossed himself.

Hutch was telling Pharoah, "Her doctor was some East Indian named Singh Bebbisingh. He's typing up a report for us. But, he can't hurry it up. He's only using one finger. It was ricin. No idea how she got shot." He paused. "Something that shoots pellets. The body's going downtown to the Pagoda of Heaven." He filled Pharoah in on the details.

Pharoah told Albert and Christy, "The *gonser meshpuchah* were on hand for the send-off." He explained to Christy *gonser meshpuchah* meant the whole family.

"You're such a show-off," said Christy.

Pharoah said, "Hutch is hanging in until he can pick up the doctor's report." Christy nodded approval, and Pharoah relayed that to Hutch and hung up.

Christy asked Pharoah, "How'd you leave it with Lena?"

"Well, I left it that no matter how she shakes the dice they still come up aiding and abetting. But of course now that you tell me she's on our payroll . . ."

"We take her off the payroll," said Christy. "I want that book and I don't care how dirty we have to play to get it. All those men at the conference today, Gai Kiong, Tai Liang, Willie Lau, they are very powerful men."

"So why don't they do something instead of yelling at us?" asked Albert.

"They're afraid their relatives will be murdered," Christy said impatiently.

"These guys are rich. Why don't they just pay the ransoms?" asked Albert.

"Remember Hugh Shanxo? He's the publisher, in case you forgot. He paid for his wife's sister's family. Five of them. It took weeks to recover the bodies from Barnegat Bay. Turns out Hugh's sister-in-law had heard too much. Her kidnappers knew it. The whole family was sacrificed. *And* Hugh Shanxo went bankrupt."

Albert looked at Christy quizzically. "Then what the hell are we up against? All the kidnap victims are goners."

"Not if we have that book with the locations of the hideouts and sneak up on them very quietly and rescue them just like they do in television movies."

"We have better dialogue," said Pharoah. "Christy, I don't think I have struck Lena with the fear of God. I mean she swore she'd do her nut to try and figure out where the book's stashed, but the thought of doing time doesn't seem to bother her. Have we ever checked to see if she has a record?"

"She's been on the books once. Beat the shit out of some woman she caught cozying up to her femme."

Pharoah felt as though there was a glaze forming over his eyes. "Her femme?" Did Christy read *The Advocate*?

"Why, Pharoah, you're behind the times. Her femme. Her One and Only. Her Essential Other."

"How long ago was the arrest?" asked Pharoah.

"Long, long ago. She was like maybe nineteen or twenty. Case dismissed. She got off clean. The victim was a well-known politico and of course didn't want that kind of publicity."

"Who's Lena got now?"

"Nobody that I know of," said Christy. "She brings me information, not confidences."

"I was just hoping for some ammunition," said Pharoah.

"Like I said, boyo," said Christy, "she's a straight shooter. She's plotting some way to get to the book. There's probably a diagram layout of every inch of the Warehouse in Kao's office. She'll find a way to lay her hands on it."

"And then what?" asked Pharoah. "There's a convenient little red X marking the spot where the book's hidden?"

"There must be a way to get the fucker," said Christy.

Pharoah was staring at the ceiling. "Kao has this astrologer."

"Madame Khan," contributed Christy. "I told you, we sometimes use her to give Kao misinformation."

"Isn't she also supposed to be a psychic?" asked Pharoah.

"Sure," said Albert. "She's been known to direct people to the nearest supermarket."

Pharoah asked wistfully, "Albert, when did you lose your girlish laughter? Where's the Albert of let's kick the door down and rush in with our guns blazing? Where's the Albert . . ."

Albert was on his feet and walking out of the room. "You'll find Albert in the men's room and you'll find Madame Khan in Christy's Rolodex. But if you want that book real quick, I'd think about smoking it out."

CHAPTER 19

It was the story of Rhea Lee's murder on the early news that made Cylla Mourami come to one of her snap decisions. By phone she summoned Hiram Wiggs out of his office and to her side. While he rolled from side to side in the speeding taxi, the driver ignoring his plea to slow down, Hiram could see the evening's planned adventure being shot down in flames by a billionaire of a markswoman. This was one nimrod whose aim was infallible.

In the mansion's drawing room, Cylla was giving Goren, the butler, a series of orders concerning the shuttering of the town house. Against a backdrop of *The Tales of Hoffmann*, Goren made notes in the loose-leaf folder devoted exclusively to the household while Cylla went through desk drawers finding pieces of paper that would associate her with Kao Lee and possibly prove incriminating. She piled them atop the desk and every so often consigned them to the fireplace. She was closing the house. And most certainly also the house on Long Island where the small boats were moored. Those would have to be moved, and Cylla ordered Goren to make a note of that. The staff in both houses were to be given notice and four to eight weeks' severance pay based on the amount of time they'd been in Cylla's employ. She was always generous to her staff, something her father had drilled into her during his last months of life.

They heard the doorbell, and Cylla assumed it was Hiram Wiggs. She dispatched Goren to the front of the house, where he opened the door and admitted the lawyer. Goren directed him to the drawing room. Wiggs followed Offenbach's melodic "Barcarolle," which led him directly to his client.

"What's going on? Have you gone mad?"

"No, dear, I've gone sane. I suppose you haven't heard—Rhea Lee's been murdered."

"No!"

"It was on the early news. Kao's running amok." She was riffling papers in another drawer. "He's snapped."

"Don't be ridiculous."

"When he murders a brother or an errand boy or nuisance rivals, that's a kind of expediency I understand and appreciate. But when you murder your wife, my dear, especially a wife you care nothing about, that's a signal for anyone in the immediate vicinity to make for the hills and as quickly as possible."

Wiggs huffed and puffed. "He wouldn't dare murder you!"

Cylla's hands were on her hips. She addressed Goren, who was standing in the doorway, ballpoint pen poised, awaiting further instructions, "Goren, have the maids take an inventory of the linens and the napery and then lock the closets." He started out. "And Goren!" He paused. "I'll want my usual overnight bag."

"Yes, madam." He didn't need to inquire about clothing and accessories. Cylla Mourami had duplicate wardrobes in all her residences across the world. That's what having billions was all about. Cylla waved him on his way, and when he was out of sight and presumably out of earshot, Cylla resumed her conversation with Hiram Wiggs.

She propped herself up on the desk with her hands. "Kao's world is about to come crashing down around him and I have no intention of participating in the debacle. I'm off to my enchanting little island in the Mediterranean, where I shall stay reclusive until this all blows over. I have no taste whatsoever for scandal and notoriety and my face plastered all over the front pages of those supermarket tabloids. I've checked my bank accounts across the world, and they are all in excellent order, my deepest thanks to you, Hiram."

"You pay me lavishly, my dear, most lavishly."

"And I shall continue to do so. By the way, who takes over in case of your demise?"

"My demise? What demise are you thinking of? I'm in perfectly good health."

"Perfectly good health has never been a deterrent to Kao Lee. Actually," she murmured, "I think it's something of a challenge. I sometimes think the healthier you are, the more mortal you become. Now, really, Hiram, do something to protect yourself. Hire some bodyguards. Better still, go into hiding. You still have that hunting lodge in Scotland?"

"Yes, I do. In fact, I was planning a trip there shortly." He paused. "No matter where we go, we can always be found. You realize that, don't you? Interpol will always sniff us out."

"I have friends with Interpol, so it won't come to that. And with the CIA and with the FBI and of course with CAA."

"What's that?"

"One of those cunning agencies in Hollywood I should have bought into when I had the opportunity." Exhausted, she sank into the desk chair. "I'm going out to my house on Long Island. My yacht is moored there. A crew and a staff are being hired now, and if God is with me we shall be under sail with the tide at midnight."

Wiggs pulled up a chair and sat opposite her. "My dear, my dear. Shall I never see you again?"

"Of course you shall, unless something unforeseen . . ." She shrugged. She leaned back in the chair. "Little Rhea. I suppose he felt she posed some sort of a threat to him. What's so tragic is, all these executions are so senseless. Listening between the lines with those detectives this morning, I foresaw Kao was already walking the plank." She laughed. "I assume the money I lost with him is tax deductible."

"Leave it to me."

"I'm leaving just about everything to you. Business, that is. I caught a glimpse of Rhea today. She was at her sister's store. She seemed at peace. In good spirits. She chatted briefly with Lena Wing and what appeared to be a teenage Oriental sexpot."

"You still remain in Wilma Joy's bad graces?"

"Good God, yes. Wilma never forgives. Under that very cold facade of hers lies a broad bed of cruelty. You know, she and I should have been friends. But from the first, Wilma kept me at arm's length." Her tone of voice changed. "I was always very nice to her. I invited her here. She accepted at first and, I thought, with alacrity. She never had an escort, though once she came with that woman who works for her, Chana Ritch." She thought for a moment. "You adore gossip, don't you, Hiram?"

"Oh yes! Have you something juicy to tell me?"

"Have you ever heard any gossip about Wilma and a man?"

Wiggs leaned forward hungrily. "What man?"

"*Any* man."

"Oh." He gave it a little thought, then shook his head from side to side. "In my book she's clean. There was a hint that some years ago she showed interest in Kao Lee, but I find that a bit much to digest."

"Why not? He's an attractive man if you're drawn to that kind of look. And of course years ago he was younger and we must assume even better looking."

"Well, whatever, that was then. This is now. Cylla?"

"Yes?"

"Won't you be terribly lonely on your island?"

"Possibly. But you know how self-sufficient I am."

"I was just thinking. Perhaps if I—"

She interrupted him in mid-sentence, "Hiram, Confucius say he travels fastest who travels alone."

"I sometimes think Confucius say too goddamn much."

If you want that book real quick, I'd think about smoking it out.

Christy, Pharoah and Albert were now in Pharoah's office. "That exit line of yours when you went to the john . . ." said Pharoah.

"What exit line?" asked Albert innocently.

"About if we wanted Kao's book real quick we should think about smoking it out."

"Well," said Albert, "I'm so pleased you noticed! Here's my thinking: If we can't get what we want fair and square, then let's torch the joint. Once somebody yells 'Fire!' and the alarm goes off, Kao is bound to go tearing off to his secret hiding place to retrieve the treasure."

"Supposing he isn't around when this hypothetical conflagration erupts? Then the evidence goes up in smoke along with everything else and that leaves us holding the bag," said Christy.

"A smoking bag," added Pharoah.

"You make sure Kao is on the premises before doing anything. He's there more often than he's anywhere else," said Christy.

"Unless he's in Tisa Cheng's suite creating a little heat of his own," said Pharoah.

Christy threw his hands up. "Are we nuts or something?" He turned in his seat to make sure the door was shut, which it was. "Three respected officers of the law plotting an act of arson! Have we no shame? Have we no sense of ethics? Do we want to be fingered as rogues? Supposing we're caught and drummed out of the regiment?"

Pharoah said, "I'll plead insanity."

"You'll be believed," said Albert. Then there was silence among them.

Pharoah broke the silence. "We get somebody to do it for us. Lena Wing. I hear she strikes one hell of a match."

"Supposing she gets caught?" asked Albert. "She implicates us."

Pharoah said to Christy, "I thought you said she was a straight shooter."

"So far."

"A straight shooter doesn't rat on her buddies," said Pharoah.

"She does if she's got a stiff stretch unwinding ahead of her," said Christy.

The phone rang. Pharoah picked it up and listened. He said to the others, "Michael Lee to see me." His fellow officers reacted with surprise. Pharoah told the desk sergeant to send Michael in. Pharoah went to the door and opened it. Traffic in the hallway was heavier. Officers of various sizes and genders were rushing about their business as though their cases were the most important on the calendar. The hum of voices gave Pharoah a certain warm, wonderful feeling he felt only in a precinct house. Everyone looked squeaky clean and honest, but Pharoah knew there were some bad apples. In some precincts there were barrels of bad apples, like Harlem's Thirtieth. Pharoah sometimes wondered if there was an isolated bad bone in his body, the one that might someday cause him to go bad. Well, if there was, it had better lay dormant or his mama's ghost would come zeroing in on him from her own special cloud and give him what for.

"Hello, Arch." So deep in thought had Pharoah been, he hadn't realized Michael was standing staring at him.

Pharoah held out a hand. "Long time no see since yesterday." Michael shook his hand. Pharoah smiled and said, "Buddy, if you hadn't shook that hand, I'd have crashed my head against the wall. Come on inside. We're having a powwow." He introduced Michael to Christy. Michael and Albert knew each other from the Warehouse. Pharoah offered Michael a seat and coffee. Michael accepted the seat. Pharoah thought, He's not looking good. He's having trouble keeping control. Oh, no. Oh, Mary of all the mothers, he's going to start blubbering. Pharoah couldn't cope with other people's tears. He never knew whether to offer solace, a tissue or a chocolate bar with almonds.

Michael fought back the tears. Not a word was spoken. Pharoah knew when a break had dropped into his lap. Michael Lee was here for a reason; this wasn't a social call on his old shipmate. Michael finally said, "You know my mom's dead." Pharoah nodded. "He had her killed. Kao had her killed," Michael almost wailed.

"Why?" asked Pharoah. He could guess why, but he wanted Michael's version.

"She was leaving him. She was going to settle in Switzerland." Pharoah tried to imagine an Asian in Switzerland, then reminded himself there were plenty of Asians in Switzerland, especially Japanese. They were making excellent Japanese watches in Switzerland. "He didn't trust her not to talk."

"About what?" asked Pharoah.

"About everything Kao was involved in. Smuggling aliens. Extortion. Kidnapping. Murder. Always murder. Kao takes great pleasure in ordering someone's death. It's like you and I would select a particular material for a suit."

"He ordered your father's death," Pharoah said, although come to think of it, he probably didn't have to remind him.

"I didn't tell you in as many words on the ship, but it's a shame I have lived with for too long. My mother thought Kao would leave me his empire, but when I learned from Kao that my mother was as much a conspirator in my father's death as Kao was, I did not know what to believe. I have been crossing through life over an evil bridge of lies and deceit. I couldn't believe that my mother was a willing conspirator, in Kao's words, the one who urged him to have my father killed. I once tried to talk to my Aunt Wilma about it, but she professed ignorance. She was lying, because for a long time now I've suspected that Kao provided the bankroll for Wilma's business."

Christy interrupted, "Your Aunt Wilma is down in the books as a very clever lady. I hear she has great connections."

"Great wealth leads to many friendships," said Michael.

Pharoah said, "You found that in a fortune cookie."

"It is the truth," said Michael.

Pharoah suddenly remembered Tisa Cheng. "What have you done with Tisa?"

"I've done nothing with her. She is now under my uncle's wing."

Pharoah explained to Christy, "A form of protective custody."

Christy was more down-to-earth. "You mean now the uncle's screwing her."

"She wants to be a movie star," said Michael.

"No pun intended," said Pharoah, "but in a way, she's got a head start. Where's your mother reposing?" How archaic, thought Albert, as he raised an eyebrow.

"The Pagoda of Heaven. She should be there by now."

Pharoah couldn't resist asking, "The family sitting *shiva?*" Christy smiled. He knew *shiva* was the Jewish period of mourning, when the orthodox sat on wooden crates and presumably wept and wailed for six days, with Saturday off for good behavior. But mostly they ate and drank because friends and relatives kept them well supplied when not poking around in the deceased's belongings to see if there was anything worth claiming.

Michael didn't understand Pharoah, his mind occupied with the reason he had decided to present himself to the police, in particular, to Pharoah, the erstwhile Archie Lang, who was such a fine companion and confidant. "It's hard to call you Pharoah when I've known you for so many weeks as Archie Lang."

"What both Archie and I want to hear," said Pharoah, "is that you've come here to help us."

"Should I call a lawyer?"

"Do you have one?" asked Pharoah.

"No. I don't know any. Kao's got a lot of them, but I don't trust any of them. I'm so dumb about the law. I'm so dumb about so many things." He produced Rhea's keys. "See these? My mother's keys. They're for her personal things hidden away from Kao, her safety box. But instead of digging them up, I came here. You'd be coming after me pretty soon anyway. My part in the *Green Empress*. Working for Kao. Aiding and abetting, isn't it?"

"You'll plea-bargain," Pharoah said assuredly, while Albert wondered if Pharoah was planning to appoint himself as Michael's defense lawyer. Albert wouldn't put it past the nut.

Michael asked, "Will you deport Tisa?"

"Do you give a damn?" asked Christy.

"She's a good kid. She deserves a break."

Pharoah told him, "She'd have to request political asylum. But from what I know of her, she needs another kind of asylum. Michael, you know about the attempted robbery at Kao's Mandarin shop. What you don't know is that the four kids were after Kao's private book, the one in which he lists the persons he's had kidnapped, what they owe, where they're being held."

"He kept it in the office safe. Did the kids get it?"

"No," said Pharoah, "we've got the kids upstairs. Kao moved the book to the Warehouse. Do you know any particular hiding place he's got there?"

Michael thought, a process that did not come easily to him. "That's a lot of real estate, guys. I mean there's all sorts of nooks and crannies that only Kao would know about."

"We have to find that book," said Pharoah. "Tell us about the pellets. Who makes them for Kao?"

"There's a lab in New Jersey. Just across the George Washington Bridge in Fort Lee. It's camouflaged as a dress factory." Albert was taking notes. "Fujian Frocks. The lab is in the basement."

"Let's get Fujian Frocks looked into," said Christy. He was remembering that he had told Pharoah earlier a precinct can't have too many informers. He smiled at Michael Lee like a benevolent uncle seeing his nephew coming of age and regretting not having a nice new fountain pen to bestow upon him.

Michael continued, his voice now a drone, "Kao got the idea for the ricin when he was on a business trip to London and some diplomat was murdered with a pellet shot from an umbrella tip."

The three officers exchanged looks. Pharoah asked Michael, "Kao has a similar queer kind of umbrella?"

"It's green," said Michael.

"Something lethal for a rainy day," said Pharoah. "Nick Wenji's the shooter, I suppose."

"He is the only one Kao trusts with that umbrella."

"Michael, there's a lot we want, and you're going to help us get it. We want that umbrella, we want that book of Kao's, and we want a sworn statement from you. Albert, you confidential sweetheart, you made notes?"

"Here I sit. Good old reliable Albert. But we'll need a secretary to take his formal statement. Michael, you're going to have to repeat just about everything you've told us. I'll be right at your side refreshing your memory. Why, here's old buddy Hutch Casey." Hutch said nothing.

"Is that the doctor's report?" asked Christy. Hutch crossed slowly to

Christy's desk and laid the envelope he was holding in front of his superior. "You know Michael. He's being a big help to us. What's the matter, Hutch? You got an upset stomach or something?"

Michael said, "I guess he's afraid I've been telling you he's paid by Kao to snitch on you guys."

CHAPTER **20**

Hutch stared at Michael. Hutch looked like the kid who'd been caught with his hand in the cookie jar, except in this case the cookie jar was hiding some of the family's cash assets. The other officers were expecting to hear a heated denial from Hutch, but none was forthcoming.

"Well?" asked Christy.

Well? thought Pharoah. *That's all? Just Well? No hellfire and brimstone? No lunge at Hutch with a right uppercut to the jaw? No cursing? No nasty names? Although I suppose, considered Pharoah, it* would *be a bit* de trop *if I slapped Hutch's face. Because then what? Challenge him to a duel? Shrimp forks at twenty paces?*

"What do you expect me to say?" asked Hutch. The man actually had the nerve to sound slightly peevish.

Pharoah asked, "Did you know about the umbrella?"

"What umbrella?"

"The green umbrella."

"What green umbrella? I don't own any green umbrella."

Christy momentarily rescued Hutch. "Put your badge on the desk." Hutch complied while Christy continued talking. "You're suspended without pay until you can be brought before the board to answer the accusation. Clean out your locker and get the hell out of here before the word spreads and somebody might decide to make mincemeat out of you. And don't go running to Kao."

"I can't. At the hospital he told me my services were no longer required. Well"—with a brazen smile that repelled his former brother officers—"I've got a wife and family to support. I'd better file for unemployment insurance." He sauntered out of the room.

Pharoah was appalled and let his feelings be known to Christy. "You didn't warn him not to try leaving town! You didn't ask for his gun!"

Christy waved a hand impatiently. He looked profoundly depressed. "Let the son of a bitch leave town. The farther away the better. And the gun's his. Maybe he'll use it on himself." At the moment, Christy looked like a serious candidate for suicide himself. He finally roused himself to say, "Oh, all right. I suppose if that scumbag scarpers, the commissioner will chew my behind off."

Pharoah made a face at the repulsive thought. Christy sent Albert after Hutch. "Don't put him in a cell. Put him in your office."

"What about *his* office?"

"He's probably there right now removing anything that's incriminating. Get after him." Albert hurried out.

"Holy Saint Genesis," cried Christy. "If I'd a been a priest I'd be hearing his confession and assigning him a wide assortment of Hail

Marys and Stations of the Cross and I'd be done with him." He paused. "I feel like visiting a topless bar."

"Please do not stupefy us with your perverse suggestions," said Pharoah as he patted Michael on the shoulder. "Michael, did you know Kao was planning to bounce Hutch?"

"Is Hutch so important? He's just another sneak."

Christy winced. Hutch Casey a sneak. One of his best men. Correction. Formerly one of his best men. Was there anybody else? Christy said suddenly, "I suppose there's big bucks in betrayal these days." He exhaled. "What a world. What a life. We ain't even got any more heroes." He mused on this thought for a moment while Pharoah and Michael watched. "Pharoah, why do I get the feeling Kao is quietly closing up shop?"

"If he is, it's not his own idea. There's a celestial being sitting on a throne and hurling thunderbolts. Kao wouldn't close up shop on his own. You think he's about to unchain his prisoners without a concerted effort to collect more of the big bucks owed him? Kao's a very greedy little bugger, right, Michael?"

"It would mean giving up his real estate. The Warehouse, the hotel, the Mandarin shop and some other parcels of land I suspect he owns. He's got a big piece of a Chinese take-out chain."

"And yet the rumor's around that he's got a big money-flow problem." Pharoah scratched his cheek. Then his eyes widened. "Sure, he's got a money problem. Because all this stuff isn't his."

"You know that for sure?" asked Christy.

"I don't know anything for sure. I'm deducing! I'm a detective and detectives are supposed to deduce! We did a great job together last night, let's try to top ourselves. Kao Lee is a front. Are you with me?"

"With you and right behind Kao Lee."

"Everything Kao Lee represents, the Chi Who gang, the rackets, everything . . . is somebody else's property. For simplicity's sake, we'll call this person Mr. X. Kao's the front, the facade, and he's been doing a damn good job for a long time. Worth his weight in taels. But for some time now he's been falling down on the job. Maybe siphoning off some of the cash and stashing it. Possibly offshore."

"He does have interests in Nassau and Bermuda," contributed Michael.

"That's positively offshore," said Pharoah. He was pacing the room. "I'm getting warmer. I can feel it. Kao's rid of Rhea. Sorry, Michael, no offense intended. Does Kao have some hideaway that you might have heard of? Some island, some country, some city, someplace in South America? They're terrific at hiding criminals in Latin America. Look at how many ex-Nazis they protected for decades. If he's planning to take it on the lam, then he knows the FBI's very close to making a pinch. He's probably got a spook in the FBI. He does, doesn't he, Michael?"

"I only know of one. You met him this morning. His name is Malone."

"Oh." Pharoah and Christy looked chagrined, then Pharoah recovered quickly. "I thought he looked suspicious." He turned to Christy. "We turn them in, right? What else? Michael, what were Kao's plans for the rest of the day?"

"He and my aunt were going to the Pagoda of Heaven to finalize the plan for my mother's funeral. Then he said something about taking Tisa Cheng uptown, someplace fancy, and show her off."

Pharoah added cynically, "After which he just might show her out."

"No. Not this one. Not Tisa."

"Well, she wants to be a movie star," said Pharoah, "is Kao thinking of hiding out in Beverly Hills? He'd be hard to find if he went to William Morris."

"Or maybe he'll hide in plain sight." Christy shrugged. "It's worked before. Stay put right under the noses of authority and they just might not notice you."

"The hotel," said Pharoah.

"He's got a very cozy nest there," said Michael.

Albert rejoined them, carrying what they assumed was Hutch Casey's gun.

"Did he put up a struggle?" asked Christy.

"No, I think he was glad to get rid of it. He might have gone disconsolate and been tempted to blow his brains out."

"That's always a problem solver," said Christy.

"Not in my office!" exclaimed Albert. "They just cleaned my carpet. Now what have I missed?"

At the Pagoda of Heaven, the funeral director was serving tea to his illustrious guests, Kao Lee and Wilma Joy. They discussed several of the director's appealing burial packages, with Kao favoring one that included a number of professional mourners and an assortment of Chinese hors d'oeuvres. Wilma helped Kao choose a simple pine coffin and the funeral director had a resident Buddhist priest available as of the next day, when he'd be finished shooting a television commercial he'd signed to do a few weeks ago. There would be joss sticks and incense supplied, as a matter of course, and limousines to transport the funeral party to a cemetery near Passaic, New Jersey. Wilma kept looking at her wristwatch, and Kao tolerated her impatience. Wilma was always impatient.

A young man in a black suit that sported a white carnation drifted in almost on tiptoes. He begged them to excuse the intrusion and then asked, "If you care to see Mrs. Lee, she is prepared and ready to receive." Wilma bit her lips to choke a laugh, and then she and Kao dutifully followed the young man into the viewing room. Rhea lay on a white bier swathed in a shocking-pink shroud, which would be replaced by her burial clothes. She looked so tiny, like an expensive doll on display in one of the windows of F.A.O. Schwarz. Religious temple music emanated from a hidden speaker, consisting of much subdued wind chimes and tinkling of bells. There was a hint of an aroma, which Wilma thought might be heliotrope, a pretentious scent suitable to such a pretentious funeral parlor as this one. Kao dabbed at his dry eyes with a lace-trimmed handkerchief while Wilma once again referred to her wristwatch. She knew Chana would be worried after not having heard from her for several hours. She whispered to Kao she had to leave. He followed her into the foyer, where the funeral director awaited them. They told him the deceased's son would probably be dropping by before the evening was over and that was about all the prospective attendees they seemed to be able to muster.

In the street while Kao tried signaling for two taxis, as they were now headed in opposite directions, Wilma stared as he flailed an arm. A cab pulled up. Kao opened the back door.

"I will see you at the services." It sounded more like a question. She did not respond. He shut the taxi door behind her as she gave the driver the address of the Madison Avenue store. Kao flagged a cab for himself to take him to the Warehouse. There was much to do. A great deal to be taken care of.

Night was descending, and in the twilight, the Warehouse looked eerily supernatural. It was an ugly building that no amount of renovation would improve. Kao had sent Nick Wenji back with the Cadillac as he didn't want the gaming unattended for too long. Nick was formulating plans of his own. A getaway to some zone where there would be very little rain and therefore little need for an umbrella. The roundup would soon begin. Any day now. Maybe any hour. Any minute. Any second. Maybe right now they were drawing up the warrant for his arrest. Walking from the garage to the Warehouse, Nick was thinking of maybe Panama or Ecuador. He had connections in both places. They owed him. It was time to think of calling in his markers. He had no cash problems, not like Kao did. Kao thought the good life would go on forever, like this was all a fairy tale and like the bottomless pitcher of milk there would be a steady flow of wealth and hedonistic pleasure.

He walked slowly. Rhea was on his mind again. He never before had murdered anyone with whom he'd had an affair. It filled him with a strange feeling of ingratitude. It was even stranger for him to be filled with any kind of feeling. He must have felt something for Rhea. Certainly when the affair started. It couldn't have been love, because Nick couldn't remember ever having experienced that emotion. Although he'd heard once that love means being able to say good-bye, he must have experienced love lots of times because he was always saying good-bye, especially after knocking them about a few times. He never hit Rhea. That would be like hitting a nun, and there was something religious about Rhea. She herself could have been an icon. The Pagoda of Heaven. That's where I heard them say she'd be. Maybe I'll go over later and say a last good-bye. Maybe even stop at a florist and steal some flowers.

In Kao Lee's office, Lena Wing was rifling through the one last drawer that remained to be examined. Nothing. No book. Some pornographic material. She flipped through the photographs. Why do so many men go bananas over pornography, especially Asian men? She stuffed the photos back in the drawer. She stood and looked around the room. Where is the book? If it's not someplace in this office, then where is it? Aha! She snapped her fingers. The umbrella stand. She crossed to it and lifted out the green umbrella. She laid it across a chair and then ran a hand around the inside of the umbrella stand. Nothing. She was dejected. Wait a minute. The bottom. It could be a false bottom. She upended the umbrella stand. She knocked at the bottom. She poked at the screws holding the object together. Nothing. No secret compartment. She righted the stand and then lifted the umbrella from the chair and sat. Strange umbrella. Pretty shade of green. Carved head. Fine craftsmanship. Oh Christ. What kind of a book am I looking for? It couldn't be ledger-size. Much too big. Maybe it's one of those cheap little notebooks people used to jot reminders. Kao wasn't big on statistics unless he was reading them on a computer screen. The computer! Maybe he's transferred all the information into the computer. Umbrella in hand, she crossed to his desk. She placed the umbrella down across the desk and sat in front of the computer. She rubbed her fingers together, a yegg about to try to crack a safe.

The door opened quietly. Nick Wenji stared at Lena Wing. He saw half-opened drawers with objects protruding from them. Lena's looking for something. He wouldn't mind knocking Lena around a bit. She often rubbed him the wrong way; he wouldn't mind rubbing her the wrong way.

"What are you looking for?"

"You almost gave me a heart attack! Why didn't you knock?"

"I listened at the door first. It was quiet. I knew Kao wasn't back yet. So what are you looking for?"

"Some data I punched in a couple of days ago."

"You've been going through his desk drawers. And the filing cabinets. What are you looking for?" he repeated.

There was no mistaking the menace in his voice. Lena pushed the chair back quickly. His right hand was forming a fist. She grabbed the umbrella by the handle. "Don't try anything or you'll have a crease in your skull!"

She was fascinated by how quickly her threat seemed to have taken effect. There was a look of fear on his face, a look she'd never seen before on anyone's face, and she gloried in her sudden power. She took a firmer grip on the handle and made a threatening feint at him.

"Don't!" he yelled.

"You lily-livered bastard. What are *you* looking for? Maybe a little notebook with names and numbers and locations, huh? Is that what you're looking for?" He lunged at the umbrella, trying to hit it out of her hand. She fell backward, squeezing the handle. Something gave.

Nick cried, *"Ouch!"* and clutched his left shoulder. "You stupid bitch! You've killed me! You stupid bitch, you've killed me!" Bewildered, Lena turned the umbrella around so that she was pointing it at herself. She looked at the tip, the hole in the tip. Came the dawn. Her mouth formed an O. Nick staggered out the door.

Lena chased after him shouting, "I'll take you to a hospital!" Downstairs, the bartender, a dealer and a croupier plus a handful of patrons looked up to see Nick stumbling down the stairs, behind him Lena holding the umbrella and anxiously offering Nick help.

The bartender shouted, "What's the matter with Nick?" Lena had torn past him, ignoring his question. A croupier said, "Place your bets," while a midwestern tourist whispered to her equally tastelessly dressed friend, "Lovers' quarrel. So emotional, them Chinese."

"I thought they didn't show any emotion at all."

"Don't you believe it. Haven't you read Pearl Buck? Read Pearl Buck. *The Good Earth* or *Sons*. *Very* emotional."

At the Fifth Precinct, Hutch Casey was the centerpiece of a highly emotional news conference. The Commissioner of Police was talking into a microphone and commending Christy Lombardo for finding the bad apple in his barrel of police officers. Hutch Casey stood staring straight ahead, seemingly oblivious to the seriousness of the charge. In his office, Pharoah with Albert's assistance was dictating arrest warrants for Cylla Mourami, Hiram Wiggs, Nick Wenji, Kao Lee, Michael Lee, Lena Wing and the usual assortment of John and Jane Does. It was a familiar formality to the secretary, Angie DeVito. She knew they'd all be out on bail in no time, give or take a few who might be aware they were on a wanted list and had already skipped town.

"What about Tisa Cheng?" Albert asked Pharoah.

"Oh, sure. Let's bring her in. Someday when she's a big star in Hollywood, she'll look back on all this and tell her vast, loyal following how she beat the rap."

"How did she beat the rap?" asked Albert.

"She'll think of something." He was jotting notes at his desk. "The Fujian Frocks. Fort Lee, New Jersey. We getting a line on them?"

"In the works."

Lena Wing burst into the room brandishing the umbrella. "Help me! Help Nick! It was an accident! I didn't mean to hurt him. I shot him with the umbrella!"

The very tired Angie DeVito slammed her hand on the desk. "Now if that don't the cake! What are you on, girl, what are you taking? Sounds heavenly! Let me in on it!"

CHAPTER 21

A few minutes later, Pharoah, Albert and Lena were in an unmarked police car headed back to the Warehouse. Lena said, "I don't think he'd go back to the club. He was in shock, panicking. Maybe he went to Downtown Hospital. I know! Kao's doctor, Han Yu-tang, he's nearby on Mott Street. That's where Nick would go. Dr. Han asks no questions."

"Doesn't he even ask you to say 'Ah'?" asked Pharoah. Lena shot him a look as she gave Albert the doctor's address. Albert skidded around the next corner barely missing striking a street peddler who was out too late for Pharoah's satisfaction. And probably unlicensed too, thought Pharoah. They arrived at their destination. The doctor's storefront quarters were dark. Albert rapped loudly on the door. The windows were covered with vertical blinds. Albert continued banging. A window overhead shot open and a middle-aged man stuck his head out cursing loudly in a dialect with which Lena was unfamiliar.

She apologized profusely, claiming herself unworthy and under the spell of an angry god and finally hoped he understood when she asked if he knew Dr. Han's whereabouts.

The man shouted obscenities, in between which Lena deciphered the doctor was in jail for having sold prescriptions for drugs otherwise unattainable. The three piled back into the unmarked car.

"Now what?" asked Albert.

Pharoah said, "The nearest emergency room is Downtown Hospital. And that's too far for someone shot full of ricin." He asked Lena, "Do you know of some clinic nearby that's on call all night?"

"Madame Khan."

"The astrologer person?"

"She also dispenses herbal medicines. Her place is on Cherry Street. It's a popular hangout. A lot of gossip and information gets traded there."

"Along with some predictions, I assume. Tell Albert how to get there."

They were there in less than five minutes. The curbs were jammed bumper to bumper, so Albert double-parked. Madame Khan's store looked like any mom-and-pop store you would find in an ethnic neighborhood. Pharoah opened the door, which chimed. There was a heady, mystical aroma of herbs and leaves, and Pharoah delighted in them. It reminded him of his childhood in Canarsie and a store that specialized in a variety of brands of coffee beans, tea leaves, such condiments as Hungarian paprika and sesame seeds surrounded by huge blocks of Greek and Turkish halvah. Here customers were navigating among baskets stuffed with multiple varieties of leaves and bowls filled to the brim with seeds and other colorful wares that Pharoah and friends were ill-equipped to identify.

A middle-aged clerk wearing a pince-nez and looking impressively scholarly was telling a couple, man and wife presumably, "Marigold clears the skin. And here is horsetail to soothe your rheumatism if you are sadly afflicted. Here is hawthorn to calm the nerves."

"That's what we need," said the woman, "we need hawthorn. My husband's a mess."

"Stop saying that!" the husband shouted.

At the back of the store Pharoah spotted a door which was marked "Clinic" and gestured for Albert and Lena to follow. As Pharoah reached for the knob, the door opened slowly. If he'd been a head shorter, Pharoah would have been standing nose to nose with Madame Khan. Taking a gamble that this was the celebrated prognosticator, Pharoah reached for her hand and held it, the palm open. He stared down at it in concentration. Madame Khan was the soul of patience. Clowns amused her, professional and otherwise.

"You will meet a tall, dark stranger." Albert admired Madame Khan's forbearance while Lena shifted impatiently. "He will mug you. Madame Khan, I presume?"

"You are a detective," she pronounced solemnly.

"An admirable deduction."

She looked at Albert. "And here is a brother under the skin. And here stands my dear friend Lena Wing. And Lena is most anxious and very troubled. Come inside."

They followed her into a large reception room, beyond which Pharoah assumed were examining booths and possibly an office. The place was spotlessly white.

"To what do I owe this unexpected visit?"

Pharoah while listening was looking around, wondering where she composed her astrological charts.

"I do them upstairs. In my apartment."

Pharoah's mouth was agape. "You're also a mind reader?"

"The way you were peering around with such obvious curiosity, I assumed you had my gifts on your mind." She asked Lena, "Has Kao been brought down?"

"Not yet, but it's on the way."

She sighed. "There goes easy income. Why are you with detectives?" Lena explained about Nick and the umbrella. Madame Khan had heard of Rhea's murder and murmured something that would probably pass somewhere as sympathy. She indicated they sit and sat herself at a desk from which Pharoah assumed she dispensed her clinical advice.

"That's right, I do," she said,

Pharoah said, "Now you cut that out!"

Madame Khan smiled. "You're so expressive. You're so easy to read."

Pharoah asked, "Want to go dancing at Roseland?"

Madame Khan ignored this. "That accursed umbrella. I'm afraid I'm guilty of bringing the weapon to Kao's attention. I saw it demonstrated when I visited China several decades ago. I was most impressed. Upon my return, when I met Kao through a mutual friend, I told him about this weapon. I must now assume he ordered one from China for his personal use."

Pharoah told her, "His is a green umbrella."

"Oh no no no. What a terrible mistake. Green is bad luck. Better purple or a medium shade of orange." She sighed. "It is too late now. Where is the umbrella?"

"Back at the precinct," Lena told her, "on Christy Lombardo's desk."

Madame Khan looked at the ceiling and must have seen something that eluded the others. "Where does Rhea Lee repose?"

"She's at the Pagoda of Heaven," Lena told her.

"It is possible Nick is also there. To humble himself before her and beg for her forgiveness. You have of course heard they were once briefly but passionately lovers."

Briefly Pharoah understood, but *passionate*, he couldn't see it.

Madame Khan's eyes pierced into Pharoah's face and it was one of the infrequent moments he was feeling uncomfortable. He flashed her a smile. The killer of a smile that once worked its instant magic before the emergence of the killer disease AIDS.

"I am trying to help you. To make you unlock some inner resources that are jailed behind a wall of worthless information. I did not hear your name."

"It wasn't mentioned." He introduced himself and Albert.

"Pharoah. Egypt." She closed her eyes and Pharoah was wondering if she was mentally pirouetting among the pyramids while also wondering whether she would tell him his mother had misspelled Pharoah. She opened her eyes. "I have been told I am the reincarnation of an ancient Egyptian diviner." How, thought Pharoah, did you make your way to China? But he thought better of asking. He was looking at Albert. He wanted to get to the Pagoda of Heaven. "Fujian."

"I've been there," Pharoah told her. "What about it?"

"Fujian Frocks. A factory in Fort Lee, New Jersey. Just over the George Washington Bridge."

"As the crow flies."

"As the flippant police should fly. Don't you know a smart suggestion when you hear it? Kao's laboratory is there. They make the ricin pellets, among other things. You might think of having it investigated."

Pharoah took her hand and kissed it. "Very soon. Roseland. My treat." He patted her cheek. "May I use your phone? Urgent matter." He called Christy Lombardo. He urged him to get in touch with the Fort Lee police. Crash Fujian Frocks. Lab in the basement and who knows what else they might find. Send a patrol car to the Pagoda of Heaven, possibility that's where Nick Wenji might be found. Don't forget to bring a warrant. "We're going to the Pagoda and then the Warehouse." He slammed the phone down before Christy could ask any questions, blew a kiss at Madame Khan and hurried out the door followed by Albert and Lena.

Meanwhile, at the Pagoda of Heaven, a strange drama was in progress. Nick Wenji was in Rhea's room of repose, kneeling beside her body. Across her chest lay a beautiful red rose he had placed there, stolen from an unsuspecting street vendor. The funeral director assumed this was Mrs. Lee's son Michael, as he'd been told there was the probability Michael would visit to pay his parent the respect that was due her. But when Michael arrived accompanied by two slovenly plainclothesmen and introduced himself, the funeral director was understandably confused.

"Then who is the man who is kneeling and muttering words I do not understand?"

"He is Nick Wenji. He is wanted for murder. These two gentlemen escorted me here, as I am also under arrest. Do you know any good lawyers?"

The funeral director was mesmerized. "Who did this man murder, if I may be so bold to ask?"

"Oh, very many people. Among them, my sainted mother."

The funeral director was feeling faint. "He murdered your mother? And now he is here kneeling before her? Doesn't he realize he's about to be apprehended?"

"It doesn't matter. He has also been murdered, although not deliberately."

The plainclothesmen caught the director as he started to collapse and helped him to a sofa. Michael saw his opportunity and took it. He slipped out of the room, out of the mortuary, hailed a taxi and directed the driver to the Warehouse. Albert, Pharoah and Lena arrived, and Pharoah insisted it was Michael he saw getting into a taxi. They hurried into the mortuary as the plainclothesmen came out of Rhea's room of repose.

"Which way did he go?" one of the slovens excitedly asked the new arrivals.

"You should be embarrassed," said Pharoah. "If you mean Michael Lee, he's in a cab probably headed for the Warehouse."

"Oh, good," said the plainclothesman, "they'll catch him there. It's being raided tonight." He mopped his brow with a handkerchief. He was rather portly and just eight days away from retirement. This mortuary made him nervous with its wind chimes and its strange music, which couldn't possibly be from Muzak.

The plainclothesmen did proudly announce they had Nick Wenji, which as far as Pharoah and Albert were concerned wasn't all that much of an accomplishment, as Nick was already on his way out if he hadn't already gone.

He hadn't, but he had weakened considerably. His head rested on the bier and Rhea looked as though she just might put an arm around him and cosset the dying man. It was a striking tableau. Lena found the sight touching. Pharoah was admiring Rhea's makeup job, especially the eye shadow, and Albert, who had never paid much attention to Nick Wenji until now, wondered if what he was wearing was from Giorgio Armani.

"Rhea," Nick whispered, as they strained to hear what he was saying, "is this what I am feeling, is it love? Is it really, truly love?" Lena tried stifling a sob, but it was no use once she saw a tear slowly making its way down Nick's cheek. Pharoah sent Albert to phone for an ambulance. Then he returned his attention to Nick Wenji. The bastard. An executioner, and he wants to be loved? What is it with these killers? They have such chutzpah.

●   ●   ●

Cylla Mourami's stretch limousine made its elongated way to the Hamptons, the chauffeur having been instructed firmly and in no uncertain terms to go at a breakneck speed, which made the man giddy with recklessness. "The Ride of the Valkyries" blasted from the specially built stereo and Cylla was almost inspired to let loose with a few of those ear-splitting *yo-ho-te-hos* that she remembered from soprano Kirsten Flagstad's memorable recording. Poor Hiram Wiggs was left behind to cope with the authorities unless he managed to make it to the safety of his lodge in Scotland. But when the phone tip arrived that warrants had been issued, it was every man for himself, and Cylla took off, overnight bag, jewel cases and a couple of hot pastrami sandwiches in a brown bag at her side.

The recording came to an end and Cylla switched to the latest model in sophisticated television sets. CNN, as usual, had beaten its rival news programs to the punch. They had superb coverage of the FBI and the police joining forces to raid gambling houses and houses of prostitution all around New York.

Wilma Joy in her palace of an apartment on Fifth Avenue overlooking the Metropolitan Museum of Art and Central Park was watching the same channel and shouting obscenities into a telephone. In the bedroom, Chana Ritch was on another phone making sure Wilma Joy's private jet would be ready to depart within the next hour. Wilma got off the phone and stormed into the bedroom. "That idiot. That fool. Are we ready? Let's get the hell out of here."

Chana said, "There'll be no one at Rhea's funeral."

"That's fine. She never liked crowds. Let's get going."

On the outskirts of Fort Lee, New Jersey, stood the factory that housed Fujian Frocks. It was surrounded by surprisingly well-tended lawns and shrubbery, a throwback to the days when it had been the headquarters of a pharmaceutical company. Detective Jack Amster of the Fort Lee Police Department was absolutely delighted to cooperate with New York Chief of Detectives Christy Lombardo. Someday Amster might need a favor reciprocated, such as fixing a ticket for speeding or illegal parking, which he frequently did when attending an event at Madison Square Garden. Amster led a caravan of three police cars, each holding three officers, for a total of nine. It was all he could muster on such short notice, although neighboring townships had been alerted to stand by in case of the need for emergency assistance. Amster hadn't been this excited since he drew five numbers in the state lottery several years ago.

Arriving at the site, Amster assigned his men to strategic positions in front and in back; fortunately there were no side exits and entrances. Amster announced the raid through a loudspeaker and was amazed there was no resistance. The front door was opened to them by a slender Chinese youth who bowed and smiled them in. What they found appalled them. There were rows of sewing machines at which sat an assortment of what would later prove to be illegal aliens, most of whom looked half starved. In the basement there was indeed a laboratory, although the technicians had all gone home. Unfortunately, some heavily armed Chinese guards decided to defend to the death the empty lab, and there was an immediate exchange of gunfire. Amster immediately radioed for backup, watching with dismay as the sweatshop workers panicked at the sound of gunfire and stampeded toward the exits. He winced as he watched several fall and be trampled.

In the basement, two Chinese youths were mortally wounded and one of Amster's men had taken a bullet in the buttocks. There was heavy pounding coming from under the basement floor. One of Amster's men found a wheel that opened a trapdoor. As it lifted, the stench that came from beneath was overpowering. An Asian man climbed out, followed by another and then another. A woman, tears streaming down her face, grabbed Amster's hand and peppered it with kisses. "Thank you, thank you," she gasped. Amster shouted to one of his men to get through to Christy Lombardo and tell him what they'd found.

When the news reached Christy, he shouted "Hallelujah!" and spread the word they had rescued, with some help from New Jersey police, a number of kidnap victims belonging to prominent China-town families.

And in Tisa Cheng's suite in Kao's hotel, she stood facing Michael Lee. Michael had pleaded, then threatened, then finally knocked her around a bit until she shoved a hand under the mattress and retrieved what she hoped he wanted. "Is this it? Is this it? Is this what you want?"

He snatched the small memo book from her hand. He riffled some pages. "This is it. Yes, this is it. It will buy me my freedom!" He tore out of the room, leaving Tisa to examine her bruises. Michael hurried down the narrow hallway leading into the Warehouse.

Smoke. He could smell it. It attacked his eyes. Ahead of him there were flames. The kitchen. The fire is in the kitchen; Kao had been warned someday it would happen. He was within reach of the gaming room. He held a handkerchief to his mouth and nose. He'd seen it done on TV. He staggered into the gaming room. He heard shouts and screams and then the welcome sound of fire engines.

Then two strong hands were trying to prop him up and the familiar voice of Pharoah Love demanded, "Michael? Why are you so god-damned accident prone?"

CHAPTER **22**

Pharoah easily lifted Michael onto his back and carried him out to the street fireman-style. There Christy Lombardo and what seemed to Pharoah a small army of police officers looked at the smoking building with what appeared to be chagrin and disappointment. They were supposed to be conducting a raid, but the object of their raid was on fire. Pharoah deposited Michael on the sidewalk and propped him up against the base of a lamppost. Fire fighters had arrived in what for Chinatown was record time, though they were having trouble maneuvering through narrow Catherine Slip. Several ambulances had to park at the end of the street, and medics had to elbow their way through the crowd that had gathered. One of the fire chiefs directed some men to the hotel at the rear of the Warehouse where he had been informed some women in residence might be in danger. A medic knelt at Michael's side holding an oxygen mask to his face. Michael was conscious and annoyed and pushed the mask to one side.

"I'm fine. I'm fine. I'm perfectly fine." He reached into an inside jacket pocket. "I have it, Pharoah. I have it. I have Kao Lee's book." Albert West arrived in time to see Michael give Pharoah the book.

"Why, you clever little rascal. Wherever did you find it?"

"It was under Tisa Cheng's mattress. That's where she hid it for Kao." The medic had helped him to his feet. "I remembered when he had important documents he gave them to my mother to keep for him. He insisted women were the best guardians of important documents. So I gambled he'd left the book with Tisa. It works in my favor, okay?"

"I'll do my best for you, Michael." He was turning pages in the book, occasionally giving a low whistle. "Kao was quite a businessman. Would you look at these prices he was demanding? The man must be mad."

Michael said, "Of course he is mad. Insane."

Pharoah signaled to a plainclothesman and appointed him Michael's guardian. Then he took Albert by the arm and led him away. "You look very antsy. What's bothering you?" He was momentarily distracted by the outpouring of streams of water from the city's antiquated hoses, reminding him of an old Radio City Music Hall extravaganza called *Dancing Waters*. Except here on Catherine Slip there were no mermaids or sea nymphs simulating underwater swimming and then doing precision high kicks. Albert was talking a blue streak and suddenly what he was saying took on a coherence and an urgency.

"I talked to Christy on the radio. He got something from Amster . . ."

"Amster what?"

"Fort Lee police. Those dresses at Fujian Frocks . . ."

"Oh dear. Don't tell me some of those guys gave themselves dead away and tried them on."

"Shut up and listen. They were labeled 'Wilma Joy.' There were boxloads of them waiting to be shipped."

"All over the States?"

"All over Asia."

Pharoah snapped his fingers. "That's what the freighters carried to China before picking up the illegals. Damn it, the smuggling's been going on two ways. Kao Lee actually in partnership with Wilma Joy? Presumably loathing each other but still playing footsy under the table. Damn it. I need to find Kao." He hurried to Michael. "Have you any idea where I might find Kao?"

"His plan was to go on the town with Tisa."

"Your mother newly dead and he's going out stepping? The cad. I shall break his sword over my knee. Come on, Albert, we're going to a whorehouse."

"I hope the madam has a heart of gold."

"If she did, she's hocked it. Come on. Down this alley. Don't trip on the hoses. What a mess. I shall report this disorderly mess to the mayor."

In Tisa Cheng's room, she was confronted by Kao Lee, both either oblivious to or unaware of the threat of the Warehouse fire. Kao's temper was out of control. Tisa cowered in a corner as he kept lashing out at her verbally and physically. Then an even fiercer piece of punishment inspired him. With a pocketknife he attacked Tisa's new wardrobe, slashing away at the Wilma Joy specials as though this in some way represented his slashing away at Wilma Joy herself. In his preoccupation with destruction, he did not see Tisa slip out of the room and make her escape down the hall. She had had quite enough of her golden opportunity. Smoke was drifting up a stairwell, and from the stairwell also emerged Pharoah and Albert.

"Hey you!" shouted Pharoah upon espying Tisa. "Where's Kao Lee?"

"In there!" She pointed to her room. "He's a madman! He's insane! He tried to kill me! He's got a knife!"

"And I," said Pharoah with a haughty sniff, "have ten deadly finger-nails. Come, Albert, let us scratch our way to glory." As he faced into the room, he waved the little book at Kao Lee, a matador teasing the bull mercilessly. "Is this what sweetheart is looking for?"

Kao's hands froze in midair. The left hand held a Wilma Joy blouse speckled with multicolored baguettes. His right hand held the knife. And then there emerged from the very depths of his being a roar of anguish so intense that its memory would stay with Pharoah and Albert for many months to come.

In the confusion at the Warehouse fire, Lena Wing had found it easy to separate herself from Pharoah and Albert. She made her way carefully through the alley past the Warehouse to the hotel. Outside the hotel a few of the die-hard whores were holding on to their scores.

One veteran of the boudoir wars was comforting her client. "The nice fire chief doesn't think the hotel will be too damaged. We were going great, sweetie. We didn't even hear the alarms go off." She giggled a series of squeaks that made her gentleman friend think of a cage full of mice.

Lena informed one of the girls, "I'm going up and take a nice, long, hot bath with lots of sexy salts."

The prostitute asked Lena, "Supposing the bottom drops out of this place?"

Lena replied airily, "Perhaps you haven't noticed, but it already has." She entered the hotel, eschewed the elevator and climbed the stairs to her floor, heard Kao's horrific cry of frustration and anguish, and then put the key in the lock of her door. While humming "These

Foolish Things" she made her way to the bathroom and ran water into the tub.

A girl can't be too well groomed when she turns herself in to the police.

Cylla Mourami didn't realize she was doing a bad job of playing the coquette. She should never have cast herself in the part. The police car had flagged her chauffeur down on the Long Island Expressway for excessive speeding. Cylla lowered her window and favored the two officers with an audience. They were not impressed. Not even when she invoked the names of New York's mayor, the president of the United States and his wife, several newspaper columnists and some Hollywood names, two of which she mispronounced.

One of the officers recognized the license plate. There was an APB out on it. "Hey, Skeezix," he said to his partner, "we've hit the jackpot. There's an APB on this one." He whistled. "Cylla Mourami. How about that, Skeezix. She's worth billions."

Cylla was making a great show of repairing her face while several hundred dollar bills could be seen playing peek-a-boo in the spaces between her fingers. "I hope you're not trying to bribe us, lady. We're that increasingly rare breed—honest cops."

Pharoah and Albert escorted Kao Lee out of the hotel. The fire was under control at last. The fire inspector reported two dead bodies in the kitchen. Albert hoped there was someone to mourn for them. The bartender had been found unconscious behind the bar but he was suffering mostly from smoke inhalation. The other employees and the patrons—of which, fortunately, there had been a paucity—had made their way to safety at the first sign of the fire. The kitchen was wrecked and would probably be left that way until some brave entrepreneur ventured along to gamble on breaking the law again. Fortunately for all concerned, there had been no flashover, a deadly form of fire resulting in the explosion of an accumulation of gases. Kao was deposited in the backseat of the unmarked police car with Pharoah and another officer for company. Albert gunned the motor, mentally preparing himself for what he knew would be a long night ahead.

"Home, James," said Pharoah to Albert while torturing Kao Lee by reading aloud from the prized little book. Almost as if it was coming from left field, Pharoah asked Kao, "Didn't you always know Wilma Joy was an agent of the Chinese government? Sure you did. She sent you to the U.S. in the first place. Then sent you your brother Zang and Rhea and little Michael. She was already on her way in the world of fashion thanks to China's financing. All an elaborate cover for one of the most successful network of spies and undercover agents in the United States. I'll bet she worked up that clever scheme to smuggle them in as illegal aliens."

"Like hell she did! It was my—" His mouth clamped shut.

Pharoah said, "Kao, I hate cliff-hangers." Kao said nothing. He stared out the window.

Pharoah sighed and said, "We've raided Fujian Frocks, Kao." There was a pained expression on Kao's face.

"The raid released a nice proportion of your kidnap victims. Kao, you're so mean, you may spend your life in solitary confinement. Brrr. What a horrible fate. Say, Albert. Did you make sure Michael's being brought in?"

"He's in the car ahead of us, with Tisa Cheng. She spit in his face."

"Why, the mean little bitch. After all he's done for her. So come on, Kao, be your darling old talkative self again. Shall we talk about Rhea? We saw her laid out. I was so jealous. Who did her makeup? That shade of eye shadow. So original." He said softly, "I don't think she would have betrayed you."

"No. Neither do I. She was a good woman. But we had run our course a long time ago. Wilma ordered her death. Wilma ordered all the deaths." He sighed. "I made up an awful lot of stories about Rhea.

Well, why not?" Kao suddenly laughed and then shrugged, feeling that strange buoyancy that captivity brings, when one is relieved of all burdens. "You don't know Wilma. You've never met her. Perhaps you never will."

"I will tonight. Her private jet was grounded. At least I hope Christy gave the order in time once her labels were spotted at Fujian Frocks." He poked Albert. "Do you know if they caught her?"

"She and her girlfriend are on their way in from the airport. And Cylla Mourami. Her lawyer, Mr. Wiggs, is on a flight to Scotland, but we'll get him back."

"Wilma is a dreadful woman." Kao was treating himself to one of his elongated cigars. The stench of the smoke was sickening. Pharoah lowered his window, pulled the cigar from Kao's mouth, threw it out the window, while an astonished Kao let out a wounded cry.

Pharoah said amiably, "Wilma's the older of the two."

Kao said something inaudible.

"The women didn't like each other."

"You know sisters," said Kao.

"I know a lot of sisters and some of them most certainly like each other."

From out of nowhere and for no apparent reason, Kao said, "Michael is basically a good boy. He has never killed anyone. He just followed orders. He was born to follow orders."

"You sympathize, don't you, Albert?" asked Pharoah whimsically.

"Up you."

Pharoah smiled at Kao. "Albert's my best friend. Sometimes he cooks me a *matzo brie*." A motorcycle cop whizzed by. Clinging to him tightly with her arms around his waist was Lena Wing. "And there goes Lena. Turning herself in like she promised she would." He said to Kao. "We're going to go easy on Lena. She'll get a nice, generous plea bargain and then we'll help her find the backing for that restaurant she's *plotzing* to open."

Kao said, "My employees at the Mandarin shop are totally inno-cent."

"They might as well be. We've got nothing on them. So, Kao, what happens now to your dysfunctional organization?"

"My dear Pharoah, you would have to consult Madame Khan for the answer to that one. I certainly don't have one."

The Fifth Precinct station house was buzzing with pride. Their cup floweth over with celebrities. There were Wilma Joy and Cylla Mourami recently joined by Kao Lee. Cylla jealously guarded her overnight bag, her jewel boxes and the brown bag with its sandwiches. Christy Lombardo gazed upon his captive horde fondly like a mother hen whose eggs had hatched nothing but prize bantams. He knew most of them would soon be sprung because they had money and power, but the FBI was determined to prosecute them all. Pharoah learned that FBI man Malone had been given an assignment in north-ernmost Greenland rather than an open prosecution that would invite some unwanted, unfavorable publicity. Chana Ritch glared at Cylla Mourami. The bitch wasn't even wearing a Wilma Joy. She was wear-ing a presumptuous Oscar de la Renta. Lena Wing sat with an arm around Tisa Cheng, who couldn't stop sniffling, dreading the deporta-tion back to Fujian. Kao Lee glowered at them both.

On one side of the room, Pharoah and Albert huddled with Christy Lombardo. Wilma Joy was the topic under discussion. Christy told them, "We've already heard from Washington. She's to be part of a big trade-in. You know, you can have one Wilma Joy in return for four scientists, three agronomists, two doctors, six professors and some of those imprisoned after the Tiananmen Square uprising."

"She's worth much more than that," said Pharoah. "She's real big stuff over there. Used to be buddies with the Gang of Four."

"Past tense, Pharoah. She's failed. Failure brings disgrace."

Pharoah was indignant. "How dare they! After all her years of great service and sacrifice!"

"Oh, shut up," said Albert. "She's a monster. One of the biggest criminals of this era."

"But I adore her lantern dresses. They're *really* cunning. . . ."

Wilma said to Chana, "I'll never forgive myself for this. I should have foreseen the disaster once I recognized Kao was on a path of self-destruction."

Chana said, "The barn door's closed, darling. I'm sure Beijing is at work on springing you."

"I'm truly sorry, Chana. I will do all I can to make them see you were innocent."

"Don't you dare! I have a contact at Simon and Schuster who's been after me to do a tell-all about you."

"You wouldn't!"

"I would! I call it *Wilma Dearest*."

Cylla Mourami offered Wilma Joy a pastrami sandwich. Wilma drew her furs tightly around her and turned away.

In the Pagoda of Heaven, Rhea Lee had a visitor. Madame Khan sat in a chair meditating, her eyes closed. Then she opened them and spoke softly to the corpse. "My dear Rhea. My dear friend. I should have warned you. Among other things about that son of a bitch Nick Wenji. Anyway, I foresaw his death tonight but chose not to tell him. But I am saddened that I did not foresee yours. Forgive me, my dear, wherever you are. So now you are dead, Rhea. Well, dear, there's a first time for everything."